PRAISE FOR SUSPENDED HEART

"Magical realism at its finest. Great work by Heather Fowler. Recommended."

– Kathy Fish, author of *Wild Life*

"It's a dazzling collection of magical realism, from boys made of clay and girls made of razor blades, to Philip Dick-esque replicants, to vampires and heroic parrots."

– Jen Michalski, author of *Close Encounters*

"Common emotions that come forth as literal components in the characters' lives are too good to miss. The author's fabulist style, both sarcastic and charitable, is one to be admired."

– Melanie Page, American Book Review

"Fowler's descriptions are exquisite, and her stories absorbing. Her fabulist elements intertwine with reality to create allegorical narratives that expose deeper truths about men and women, about humanity's common fixations. Her heroines are strong, but searching and consistently surprising. Fowler's stories are like spells: Through words alone, beautiful imagery, tremendous substance, and poignant feeling become palpably real."

– Savannah Schroll Guz, author of *American Soma*

"Fowler's writing itself is beautiful—her sentences are as varied as her characters, and the images she carefully paints echo Francis Bacon's statements about beauty: there's nothing pretty that isn't at least slightly bizarre in some way. This strangeness never hinders Fowler's work, and instead, increases the world she so vividly introduces us to, making her plots more believable, and just that much more fun to read. Her language doesn't flow, but laps, much like Minnow Lake, at the reader's feet, slowly drawing them into her sphere."

– Stephanie Johnson, Ampersand Review

D1563820

"Sometimes, just sometimes, from the scrolls of work I read online, I stumble across a story different enough to make me remember a name. Heather Fowler's such a writer. I encountered her work a few years ago online. It's almost impossible not to. Fresh, vivid, her prose is fluid. It flows like a river. Never static. The work moves characters and perceptions. The heart is revealed and swept away. A single story can be strange, beautiful, moving, dark, then funny. Stories that may seem quirky on the surface of subject matter have layers and deceptive depth... Such fearlessness is reminiscent of Joyce Carol Oates, yet the work is surprising, moving, and full of humour."

– Angela Readman, The Short Review

"Heather Fowler is Kafka in drag, an American Marquez... What really wins the reader over, though, is the way she tells the story."

– Bonnie ZoBell, Gently Read Literature

"The stories in *Suspended Heart* have made for some of the most twisted, exciting reading I have had in a very long time. They are read with a zealousness and momentum that is like a solid relationship, improving with age and with each re-read. I find these stories to take the idea of love and blast away any cliché notions that love is an ordinary thing. Bitter hearts will be relieved, hardened hearts will soften, and dangerous hearts will finally use caution. Each story is fresh and crisp and offers a new angle on the age-old ideas of romance and sex. The themes of lust and courageous love are never dulled by overly dramatic tales or melodramatic fantasies. The voice Fowler uses is real, and in my opinion, these stories are some of the best tales of love and its consuming ideas that have been written in many years."

– Zach Fishel, Girls With Insurance

SUSPENDED HEART

stories

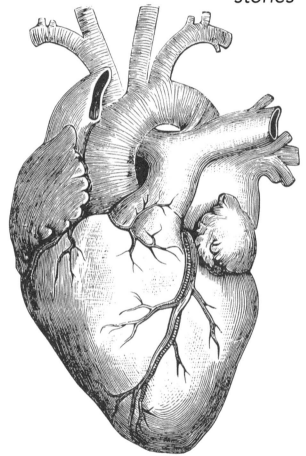

HEATHER FOWLER

pink
narcissus
press

SUSPENDED HEART: Stories
© 2019 Heather Fowler

A version of this book was originally published by Aqueous Books in December 2010.

"A Companion to Minnow Lake." First appearance: *Prick of the Spindle*. Vol. 4.3. (Fall 2010)
"Bloom In Any Season." First appearance: *DOGZPLOT* (Fall 2009)
"Cock Sculpting." First appearance: *MindKites: Perceptions on the Fringe*. Summer 2000. (June 2000)
"Dangling Now, In the Erotic City of Ghosts." First appearance: *Contrary Magazine*. (Winter 2014)
"Fear of Snakes." First appearance: *The Abacot Journal: An Online Magazine of Weird Fiction*. (Spring 2009)
"Men Like Chameleons In the Dark." First appearance: *Etchings 7*. Ilura Press. (July 2009)
"My Brother, Made of Clay." First appearance: *Zoetrope All-Story Extra 33*. (June 2001)
"The Rose Lamp." First appearance: *Underground Voices*. (Nov. 2008)
"The Time Broker." First appearance: *Fictionaut*. (Jan. 2010)

Cover design by Siolo Thompson

Published by Pink Narcissus Press
Massachusetts, USA
pinknarc.com

ISBN: 978-1-939056-15-3
First trade paperback edition: May 2019

CONTENTS

DEDICATION

For all the beautiful women, inside and out, who have struggled for life in the name of love. My best, most healing magic to you always.

SUSPENDED HEART

The suspended heart became an oracle of sorts. Hung from a string, immersed in the kind of glass container in which tulips grow, it was located between Bath and Body Works and Kleinfelter's Jewelers at the north entrance of the mall. Someone had lost it, and when this happened, it was tied with a string, much like a butcher's roast, and hung up high to avoid the encroachment of traveling feet. Originally, there was no water in the jar, but the janitor noticed its dryness, and he and a few other members of the cleaning staff came up with the idea of submerging the heart in a large glass vat of sterilized water.

But it went unclaimed for months, and when people started to notice its presence, it became a source of speculation. Mall rats regarded it with pity and then interest, sometimes stopping to scrutinize its bodiless, constant beating and wonder how, in a mall pealing with Christmas carols and corporate announcements, it could continue to thrive or even function. Then they noticed its love connection and greater abilities with divining.

The girl who lost this organ had no idea it was gone, which is to say she knew she missed something, but had no idea it was something vital. In general, her head felt clearer, her step was lighter, and despite entering the mall via the northern entrance on the day she grew so happy, stopping briefly at the jeweler's and then rushing back to her store on the western end, she was completely clueless that her heart had, abruptly and without warning, fallen out.

As the days passed, couples increasingly came to view it, hearing the rumor that if they stood before this heart with their beloved, a sudden, vigorous throbbing would mean it sensed their intent and that love was true for both parties. If it stopped beating altogether, one of the parties was false or cheating. If no love, no romantic inclination, were present, the heart would beat as usual, and one would feel that everything anticipated in the world would conform to this expectation, that life would meander on, and that a person who inspired no change in the rhythm of the beats was not a victim of heart-led fancies. Such a heart, some speculated, could not be expected to weigh in on petty squabbles or non-love quandaries like landlord spying or familial spats. People were full of questions, but it was answers they sought and, for these, they were ravenous.

The heart solely covered one topic.

—

Christmas carols rang through the mall every day now. Everyone spoke of generic love and kindness or bad parking and ludicrous off-site shuttles while "Silent Night" or another timeless holiday tune blared through the loud-speakers, both shoppers and employees frequently pulling brisk strides through the arena's walkway mazes, though it was only the romantic couples that made the heart a destination. When a reporter got wind of the heart and visited, newly learning her partner of ten years manifested a strong desire for the man who lived next door, the subsequent *Tribune* article only swelled the crowds. Travel agents advertised, too: "Live, beating heart suspended in Coppendale Mall. Measure your lover's love for free! Will your match prove lasting? Only the heart can tell!" and the arriving lovers, swallowing such promises like desire's last gasp, tripled.

At first, the janitor felt terrible for allowing visitors to throng around the organ. To his wife, he confessed, "I only meant this display as an easy way for whoever lost their heart to find it again, for it not to get lost or trampled in the traffic. I didn't intend on it becoming an attraction."

"You should get a raise," his wife said. "Who else brought in such a ringer? Mall profits are through the roof! As usual, Husband, you innovate, and they do nothing to reward you!"

It was a strange sight, he admitted, to see couples of so many varieties queued up for this heart's assessment while he emptied garbage cans and swept floor tiles. There were the rich and the poor, people on holiday, people on Quaaludes, people who drove to Coppendale on their last tank of gas and risked a failed return just to find out what they could not determine from the privacy of their own homes.

"I suppose knowing the true contents of your lover's heart is worth a lot," his wife remarked one day. "And, like the best reclusive things in life, it's free. Because nothing is free anymore! Of course they love it!"

She went on to talk about how life is an elective series of choices about time and well-purchased commodities, although no one gets a free lunch and most people pay therapists to figure things out, but when she grew enthusiastic about accurate divination from elsewhere, the Godsend of Godsends, "Not everyone wants to know what this heart can tell them," he said, dampening her enthusiasm.

From his main janitorial supply station, he saw often what he began to label "The Avoiders": People who did not line up to visit the heart, but instead hurried past, some clenching a lover's hand and staring at the pavement, taking no risks that the heart might engage them, some involved more in pocketbooks or gadgetry as replacement therapy for love or any affiliated vice, but the heart noticed them all. Had they only looked up, they would have ascertained plain and simple what they did not want to know. Of this, the janitor was sure.

Meanwhile, the girl who lost her heart only thought: *What a calm life I now have! Oh, how strange! Some say there's a beating heart on the other side of the mall that tells fortunes for lovers, but I simply do not care! It's good to be free of romantic concerns. I do not need a lover! This is the best period of my entire life. I am so happy alone.* Meanwhile, she was selling E- and G-sized nursing bras to pregnant ladies at Motherhood Maternity, panel-top jeans and stretch-belly pantyhose, dresses sewn with a longer panel in the front to accommodate swelling bumps. She sold cocktail dresses and bright-colored leggings and long T-shirts, jacket clips, and belly-itch crème. She felt fine and glad. She discussed her customers' growing concerns with their bodies, though she had never been pregnant, instead conveying former shoppers' carefully gleaned wisdom. She Windexed displays with industrious satisfaction. She asked about proposed baby names. She smiled widely, pleasing her customers and herself.

The heartless contrast of her new world heartily pleased her. There had been a time when her chest hurt each day, when her eyes burned with spent tears and she had no idea what to do with the rest of her life because a man she loved had abandoned her, and her heart, she came to know, formed strong attachments quickly, but did not let go easily, which was what made her so terrible at love. During the period of her great and depressive malaise, she'd begun to feel she would never know joy again, that her every waking thought was self-eviscerating torture, accompanied by questions regarding: How she made the last incredible mistake; how, if she had the chance again, she might reverse it; how she could not institute such reversals, ever; and how, in her lifetime, love and its games of spirit-mashing, soul-deep annihilation were now destined to be over, had to be over, that was if she survived the recovery this time.

So, when her heart fell out that very same day, she had begun again to see colors as beautiful—the red, red roses; the vibrant green grass; the blue of the hot day's sky. Near-strangers were newly enjoyable and she found herself saying things to Lizzie, her boss, like: "Oh, look, Lizzie. That heifer standing there with five fighting children—she wears the most beautiful hat! Wonder where she bought it!"

Whereas crowds had bothered her before, in her perceived solitude and estrangement, now she considered the rapid here-and-there of commerce participants a necessary flurry, keeping her employed and carrying their lives and goodwill into these corridors and shops. The mall was a fantastic place.

Yes, after her heart fled, she felt like skipping from store to store. She liked pregnant women again. "What has happened to me?" she often asked. "I feel so very glad!"

"You seem happier," her friends said.

"Your eyes look better," her mother said. "Ugly bags less often."

"You're selling more," her boss admitted.

"You look beautiful, Shopgirl," the lecherous husbands of her pregnant shoppers said, but this sort of advance was unwelcome, coming on the heels of other women's burgeoning bellies and usually while knocked-up partners fought for space to yank on garments in tiny fitting rooms.

And if there was a slight chill she now felt constantly, and a lack of complete conviction regarding her own emotions, this was to become her new era of action—one of getting things done, of moving forward with difficult decisions, of life's agendas either advanced or backtracked based solely on relevant thoughts and not ridiculous emotions. Her mind itself felt powerful. She thought of the abandoner, of course, but the idea of him was then a distantly painful memory, deliberately immersed in forgetting, as if her heart, like the one across the mall, was submerged in a glass vat of chilly water, or also tied tightly with binding string. She did, she mused, kind of want to see the strung-up heart.

Most often, she parked on the west end, entering between Cinnabon and The Sharper Image. It was only when she received a call from the jeweler to say her ring was ready that she decided to venture to the other side of the labyrinthine maze to take a gander at the strange heart. At her request, the contracted jeweler had replaced her ring's original diamond with a peridot, her birth stone. The diamond she had arranged to be set in a golden pendant, to hang from a fine gold chain.

Nonetheless, when she saw the line to the strung-up heart, directly in front of the jeweler's shop, she shrugged and decided to forego seeing it, muttering, "What a wait!" and, "I don't care enough for a glimpse to wait that long."

But the janitor noticed how the heart swayed toward her when she walked past. He saw it jump and remembered how even after they had agreed upon the glass container, they had not removed the string around the heart itself, because, in test runs, it had hopped out of the water-filled vat to make a liver-on-the-counter splat as it tried to navigate the floor—though it had not leapt in any capacity for quite some time. He might say, until now, it had been sluggish. Although as she walked past, he not only saw it lurch, despite the string, but seem to follow her in the arcing radius of the jar.

Oblivious to the janitor and the heart, the happy girl entered the jeweler's shop, and the janitor, feeling the purpose of the hanging heart had been resolved, *shooed* away the lines of waiting observers, mentioning it needed a rest. "It's on a heart-break now!" he called out. Then he retrieved his ladder from the utility closet, climbed up, and cut the frantic heart down.

The woman he watched stood inside the jeweler's a long while as he held the tulip jar in his hands. First the sales-girl brought out her new ring, which she tried on and admired. Then another chic salesgirl with blonde hair and a violet pencil skirt brought out a necklace so fine that that all within the store gathered around and gaped. It was while the girl he watched paid for her purchases, as they were packed and sacked, that the janitor looked down at the heart in the jar and spoke to it consolingly, stroking it with his free hand, for it beat so fast it nearly sprung out, and he held its container against his chest gingerly while severing the inner restraining strings with his Swiss army knife, whispering, "Don't bleed. Don't bleed, now," as if he encouraged a reti-cent child or a fearful animal.

It did not bleed. The indentations of the butcher ties showed a bit, but as he brought the heart to the door of the jeweler's shop and waited, its smooth tissue seemed to flush redder than before, thickly beating with a rhythm like sleep, staid and docile. "You're a happy heart now, aren't you?" he said, having developed the habit of speaking to it like a cher-ished pet or kindly relative.

When the girl stepped out, fit to pass him, he blocked her. "Have you been missing this?" he asked. He could not help his aggression, his forceful proximity. With all his tender ministrations, it now seemed almost his heart.

"Is that the beating heart?" she replied.

She was pretty, he noticed. In a subdued way. "Yes. It followed you just now, so I thought it might be yours. I'm here to return it."

Between the two of them, there seemed a long unspoken history, a glimmer of an open-ended conversation that almost was, but he held the jar out toward her silently, like a supplicant, as she felt her blouse slide open where a small aperture in her chest appeared. She looked at the heart and then at the pale opening of skin, gaping, that seemed to want the organ back. "Guess that heart's mine," she said. "But I don't want it." Hysteria grew within her like a bee-storm. "I didn't really, not till this instant, realize it was missing—" she confessed. "But I don't want it now. I am happy."

The janitor shifted from foot to foot, staring at the legs of his green pantsuit. "But if it's yours..." he insisted. "Shouldn't you take it back? Isn't it your obligation?"

She stared at her slim black shoes.

"What if it dies here?" he said. "Or you die? Something could die, and it would be your fault."

She looked to him as if she were about to say, "So be it," but said, instead, "I've been doing so much better without it, so much better. I never really missed it," her cheeks turning red, the necklace glimmering under the mall lights like a sparkling diamond tear on her neck. She looked at the bodiless heart, which bounced up and down in the water for her attention. Once it was gained, the heart seemed to communicate with her wordlessly, the janitor standing before them, baffled, as he watched her initiate and prolong an animated argument, throwing her hands around, saying things like, "I can't!" and "What do you want from me?" and "What good did you ever do for me?" and "No, I won't have you back! Not today! Not ever. I don't want any more of your messy failure!"

But her heart was tricky, something both he and she already knew, slowly descending into the tulip jar he held, as if it would stay down, rather forlornly, and then, before she could repair the open state of her blue gingham blouse, both watched it jump like lightning from the jar and fall back into its cavity in her chest.

A lingering crowd gathered nearby, waiting for the heart to determine who was truly in love, some people looking certain it would confirm them, some looking green, but there would be no more soothsaying from the clear water that lingered in the empty jar. "I'm sorry," the janitor told them as he turned away from the girl, who shivered and shook, seeming as if she'd just been hit with a seizure of maladroit or smacked in the head with a curbside brick. In his peripheral vision, he noticed she fell to the ground, weeping.

Assuming his role of organizer, he then returned his attention to the remaining crowd, announcing in a loud, firm voice: "The Coppendale Mall's Divining Heart has disappeared. It's gone. Try Victoria's Secret or See's Candy for love stuff."

But when he returned his gaze to the floored girl rejecting her reabsorbed heart, she was prostate on the tiles, beating her fists against the dirty ceramic tile, before hugging herself into a ball and moaning and sobbing like she couldn't have cared less who saw or heard. "It's back!" she exclaimed again and again, interspersing her announcement with assorted expletives, but these utterances were so convoluted with sobs, they were difficult to decipher.

When he tried to help her stand, she leveled him with her gaze and resisted, clinging to the ground, murmuring, "Haven't you done enough?"—her aggrieved tone making him feel like he'd killed a crippled and helpless thing. "I didn't want it back!" she reiterated.

But she stopped looking at him then.

He let her be.

And he cleaned the mall that day, starting with the west wing. By the time he returned to the northern entrance, she was gone, but he found her diamond necklace, chain broken, beside some fast-food wrappers near the trash. He picked up her jewelry and took it home.

"Maybe she was on a little break from her heart," his wife said that night when they discussed the situation. "It needed to do a tour to help others because it was of no use to her, perhaps. Lots of women feel that way. You shouldn't have cut that string, Honey—should have just let those people go see it. But you had to play delivery guy. Now what will happen to your raise? No more free heart at the mall!"

"I just wanted to give it back," he said. "It was so happy to see her. It jumped and throbbed."

"Just because something wants us doesn't mean we want it," his wife responded, cracking her knuckles and putting her hands behind her head, before muttering, "That poor girl. Her heart made her miserable! You returned a burden. You say she was in tears?"

"Right," he agreed. But he looked so tortured then that his wife smiled, as if to soothe him, touching and handling the sparkling diamond pendant of the girl who had lost her heart. Though the slender chain around the young girl's neck had been destroyed at the mall, within moments of his wife's receipt of the pendant, she had restrung it on a thicker, sturdier chain, and in the heavy gold-and-yellow light of their living room lamps, the white stone sparkled beautifully.

"So, you did wrong by confronting the girl," his wife told him. "But you meant well. And I love my new necklace. A lovely yule present!" She stared into his eyes, which focused on a dying Venus fly trap on the sideboard. "Too bad she didn't have a man like you," she told him. "She might've wanted her heart back."

"Or never have lost it in the first place," he replied. "But then again, maybe that's speculation. I admit, I'm no miracle."

"But you say she was crying as you left?" his wife asked.

"Yes, crying," he replied. "Torrents. Laid out on the nasty mall floor like a homeless person."

Both shook their heads, considering for the length of a beat what ideas could make somebody crazy enough to lose their very heart in the walkway of a public mall. He kissed her. She kissed him. They leaned in close, side by side, comfortable in the other's near heat, yet each already retreating into private branches of meditative thoughts, before settling in lightly for the night.

BLOOM IN ANY SEASON

Deal was the lover I took up with time and again. For him, I wanted to bloom in any season, to create a non-annual flowering that bore the healthy radiance of well-kept perennials, but with more color. In spring and summer, on my thighs, magenta roses bloomed; Gerber daisies covered my breasts, encircling my nipples. Enormous hibiscus blossoms grew from the crack of my ass and a dappling of heathered groundcover spread from my shoulders down my back, intersecting with an occasional grouping of forget-me-nots and a scattered dash of bachelor buttons.

I could not hide my color when it sprang forth this way. At times, it was embarrassing. I could not work nude. I could not wear clothes without crushing the flowers. I could not crush the flowers without conceiving their wilting corpses like bedraggled, ill-used ladies in the evenings, creased by the borrowed age of the weight of cotton or linen or rayon or wool. All day on the job, there was the sensation of their petals shifting, growing mangled, twisting and pinching against confinement, being ravished by a cruel invisible foe beneath my garments—my own motion—but the other ladies whispered if something pink or blue popped free, speculated endlessly on my loose living, and only accepted me again when I looked as bewildered as they were, as joyless, wrecked, and tired.

Amidst the other admins were those with pine-needle hair, those with sweet-grass lashes, those with any number of variations of plant or water life entwined with their features. But I was afraid to show my full bloom because they taught me fear with their jealousy: "You don't belong here," they would say. "You will outwork us. Why are you here? Shouldn't you work where the fancy people are? Go find your own kind." But by fancy, they meant trashy. By outwork, they meant upstage.

I came to know that, like social workers, they always meant a worse word than the one they used. But I looked like them in shadows. In partial views. Seated at my desk, answering the phone again and again: "Ingénue Enterprise. How may I direct your call? Please hold."

Yes, there were the year-round strangling ivy vines that did not cease from my elbows to my fingertips. The morning glories wrapping my legs from knees to ankles that seldom bloomed. But when I got home from work each day, in the blooming, in the spring and subsequent season, nearly always, there was the lover. He was seasonal, like fruit, like me.

He had dark brown hair with summer-blue tips. His lips fit my fingers, my elbows, my groin, my face. He came to me most often in April, saying, "I'm back," as if we had agreed each year he would come just as casually, as if he were a migrating bird flying south for me, as if I had not cried and pulled my hair out the last time he left, swearing he could rot in hell before finding his way back into my bed, which was soil and cocoa bark, which I swore would be forever closed to him—which had been empty but was full again when he arrived—because he knew how to make a woman wait.

He counted on the months between these absences to soften and confuse me, exclaiming, shouting, singing, "I'm back! I'm back!" on his return, his refrain always announcing his arrivals like they were the Roman holidays of my life-time, like I should say something delighted or embrace him as if his last absence were solely an eight-month trip to the distracting grocery store of someone else. For milk. For more flowers. For fresh meat. For good cream.

"You're back," I'd say. "That's nice. Did you want to come tell me again I taste like earth and moonlight? That was last year's line." Sometimes, I'd say, "I'm tired. I'm bored. I've been working all day, and I did not order take-out boomerang dick for dinner, as far as I know, so why don't you leave?"

He would smile like I was glad to see him, like I had said something endearing. This was his winsome charm. "I came to touch you," he would say, coming so close I felt him brush the flowers, their pistils, their stamens, the thin tips of their petals. I would say, "No," as he leaned closer. But he would keep touching me, which I could not resist, touching me so well even the bruises on the flowers trapped all day under blazers and fine button-up blouses would relent and freshen.

Invariably, after days of his attention, I would let him close, stop sniping, and show him the joy face I guessed he wanted. He knew what to do with a woman who blossomed. Sometimes, he sniffed my skin and sighed, touched my flowers ever-so-lightly, or shook them between his thumb and index finger to move pollen from one to the others, but at other times blew warm breath across the blooms on my lower back as if his exhale alone could spread the pollen like a sunlit morning breeze warming my meadows and vales.

"Thank you," I'd say. For months, we would continue making love until I worked, which was when he waited and bathed and did crosswords and cooked himself udon and dreamt his wayfaring dreams—and then we made love again, nights falling softly into days, entranced with each other, one after another, until I could hardly concentrate at work, until I could not tell his body from my own, until his hands were extensions of my heart's desire and quiet whispers, until his eyes were the mirror I most preferred to see me by. His body was hard and cold, like stone.

Sometimes, he crushed me. Often, "You're blooming," he'd say. "I love that."

Then on weekends, he'd play my grandmother's upright piano and make us carrot soup and lobster salad. He would dance with me all night, especially through the month of July, me nude save the flowers, him in a light T-shirt and ripped jeans, as we stood in the garden behind the green split-level house in which we met, the one I bought from him, and where, during the protracted transaction, we fell in love.

Then winter came, and my flowers died. I tried to prolong their life, whispering to my skin, "Please. Please..." But they would not stay. The arm and leg vines persisted, but across my body, brown brambles, the texture of branches, a wood like rasp, proliferated. "You are too hard. You scratch now," he would say, packing, picking up the handfuls of shed, dying petals from the hardwood floor, lifting them to his face and smelling them almost nostalgically, before looking back toward the door he intended to walk through. Moments later, he would go through that door, and he would be gone. Considering my recent loss, I would wish to bloom for him in any season. I would curse him, waiting through the rest of the year's hard, cold months when the ladies I worked beside grew fonder and kinder, seeming to like me more in heartache, in dull ache, seeming to know that my bloom had fallen from the bud.

And bolstered by their platonic, nurturing love, I would swear myself done with his irrational leave-takings. I would look for more perennial and durably rooted men— those for whom my vines would suit all year long. I would find them. They would bore me. As the months passed I would forget the lover, forget how it felt to have him cease to darken my doorstep, cease to dance with me all night long, pressed close, naked in the yard he once owned and then sold to me. I'd curse him for how the ephemeral textures of his stays had thwarted all measure for regular happiness, making all kinds of lists for myself about how and why I would never take him back.

But winter would end and spring would near as the hurts of the previous year grew muted enough to numb, though my mental affliction remained, when I'd be virulent with conflict, loving, hating, mild, and dismayed—flying through light spectrums of his defense and his evisceration, alone in my bed of soil and bark, saying, "I hope that sono-fabitch never returns! I barely survived the last time! He doesn't love anyone! Love lasts longer than a spring and summer. Sniffing my dead flowers? Such a pity! Such a shame! I'm still here, damn it! Look at me and stay this time, you bastard! Heaven preserve me from the hard crush of a man who cuts my heart out every year and returns it to me smaller! He is a murderer. A flock of crows paused on odd numbers! I never want to see him again!"

But, as April neared, I'd be looking out the door he so often entered through, my riotous body hovering near the jamb, feeling the flowers grow and flare across my body to paint me bright like a carousel of color, like an effervescent chorus, feeling their petals whisper and flush across my chest with a new sensual abandon, decisively unfurling as the caterpillar thermometer on the outer garden wall inched up through the ides of March... when I would hardly remember what he had done. Or that he had hurt me.

Had he hurt me? Yes. And yet, I would crave him and his cunning crosswords, his carrot soup and lobster salad, his hands that danced with knives, seasonal lovemaking, and other sharp-edged things.

I'd be listening for his return.

CAT/BIRD LOVE SONG

Megan took a job as a greeting card writer when the going got miserable, after her last boyfriend left and she bought a bird, three years ago when all waitressing attempts had failed, when her customer service efforts were bleak, and when, though she had never considered herself an expert at deciding upon pithy expressions of love or romance (especially after the nasty break up that ground her heart in a blender with Tabasco), it turned out such expertise was not necessary to be a Love Sentiment Specialist. It was not as though the company didn't have hundreds of thousands of examples of successful cards on research files, so more often than not, her job was to subtly adjust pre-existing cards so the message would seem caring and heartfelt, albeit slightly different from the preceding year's crop.

After a short while, possessing no natural affinity for such leanings, she came to depend on the ability of her talking parrot, Max, who proofed her earnest attempts with subtle revision and accompanied her to work to tell her how to alter new and consoling or glorifying messages to make them sing. Max was an expert in love. And song. Like most birds.

Turns out, birds and cards went together as naturally as birds and singing.

Megan often said Max should have been CEO of Tried and True Greetings, Inc. But a few years into their work together, Max stopped flying home. He had, he admitted upon repeated questioning of his bashful looks and faraway demeanor, fallen in deep and sustaining love with a nearby cat. Never a typical parrot, able to whisper in Megan's ear, able to recite not just memorized lines about crackers or other such parrot-speak, he created his own verses for his beloveds, and, because she fed him, stroked his lovely feathers, and affirmed his self-confidence, he gave these verses to her, truncated and dumbed down for the packaged love market—the wondrous aisle of cards populating grocery stores everywhere from there to Des Moines.

She and Max, in their work, had a system. There was the issue of letting him out to relieve himself several times if the workday became too long (only occasionally, in emergencies, did he use her office trashcan, though she hated this practice), but she had a convenient window in her office and an office rather than a cubicle, unlike other colleagues, so this peccadillo had been navigated without a hitch.

Max was an African gray. The cat he loved was the same color. For weeks Megan had been hearing about this creature and did not mind, as the company's cards lately included more felines. "A theme!" she told her boss, Eugene. He liked it.

"I love you like I love my cat," one card said. This card was applauded by Eugene, heartily, since he cited many lovesick women, who bought the most cards, had cats they loved too well. Eugene thought both the target market and content was effective.

Another card Max conceived was, "Let me wrap you in the soft fur of my love. Clipped claws make for an amiable me." There was a goofy, love-struck bird on the inner flap. Megan drew the art, only a mock-up, and the bird shrugged in the cute, yet timeless, way of embarrassed shrugs.

Of course Megan heard many cat-bird ideas as Max

fell deeper in love with his cat. He said he found her fur so sleek he wanted to lie on it always. He also admired her ability to ambulate on all four legs. Apparently, she was owned by the neighbors five doors down, and he talked to her often. Her name was Pearl.

Pearl! Her claws were not clipped, but neither were his talons. Still, he said she liked when he preened and stroked her with his beak—and that she was a good size for him. One day, before leaving for work, Megan saw Max perched on Pearl's back a few yards down, and they did look oddly well-matched, gray bird on gray cat.

"She's amazing!" Max said that night. "The best creature I've ever met!"

For weeks, Megan allowed for Max's sporadic or lackluster attendance at her job so he could spend more time on what he called "the important things." He was, he said, wooing Pearl with bird poetry. But after the first three months of Max's absence, Megan's boss, observing a breech in the goldmine that had characterized her former work, began to hover at Megan's doorway, second-guessing her cards.

"Camping?" he said. "Who wants a card while they are camping? Where's the M.O. or P.O. box for that?"

I know about camping, Megan thought. *Not love shit.* But she didn't say this to Eugene, a man in his late thirties who appeared forty-five due to his moles, his scowls, and his deeply lined face. A fine sheen of sweat settled on his brow, as if he were working too hard and was always nervously displeased. One day, at the height of his resistance to her new cards, he came into her office instead of glowering from the door. He sat directly across from her to say, "What has happened to your talent, Megan? A sorry-you're-traveling card? Where are the cats?"

"I'm done with cats," Megan said. "This card is for wives whose husbands are always away on business. There are a lot of those. A big market!"

"I understand the concept," Eugene said. "But on the cover the card says, 'In a better world,' and then the inner flap reads: 'You'd be raising our children *with* me.' Maybe it's blamey. Just a little? Ya think? The italics alone!"

"I think it's accurate," Megan said, crossing her ankles.

"Cards are not about accuracy," Eugene replied, wiping his forehead with a kerchief that did nothing to dull its perma-shine. "Greeting cards are about guilt. Gift cards 101. But it has to be subtle and loving guilt. Try harder. Try again."

"You're quite petulant, encouraging, and subtle with your guilt, Eugene," Megan then said. "I prefer your mean approach."

He tried to touch her, but she pulled away. Once, two years ago, she had endured a brief fling with Eugene, when he told her he loved her beyond reason and had to have her, but now she maintained a happy professional distance. Still, she missed her parrot when Eugene came close for his encounters, suspecting as she did that Eugene had never quite dropped the torch their one kiss in the cleaning supply closet had engendered—and that he was deathly afraid of birds. It would be very like him to harbor such an irrational phobia. Birds. Paperclips. Maybe even unclean panties. Touching the door handles of strange people's cars.

"Where's your bird?" Eugene asked, as if aware of her mental dissection. "I haven't seen it in a while."

"It's gone," she said.

"Oh, good," he replied, and walked to her doorway.

"You can leave now," she said. "I need to work." Because Eugene stood there, Megan realized she was happy alone—but happier with Max. She stared out the window, hoping he would return, missing as she did the weight of him on her left shoulder and how he could probably have come up with a better reply regarding her excellent traveling card than she had because Eugene was still staring at her, over his shoulder, standing half in and half out of her doorway. "I have cards to write," she reiterated, deciding her next remark would be, "So, get the hell out."

"Do you want to move to the humor side of the greeting division?" Eugene asked, floating back in a little, leaning on the doorjamb and crossing one leg over the other.

"You think I'm funny?" Megan replied, surprised.

"No," Eugene said. "That was my little joke. But your card is terrible. Make another."

She created another in five minutes, rereading the history file, deciding that the words on the front of her original card were fine, but the inner flap would now read, "You'd be at home with me. We miss you and want you here." She did not add the rest of the sentence she conceived, which was, "instead of with the two-bit Pennsylvania hooker you left me in the suburbs to fuck."

After a moment's consideration, she left the card pleasant, sweet, but opened a word file to type into and save the full-humor, ruthless versions of her newest concepts to amuse herself with later. Regarding the revised card, she didn't know the "we" who loved the traveling man, but she pictured a family with two children, maybe a dog, a gerbil, a cat or two. Eugene loved it. She hated his happy, smug smile and the way he said, rushing back in, "That's more like it. You've got it now. Keep going!" like she had just remembered how to ride a bicycle.

She thought of an I-Hate-My-Boss-themed line for the humor department, but Eugene had only been teasing about reassignment—and besides, her ideas on this topic, she well knew, were just vengeful. She needed Max back. He kept her balanced.

When she got home that night, Max sang a lively song and only stopped warbling to announce, "Pearl the cat will now introduce me to her family. They gather to meet me tomorrow night in the alley! Pearl says I should be on my best behavior to impress them with my charm. She says she's fixed anyway, so it's not like they'd expect offspring."

"That's good, Max," Megan said. "But be careful."

"I'm going to prepare a short speech for tomorrow," Max said.

"Will you be at work with me?" Megan asked. "Even for a little while?"

"I don't really like going to your work," Max said. He groomed himself for a moment, without looking back. "I like to be outside."

In response, still watching him, Megan brushed her short brown hair, pondering the split ends evident from months of neglect. She felt her tension from the earlier discussion with Eugene return. "The boss doesn't like my cards," she admitted to Max, almost losing it. "I am happy you're in love, but I need you with me for this greeting card business if we want to keep making the rent. I need you!"

"Megan, you don't need me," he said.

"Oh, yes, I do," she replied. "I could never have gotten this job without you, all your high-flung love expressions. I don't do those... I could lose my office. I could get fired."

Max, who had been doing a fantastic parrot merengue from perch to perch, a little parrot boogie with rhythmically flapping wings and syncopating stomps, stopped dancing long enough to ask, "What did Eugene say today, Baby? I would so enjoy taking a wet shit on his head."

"He said my working-traveling-husband-card idea sucked," Megan said, and put her head in her hands. "He asked if I want to work in the humor division, but he didn't mean it! The bastard!"

Max flew to her shoulder. "Megan, we've written hundreds of cards together. Can't you guess what I might have said? Listen for my voice in your quiet place. I know the session in the closet with Eugene didn't go well, but maybe you need a new love primer. And for this, you need a new lover. Can't you even think about meeting a new love? It would be better than cooking all those casseroles when you get home. Maybe it would help."

"I hate love," she said. "I hate men! I hate greeting cards! You're my only companion and I'm happy to keep things this way. Maybe if it works out for you and Pearl, she can move in here."

"Oh, Megan, really?" Max said, unable to keep himself from a few joyful trills and a new variation on the parrot dance.

"Of course, Max," she replied. "You're special to me."

"I'll come to work with you tomorrow," he said. "We'll teach you how to get through it alone. I might need some time off to spend with Pearl for our honeymoon."

"I'll try," Megan said. "I do try. But yesterday I came up with a family vacation card after the man-traveling card and Eugene hated it, too. It was a car on the road with a family and I kept thinking about all those other ads where the kids are shrieking, 'Are we there yet?' between stops at diners and what have you. So, I thought, without a motor home, most family vacations must suck. I can only imagine what those parents are going through, a horrible time, and —"

Max tilted his head. Said brusquely, "And the card flap read?"

"The card flap read, 'let's hope your car breaks down and you can go home and get back to work soon, if you like your job.'"

Max shrugged. "Rather dark," he said. "Okay. I'll go with you for half the day."

And the next day, he helped her come up with all kinds of glowing greetings. Eugene's favorite was, "Just because we're different...doesn't mean I love you less." Eugene liked, also, the one with the cat and the bird hurtling toward each other on what appeared to be a crash course and then coming to rest as a seated pair inside the card, side by side, one's head on the other's shoulder, a big heart in the air between them, the text reading, "Opposites attract."

There was also a poignant card they designed with a bird timidly entering a family gathering of cats, an expression of terrible fear on the bird's face. On the front, it read: "Just because your in-laws seem vicious..." Then on the inside, it read, "Don't forget they love the one you love." The illustration: the bird inside, unharmed, riding a tide of cats.

Between these cards, Max preened. "We're meeting in an alley," he told Megan. "The catlike meet in alleys."

"That's good, Max," Megan said. "But, like I said, be careful."

"I am always careful, Megan," Max said. "But Pearl. Oh, Pearl. She makes my heart sing in fifty-thousand ways."

"That's inspired," Megan replied. "Let's card it."

They then designed a card with a singing bird on the front. "You make my heart sing in fifty-thousand ways," the flap read, the interior bird still singing, hand-drawn notes filling the interior. "As an added bonus for male buyers," Megan said, "there's hardly any space to write inside, which is perfect because men never know what to say about love. Not to mention the card doesn't say 'I love you,' but implies it. Men like that, too. No direct admission of feminine emotion."

"You're very clinical about this, Megan," Max said.

"That's what I am," Megan said. "Clinical."

But Max was not clinical. That night, he was beside himself. "What do I say to an in-law cat I don't know?" he asked Megan.

"What did you say to Pearl to make her like you?" she replied.

"Well, I had watched Pearl for a while and I knew we both picked the same porch to sun on. I kind of eased up. It was a slow build, speaking to Pearl. But she says her family, well, her family is not as classy as she is. A little feral, that community."

"Okay, so, you say, 'What do you like to do?' when a cool cat approaches. And then you wait and listen," Megan said. "Everyone likes to talk about themselves."

She was thinking she hoped the first cat to respond would not reply, "Eat birds," because that would not be soothing. She was thinking of her upcoming holiday office party and how Eugene had told her if she generated another few top-grossing cards, she would be considered for a VP slot. She was also thinking it was cute how into Pearl Max was, but that it was also dangerous. The whole love thing was wicked dangerous. Better not to love anyone. She fed him his favorite crackers and refilled his water. He looked particularly shiny, grooming all day as he'd been. "What do you like to do?" she repeated. "That's what you say."

"That's good," Max finally said, shaking his way out of his quiver. "What else?"

"Max," Megan said. "You're the thinker. You're the lover. I am the love failure. I don't think you're asking the right person. But you should scope out high perches in case things get out of hand."

He went that night, and all the while Megan considered what could be happening. She tried to watch TV, but could not focus. She put on her wool sweater and took a stroll. *He won't think I'm spying if I check on him, will he?* she wondered. But on her way to Max's alley, she ran right into a man who was carrying four grocery bags. His sacks fell to the ground and amidst apologizing and helping recover multiple fruits, bags of marshmallows, cans of peas and carrots, and assorted cooking accessories, Megan and the man struck up a conversation. He didn't look familiar or desirable, was about sixty to her twenty-nine, but she thought about Max and Pearl. The man spoke of saving the environment and of genocides. It was uncanny how he seemed to bring up several topics she was deeply interested in, one of which was camping, and when she was done helping him with the groceries, she took his telephone number, which he scribbled on a shopping bag's ripped corner, so she could call him if she ever craved a game of Parcheesi, which she often did.

It was part of this love optimism she felt swim up inside her, for the first time in years, that made her eager to reach Max. She would say, "Max, I met a man! He camps! He plays Parcheesi! He hates packaged cheese! Maybe I can help you write better cards now. Maybe I'm not such a creature of habit."

But when she rounded the corner of the street to the alley, she heard Pearl mewling something awful as a clutch of about ten cats moved in on an invisible prey.

"Ahhhhekggee," she heard the cornered thing shriek, and she ran at the cats, kicking them aside with her sturdy shit-kicking boots, only to find Max quivering in the space she had cleared to find him, shy a few feathers, eyes dilated, and paralyzed from motion. She picked him up, and rushed him home. She shouted angrily to Pearl, "You leave my bird alone! Don't come near him!"

It's not that she thought Pearl should be implicated in Max's near-slaughter, but he was so traumatized he could not speak for days. He sat on her shoulder and pressed so close to her in his troubled sleep, she wasn't sure he would ever be the same. She called in sick for a whole week. She bound Max's broken wing. On the eighth and ninth days, maxed out on vacation time, she took him to work, but he kept calling for Pearl. Oh, his Pearl-stripped misery!

She told him he should give Pearl up, stop thinking about her. She told him maybe Pearl should have known better than allow him to be ambushed.

He said Pearl couldn't talk to him anymore anyway. It

was forbidden, *verboten*, no more, no more. "My heart aches, Megan," he said.

"Cards, Max," Megan said. "Cards."

"Here's a card for you," he said. "Never love a cat if you're a bird. She may be fine, but her family will be what they are: Incorrigible ruffians and ruiners of love."

Megan felt him there. She made the card. Eugene hated it. After a few choice words—hers—she was fired. But she landed another job the next week as a copy clerk.

Max could stay home, looking out the window, because he had no expertise in fixing copiers. It took her a good three weeks to build up the nerve to tell him about the man she met, and the whole Parcheesi idea. When she did, a glimmer of Max's old in-love-with-love attitude came back. "How momentous!" he said. "How sublime!" But then he said, "What night did you say this happened?" And when she told him, shaking his tailfeathers, a clear sign of irritation, he said, "So this is probably an omen." And followed with, "I don't know what to tell you, Megan. You've been alone a long time, but maybe this isn't a good idea." He thought deeply for a while, watching a cat slink around outside her apartment. "I have a card idea for what you told me," he said, then. "Too bad we lost that job."

"Yeah, Max," she said, watching the cat, too, a beautiful red feline. "What's the card?"

"Front flap: Odd, magnificent love is beautiful in theory," he said. "Interior: Until you live it. Better to find a good companion."

She laughed. "Max, that wails like *West Side Story*'s 'stick to your own kind' song. Don't you think you're getting morose?"

"Oh, no, Maria. No," he sang. "You should know better."

He was grouchy after that, but his wing healed within a few weeks of the incident. And she noticed him leave again right after his full recovery. He didn't tell her about the next cat he fell in love with, despite the many wild parrots that clung to the telephone wires, singing all hours of the day to impress him (as well as coming down to say *hello).* No birds interested him. "Love has to be new every time," he said. "Fresh! It can't be anything I remember."

Then she saw him and the new red cat together, but he ceased to relate the details. *He doesn't want to jinx it,* Megan thought. Still, gray bird, red cat—that's what he did. Him with that red cat all the time. The cat's name was Trixy, at least so said the metal tab on her collar.

One day, Megan woke to find that Max had not come home. She didn't know if he'd met red cat's family. She didn't know if it went better this time. She didn't even know if he was dead in an alley somewhere, and because it was rather inconsiderate of her dear friend, Max, she was slightly miffed, if not more than a little worried.

She wanted to make him a new card, one that said, "Why didn't you listen to yourself the first time you were hurt and right about love—when I had to rescue you from a cat clutch in an alley?" That would be the outer flap. Maybe the inner flap would have a few loose feathers and a cat with puffed-out cheeks, munching happily, the contours of a bird poking out from, without penetrating, the cat's neck fur, a small dialogue bubble emanating from the cat's mouth that read, "Ooops. I'm SO sowr-ry!"

"Oh, Max!" Megan said, deciding neither Eugene nor Max would have liked the card. Megan made more stews and casseroles. Chicken, beef, and tuna! She fingered the piece of paper with the old man's name written on it: Poindexter. She regarded his telephone number and got down the Parcheesi, dusting the top with a rag. She put on a soft sweater, sprayed vanilla perfume on herself, and lit a honeydew-melon candle. She almost put some Ella Fitzgerald on the record player, before picking up the rotary table phone. *Maybe*, she thought, *the fat red cat and Max had actually eloped to some fine place and were happy, happily in love!*

But just as she was dialing Poindexter, she saw the red cat saunter past with another cat! A white cat! Fat-ass happy white cat. Where was Max?

She looked at his perches around her house, and decided she missed him again and was increasingly sad about all his failures at love, he who was so much better equipped. Considering his lack of success, she then wondered: What chance did she have? *None*, Megan ventured, staring at her swollen face with a lack of recognition and confidence. *Absolutely none.*

She took Poindexter's number, opened her window, and threw it out. It had been weeks, anyway. Poindexter wouldn't remember her. Maybe he'd met some old woman at the apartment where he lived. Regardless, he wasn't thinking about her, puny Megan and her silly fixations on birds.

And at least Megan could make a fine stew. Also, Pearl had started to visit. She could stroke the gray cat's fur, wishing it were feathers, considering and discarding every thought she'd ever had about what makes for a true alliance of the heart because Pearl still wore a feather of Max's in her collar, and sometimes Megan touched it, remembering... remembering... Thinking of the sadness of the doomed alley meeting that signaled the end of the glowing beacon of Max's unusual love for Pearl, from which Pearl had not yet recovered, but from which Megan grew to conclude there was something timeless about women who owned cats buying greeting cards.

But she was out of the business now. She had no cards to write, nor addresses to mail them to. Even her companion bird had left her, though his lovelorn cat still came around, and that love-lost mewl was something terrible to hear. An atrocity of a sound. Much louder than the sound of paper dropping from a window. Louder than silent melancholy. Louder than a woman's loneliness itself, or maybe, quite possibly, the amplified sound of someone's loneliness that could also be reissued as the soundtrack for the way an abandoned soul felt when any love was lost. Any beloved. Any memory likc a scar on the switchblade-slashed face of love, complicated by a prolonged absence of the try-again spirit—when the specificity of some old love wound could return sharply, like a fresh scalpel cut, freezing that bird, cat, or person in a willful pattern of stasis. Inertia. The memory of deep pain.

So the sound of Pearl's horrifying mewl got to Megan. It did.

Maybe Pearl was crying for her, too.

CRACK-SMOKING PARROTS

In a huge colonial on the corner of Elder, a large room had been converted for two White Capped Pionuses, Berty and Bertha, to process submissions for *Squawk Talk Literary Forum*. Due to their ages, fifteen and seventeen, Berty and Bertha were deep iridescent blue with bronze on their wing tips and white-capped facial feathers. Parts of their bellies and beneath their tails were shocking pink. They were addicted to crack cocaine.

Berty sported a soft, pinky-purple tinge on his throat. Bertha did not. In breeding season, the skin around their eyes turned as orange as Berty's favorite highlighter, which he sometimes stuck in his craw like a prime Buda reefer, but both birds, undersexed and overworked, nearly never took advantage of the season. Both were rather attractive, however, especially in the sun. And they were amongst the elite. They alone made decisions that could propel a new bird to literary stardom or acclaim.

Throughout the process, often, the dull face of their human intern, Lucy, popped through the door. She addressed them with a mixture of fear and adulation. "More?" she asked.

"Yes, more," they said. She readied the toke pipe.

If asked separately, each would say they thought her a retiring girl, not talkative enough for the business, but they kept her with them because she sent out the rejection slips cut three per page from the 8½ by 11, organized the contracts, and most importantly, tapped the rock house for the jumbos she expertly prepared in the base house. "Bag bride beamer!" Berty sometimes sputtered at her if she took too long, but otherwise, the abode and the company were comfortable.

Their room was crammed with perches and water dishes. The original wooden floor had been replaced with linoleum. On this particular afternoon as everything around them melted in the summer's heat, Berty sat on the desk, squawking over the receiver at the press: "Pronto, damnit! I need those proofs. Now-a-mundo!" Then he flew to the intercom and said, "Lucy, hang up the receiver."

Lucy obliged and walked out. One month prior, she had cleared declined stories from the floor, but today there was even more debris. Yesterday, she refreshed their water containers and put seeds and vegetables in the cups.

"Thank you, Lucy," Bertha said.

"Well aren't you Mother-fucking-Teresa," was Berty's addendum.

It was August in the venerable concrete jungle, one hundred degrees outside, but the air-conditioned interior sat at a permanent eighty. Pausing on his perch, Berty pooped, thinking about Lucy and considering her primate face. Fresh shit dribbled from his ass to splatter the opening paragraph of a recently rejected story.

With only a trace of superiority, Berty announced to Bertha, "Humans are just one step shy of the ugliest creature on the planet."

"Which is?" Bertha asked.

"The hippo, of course," Berty replied. He stretched his unclipped wings and snorted, "Scratch me, Baby. Scratch me."

When Bertha shot him a disdainful look, he went to the intercom again, said to Bertha, "*Non-toucher,*" and pushed the button with his beak to call out, "Lu-cy, Lu-cy.

Spritz me, please." He hopped onto the swing, pushed off from the low sofa, and dipped his beak toward the burning crack pipe, which was bolstered between two ballpoint pens and a narrow platform in the grooves of the desk.

"The issue," Bertha said. "Let's finish our selecting."

"Tweek, tweek," he said. "I hate this arrangement. Used to be we could prop the pipe on that ruler with a book under one end."

"Shut up, you binge-fiend! Remember the fire," Bertha trilled, but in a moment of posttraumatic stress, because she always remembered things visually and the fire was at the top of her list of remembered horrors, she began to wheeze.

"Fire, schmire," Bernie said. He preened, desiring a little foreplay, and then pressed the intercom again. "Lu-cy! Lu-cy!" he caterwauled, then squawked, "Spritz me, spritz me," in an identical cadence. "Doesn't she hear me?" he asked of no bird in particular. Then he chortled, remarking, "Even while talking, I'm such a poet."

"Cat's pee's no good today," Bertha said, staring toward the door Lucy came through. In a moment of para-noia, she tilted her head in Lucy's general direction, and said, "You think she poisoned us?"

Berty ignored her. "The issue, Bertha," he said. "For the magazine. Pay attention. We need to get it done."

Bertha scanned the room with glassy eyes. "I am focused. But I tell you, Berty, I like that new story on the desk. Yes, indeedy, I do! It's a new author, but we can fit her in. Let's do."

Berty regarded his sloppy down-feathers. "No," he said, then, "Who cares, who cares," dropping herky-jerky to the floor and climbing up the side of a chair. A blue feather fell from his breast. At that moment, Lucy entered.

She walked in, head appropriately dropped in defer-ence, and squirted Berty with the water bottle. "More spritz," he insisted. "More mist. You're nailing me here, nimrod. Can't you numskull humans do anything right?"

"I'm sorry. I'm sorry. I'm sorry," she said.

He hopped away and plashed in the birdbath. "Let me be," he said. "You're bothering me."

"Yes, Sir," Lucy said, a tremor in her voice. "I'm only... It's just—are you ready to have your room cleaned?"

"Not today," Berty said. "Where's our crack? I need it."

"Here, Sir," Lucy said. "I've got a whole brick. Do you have your selections ready for Ed?"

"In an hour," Berty replied, not enjoying her presence. "I'll buzz you."

Chastened, Lucy walked demurely from the room. "I think she's poisoning us," Bertha said aloud, to no one, but neither bird cared.

Both got down to business. Berty went to the desktop and tapped his beak on the mahogany. "Ow!" he said. "My beak hurts. Okay, one story by C. Finnius Boob, check," he said. "I have it right here." He indicated left-desk.

"Ak, Ak," said Bertha. "Didn't read it. Was it good?"

"Contract's in the mail," Berty said.

Bertha hopped to the couch and screeched in his ear, "That's not what I said. I said: Was it good?"

"Didn't read it," Berty said. "Don't need to. Did you hear me? C. Finnius Boob. I'll send it up for the O'Birdy Prize after we go to print. End of story."

Bertha pondered, and then nodded. She said, "The new piece I mentioned, 'Turning Blue'—did you like it? The one about those traumatized Amazonian parrots in the jungle—did you like it?"

Berty gave her the mad, devil-dip stare. "No name, Bertha. No name!" he squawked, starting to wheeze, himself. "Would you stop already? You know the drill. One no-name a year. We pubbed one last issue. We must stay on top of the market! Now, I need a hit."

Bertha flew to the swing, but Berty knocked her off to presumably protect her, aware she was too wasted to find the correct rhythm, and crooned, "Kisses, kisses," then got on the swing himself. He hoped to take a few hits, and then offer her his exhale in the guise of tender love pecks. His beak felt further softened by beak-rot, though, so perhaps he should stop tapping it everywhere.

"Get off the swing," she commanded from the floor. "Greedy bird! It's my turn!"

"No," he said.

"I said get off, you crack hog," she replied. "You Gick monster! The rock's almost gone."

She flapped her wings and knocked him to the chair. When she began to swing, as he expected she would, she knocked over the crack pipe, and the burning rock made yet another mark on the desk.

"Lucy! Come quick!" he shrieked into the intercom. "Dumb bird!" he said to Bertha.

"Not at all," Bertha replied, but from her tone, he knew her feelings were hurt.

"Lucy?" Berty called again. "Get that rock burning steady. We need now-time inspiration!" Everyone knew White Capped Pionuses frequently viewed crack cocaine as both an aphrodisiac and a drug that allowed for heightened analysis and vision, but there was a point of excess in anything.

"Let's finish the Table of Contents, Berty," Bertha then said. Silent as eggs in a nest, Lucy entered, picked up the pipe, and replaced it, after adding a new supply of the hard rock. "Light it and leave, please," Berty said.

"Yes, Sir," Lucy said.

"All right, Bertha, let's get the TOC ready. We can't play all day."

"You were saying?" Bertha replied.

"One article by E.G. Whitaker, prominent Macaw

Essayist of the early twenty-first century, known for his fasci-
nating studies of parrot scholarship, check," said Berty.

"Fine, fine," Bertha replied.

"Two features picked by Ed. One classic reprint. Five
unnecessary and expensive writing workshop ads, three
MFA ads, and two contest ads. Three poems by those
horrible Lucindacaw sisters! Trendy! Gimmicky! But because
the readership loves them. And another story by—who was
the other story by? I can't remember."

He beaked through the pile on the desk and plucked
out a few he then opted against, discarding on the floor. "Ah,
Tunesha Reed—that wonderful piece about mango!"

"Fluff," Bertha said. "Pure fluff. Feathers on the wires.
She couldn't write her way out of an open cage."

"Harold Pecker is her agent," Berty reminded Bertha,
hoping to dispense two owed favors with a single dispatch.
"So, she's in."

Bertha again commenced to wheeze.

Bertha is dialed out, Berty thought, asking, "What in
Bird Tut's name is wrong with you?" He grinned, loving to
reference Bird Tut, the toppler of the human *ancien regime*
and reigning martyr of birddom who was said to have
poisoned state officials before flying into a burning bush. He
started snorting in hilarity.

"I want to select the stories I like," Bertha replied. "Ak,
Ak, Ak."

Berty approached her, scratched her back, and said,
"You're going soft, Bertha. What will these no-names do for
us?" He took another hit from the pipe.

"What if we discover them and they make us more
famous?" Bertha moaned. "We could reach out to rural,
disenfranchised birds." A plaintive note had entered her
voice as it often did when she decided upon some eclectic
but non-functional empowerment agenda.

"You always get sninky when we finalize the TOC,

Bertha," Berty said.

"I just want to pick what's good," Bertha said.

"Not in this business, Baby," Berty said. "We need to sell magazines. Look at the demographics. Like I said, one no-name a year."

Bertha then dropped into her mournful pose, neck bent, so he hopped to the intercom and said, "Lucy, spritz needed for Bertha, right now."

Lucy entered and hurried to comply, but the spray nozzle was set to *squirt* rather than *mist* when she first aimed, so a projectile of water hit Bertha squarely in the tail-feathers. Bertha set to wheezing again, fury in her eyes.

"I'm so sorry, Bertha. I am!" Lucy said, wringing her hands, dropping the water bottle.

Bertha flew around the room, squawking. "Twit intern, twit intern! Squawk! Ak, Ak, Ak."

Lucy collapsed in tears.

"We don't want your drama, Mama," Berty said. "Get back to work."

"You both want so much from me," Lucy cried. "You don't listen to my ideas. I'm just a crack-slinging maid. Oh, why did I ever take this job?"

"Say you're sorry to our girl here, Bertha," Berty said, then, attempting magnanimity, but Bertha, wild-eyed and enraged, still flew around in a merciless circle, pecking at Lucy's dress and arms. "Say you're sorry, Bertha," Berty squawked again, more authoritatively. "We're not vultures, after all. No need to traumatize the less fortunate. Lucy is our friend. Remember, she is our friend!"

Bertha immediately stopped circling. She flew to the couch and said, quite cross, "How dare you call me a vulture, Berty?"

"You were doing that *vulture* thing," Berty said, blinking rapidly. "What else can I say? I know a *vulture* thing when I see it. It's not a sparrow thing. Not a cockatoo thing.

No, that was *distinctly* vulture."

Both birds glared. Finally, Bertha turned her head toward Lucy and uttered a quiet apology, "I'm sorry, human."

"Leave!" Berty then said. Lucy fled the room.

When Bertha settled on the perch, Berty went to soothe her. "It's for the birds, this business," he said, meaning the publication targeted a vast array of birds, from lovebirds to bald eagles, and only a limited market existed beyond the cherished aviary known as Earth. "Take a hit," he went on. "You'll feel much better."

Bertha subsumed her wheezing. "I can't. You have me all atwitter," she said. "But I love that story about the poor Amazon parrots. Remember when they used to bind our feet with tacky blue bracelets?" Bertha asked.

It was then Berty happily noticed the orange around her eyes. "You're sentimental right now," he said. "Emotional. We need to mate. That will take your mind off things." He looked at her and cocked his head, then cockled suggestively.

"No!" she said.

"Tight feathers," he said. "*Non-toucher!* Smoke more rock!"

"Pay attention to what I articulate," Bertha replied. "I like the no-name story and I want to use it. I think it really speaks to the experience of the poor, disenfranchised bird. We were poor once, Berty. Remember when we had to scavenge for food at the outdoor shopping mall?"

Berty did not rebut, but was thinking the period she referenced was short-lived and should not qualify. It was a lark. An anomaly. Once, both had flown away from home together, true, but they were only without the comforts of a private birdbath for three days or less. Also, Bertha's idea of poor was seeds without veggies or veggies without seeds. She did not understand the poor of other drug-addicted birds who did not get top-of-the-line smack. Truthfully, she had no grasp of the concept. "I'm not doing it," he said. "For the life of the journal."

"But, the story is so good!" Bertha argued.

"Good, schmood! We can't publish every Beak, Talon, and Tweeter just because they're good. Who cares about good? Now, like I said, Bertha, take another hit and calm down."

Dutifully, Bertha climbed on the swing. "Why do we use this swing?" she asked him, then. "I always thought it was stupid. I just don't see the reason for it."

"Bertha, I've told you before, but here I go again. We swing so we take in oxygen as we smoke the pipe," Berty said. "For our own small removals. Remember how I said the drug keeps our brains functioning, but we must have oxygen too?"

His bowels felt loose. He let another shit, accompanied by loose flatulence, fly. Bertha glanced over the thousands and thousands of stories on the floor, besmirched with poop. "Each of these is another broken heart," she said, reflectively. "We break hearts for a living, Berty. All day long. Doesn't that sicken you?"

"Smoke up, White Ghost Mama," Berty said. "It's okay. It's okay."

"All right," she said, heaving toward the pipe, but with her energy depleted from the vulture-esque circling, she could not get near enough the swing, nearly collapsing with exhaustion and despair.

"Kisses?" Berty asked, gently.

Feeling dizzy, Bertha moved over. He hopped to the swing and propelled them forward. After a few selfish drags, after which Bertha looked ready to kick him off, he leaned toward her and blew smoke into her mouth. "Kisses," he said. Their hard tongues touched lightly. Her eyes glazed further. "We've got to do what we've got to do, Bertha" he said.

"Okay," she replied.

Triumphantly, he spied the story she liked on the right-hand corner of the desk. As she watched, he climbed the mahogany fixture and sent the parcel of paper flying to the piles below with a scrape of his talon.

Silently, it fell. But this was not enough. He needed to kill her want for it, so he leapt to the floor and proceeded to shit across the title page. "Try not to think about it," he said, but he needn't have worried because by then Bertha only stared at the mirror across from the perch, watching herself with a bemused expression, and replied: "You know, Berty, we could have a few chicks and get away from this mess. I'm beginning not to care what we print." She wondered how old she looked to the birds on the street, and crooned a sad, old tune, before nuzzling his neck.

"We are," he said, "the most important decision makers of the century." He dipped his claw in ink. He then scratched out the TOC as he planned to release it. Clutching the paper tightly, he flew to the intercom, calling Lucy several times. But then he saw her on the porch, tears streaming down her face, wheezing, if humans could be said to do so, in what appeared to be a fit of anxiety. He tapped his beak on the window. "Lucy, it's ready to fax," he shouted. "Another winning issue. Come and get it."

Dutifully, Lucy wiped her face and walked inside, just as Berty succeeded in climbing atop Bertha. Ignoring him, Lucy dialed the fax, the rapid bleeps accompanied by the sound of parrots mating. She then called the drug dealer.

"Yes, double the Sugar block," she said. "In fact, make it Tragic Magic this time. I'll need that right away—and a hot compress to get me through this week... I'm so sorry about your bitches-and-hos trouble. I'll come to you."

As the dealer replied with something she couldn't quite make out, Lucy tilted her head to get a better look at the birds going at it in their shared room and then turned away as she caught Berty's eye and he winked.

She hung up. Lucy imagined having a rational conversation with LeDoner, the dealer, though this was never possible. "Yes, always for the birds," she'd say, as if he cared who she bought the shit for. "Two editors. Important editors. What did you think they do?" She surveyed Berty flapping his wings and contorting in an attempt to keep balanced above Bertha, who then promptly fell off the swing.

Berty, utilitarian then, lurched to the floor to be with her.

"Oh, my!" Lucy said, before redirecting her attention to the imaginary conversation she continued with her hand posed like she held a phone beside her ear. "Yes. I'm just the stupid intern. They rejected my story, 'Turning Blue,' an hour ago, which was about parrots in the Amazon. Berty shat upon it, and now I need to leave. Soon. Yes, as soon as possible." She hung up her fake phone, which looked like *I Love You* in sign language, and closed in on the mating birds.

"Berty," she said, "I would like to resign. Can I get a letter of recommendation?"

"What?" Berty asked, still focused on Bertha and attempting a big finish.

"I was hoping for a letter of recommendation," she said. "Because I've worked hard, but I have to go now."

"Then why don't you make yourself one?" he replied. "Go to the computer and print off the template, but dear God, girl, don't bother me right now. Maybe I'll sign your letter sometime next year... Bertha, we could use her for another year, couldn't we?"

"Sure, Honey," Bertha said, her glassy eyes examining the ceiling.

"All right then," Berty asserted. "I may even provide

phone references for you then. So, it's settled. Just go away, Lucy. Go do whatever ridiculous things you human interns do. Play with the slush pile. Burn it. Throw it up in the air... As Bertha can attest, what we do is of the utmost importance for the prolonged erudition of the masses! Only pre-empted success breeds continuous success. I have no time for such quibbling interruptions! Ack! Aaack! A-ay-ah-ak!"

At these remarks, Lucy went to the computer and printed off her own reference. She stacked all stories and SASEs neatly on her desk. Then she got the crack, came back, and put not one but two rocks in the pipe, sure to get Berty and Bertha so high they could no longer converse or work. When they sat side by side for several moments after new tokes, without demanding a single spritz, she left the room.

In the other part of the office, she had an idea. Inside each self-addressed envelope of the slush pile's top fifty packets, she neatly folded an acceptance note printed on the magazine's stationery, along with a contract, and sealed these missives with Berty's signature, which she knew well by now because he had insisted one afternoon, after one of Bertha's zealous fits, that *Squawk Talk* should send more personal rejection letters, so she had signed his name so many times even he could not tell his handiwork from hers.

Lucy dropped all the letters in the mailbox, and just to amuse herself, she'd also written a lovely acceptance letter from Berty to herself, adding a glowing note about her personal talent while she mused self-indulgently about using it as a referral or for the joy of receiving something in her box other than a bill in the near future—something that, maybe, for a split second, would give her the high it seemed she was always setting up for them.

She mused too that, no matter how beautiful or powerful they were, Bertha and Berty would have a hard time explaining to all those authors that they were so cracked out they didn't know what had happened on the day the contracts and memos were mailed. Maybe one or two writers would be lucky or litigious enough that the skeezer birds, so hot off the horn, would have to publish them or risk the damning infamy of appearing not to have known what they were doing while they addressed the growing white slalom of slush from the hopeful disenfranchised. The very thought made Lucy smile.

And, really, who cared what happened after that?

THE GIRL WITH THE RAZOR-BLADE SKIN

Ginger Frank didn't start out covered in metal. One August, standing in the sweltering Texas heat that bordered on a hundred and ten degrees, the heavyset girl in the peach and ivory dress looked down to find silver emerging on her arms, on her legs, silver bulging like stretch marks from every soft parcel of her skin.

There were no blades at first; such things would come later—just the presence of horizontal lines like thin-striped mercury across the peachy forefront of her presence and underneath her drowsy frock. After one sudden, mind-blowing current of pain she initially thought was a seizure or a heart attack, she spontaneously emitted such radiance, glowing in her zebraed way, gilded unevenly as a toddler-tinseled Christmas tree.

To those who looked upon her, it was as if there were a screen in front of only the shape of her plump body and that screen, or the outline in the shape of her, was determined to light up much of her frame with silver slivers landing everywhere, except her face and the palms of her hands. Those at the Saturday baseball game took note. "You sure are shiny," her date, Rydell, said. He had just text-messaged his other, thinner girlfriend to say he'd be meeting her soon.

"She's silver," said a full-figured woman named

Carolina State in a pair of navy shorts and a nautical blouse. "Girl just graduated high school in June and now turns silver! What's the encore? What a funny elephant of events." She had many times slighted Ginger's scrawny half brother, Petey, whose inability to hit made the team lose, and Ginger had long thought her a windbag, though she had never said it aloud. Today, after the elephant-events remark, the virago merely said, "Oh, Lordy, yes, Ginger Frank, you are glowing like a sterling star."

It was true that Ginger glimmered. Not that her blades poked out fully then, for this extrusion would emerge a few days later, but in that moment, as Ginger stood on the bleachers staring out over the ballfield, the reflected glare of her was so pronounced that even the tiny outfield boys looked up from their clover-picking to point and gape. Petey, at bat, turned his helmeted head and missed his third strike. "You see that! You see that!" Carolina announced. "He needs a pinch hitter!"

No one paid attention. It seemed even the umpire, once he saw Ginger, could not stop staring at the metallic ooze of lines lingering benignly on the surface of her skin, and although there was pain during this initial surge, Ginger found the premise of such a shining delightful. She was like the Statue of Liberty of the Pee-Wee Park! A silver star!

As she left with Petey, all eyes were on her, but at home, when her unsentimental, televangelistically addicted mama spied her, she shook her head. "Ginger," her mama said. "Now, what have you done? How will you get through beauty school with this defect? What is this muck all over you?" She hovered around the girl like a bellicose gnat, touching the lines on Ginger's shoulder.

Ginger shook with a pleasure almost sexual.

"Dirty girl!" her mama said, and slapped her.

"I can't help it," Ginger muttered. Each bit of metal was sensitive, like there were nerve endings on every exposed line. "I'm not dirty. I'm just sensitive. And I'm only going to beauty trade school so you can afford med school for Petey, remember?" Ginger had long since stopped arguing about how she wanted to go to college, though she doubted any medical school would take her foolish half brother.

Even now, the little worm barely knew how to tug his own organic rope, but this beauty school/med school compromise had been arranged years before, after Ginger's mother married Petey's father, Gregory. "You won't hold me back, girl," Ginger's mother had said just before the wedding. "I need this man, though he didn't want me with children, and he took me anyway! So be glad we still support you. Trade school's good enough. You can be a beautician, make people pretty for weddings. Don't think you'll ever get married, but look how nice Gregory is. He lets me keep you, don't he? Even after Petey was born. And Petey will be working at that hospital on the hill. That's good enough. You admit, that's good enough..."

Ginger winced.

"Acknowledge me," her mother said, to which Ginger replied, in a small voice, "That's good enough." She had been a young child when the good enough question was first posed, though she found it would come up again and again. And later, it was kind of like how metal braces were good enough when Petey got Invisalign, and generic glasses were good enough when her mother got colored contacts, and a boyfriend with other women was good enough despite the fact he was no looker. But Rydell kept her, too, even though she was just who she was, so she imagined he was a fine man to date, despite that she often despised him.

Besides, all less-than-ideal aspects of her own life were things her mother seemed to desire thankfulness for, so Ginger, retiring for the most part, *obliged*. It could have been her origins in semi-squalor where a soft voice was scarcely heard above the raucous shouts of the classless people near her house. It could have been her training. But as the child of her mother's embarrassing teenage pregnancy, she did not often bemoan injustice. She said nothing when her mother and Gregory hadn't bothered to attend her recent high school graduation ceremony, despite her valedictorian status.

And Ginger's own father could never come. He was out in the ozone. A bum, her mother often said, sometimes adding that he was likely out ghosting the train tracks south of Albuquerque so he could find "some place or person more familiar," but speculating, as her mama did, that it was more likely he hoped to get hit by a train and then sue the railroads for "disability for life," which was her mother's favorite scenario. It was, for her mama, a fantasy situation. How many times Ginger had heard her say, "If only I'd lose a finger in one of those racks. Disability for life! It happened to a gal who knows a gal I know. Now this other gal just sits outside her trailer all day drinking lemonade and listening to her radio. Does her nails out there and everything."

Yet the act of leaving her finger prone in a dry cleaner's rack and depressing the finger-severing button was not yet one her mother had pursued. She disliked heavy bleeding, disliked the thought of injury that may come with a severed artery. It was as though Ginger's mama imagined that, with a yanked-off finger, her hand would suddenly squirt ruby blood on all the surrounding plastic-wrapped clothing and fixtures, and she might somehow land on the floor, where no one would find her for days. Never mind the dry cleaner's heavy foot traffic. Never mind that her mother had a mouth loud as a siren, screamed at the drop of a paper-cuffed hanger, and that right next door was a man who virtually lived in his shop of Indian sweets, snoozing most nights at his register as if trying to save himself some rent.

Another thing her mother feared was that even if she took the chance and managed to cut off her finger, some doctor might reattach it such that it would droop from her hand, all function lost yet no disability gained. "Then I'd be Limp Finger!" her mother had asserted, but now, in the living room, regarding her strange daughter, she said, "This silver skin is God telling you something, Girl. Notice how he didn't give you gold."

Ginger kindly refrained from mentioning that God was always both the bad guy and the good guy for her mama refrained, too, from making sardonic comments about how the only religion-based shows her mother watched were those featuring the sexy men the faux zealot often referred to as the "handsome part of religion."

Her mama did espouse a plangent fervor for their actions when they bent over to retrieve dropped objects, for example, or pleaded for her soul with large, wet eyes, saying: "Come to Jesus, my child!"

"I'll come to Jesus, Pastor Tom!" her mother would shout.

But now, in response to the metal, "I don't think this silver is God talking to me," Ginger said, omitting to mention that the shining did make her feel sexy.

"It is God on a mission!" her mother then exclaimed. "Telling you to fit in more. Not to make things worse!"

"How is God telling me to fit in more by making me stick out?" Ginger asked, agitated, but her mother had no answer, bowing her head in apparent prayer, and it was during this conversation that Ginger began to feel her heart race. Another surge of pain and her silver lines emerged more prominently, initiating a chilling sensation on her skin. Tingling. "Oh, wow!" Ginger said, again feeling the surge of both pain and pleasure. "I need to call Shelley. Oooh. Mama. My! That's some feeling. They're pushing out. More."

"You've really done it now," her mother said. "Fine.

Go call the gimp."

It was in this moment that Gregory entered. "What'd the dumb little bitch do?" he asked, sauntering past holding his daily forty and a racetrack rag.

"Look at her," her mother said. "She grew a bunch of tin! See it?"

"I've done nothing," Ginger said. "I'm just being me."

"Well, where'd all that metal shit show up from then, huh?" Gregory asked.

"I was at Petey's game with Rydell," Ginger replied. "Watching him. Cause you asked me to. I was standing there. Doing nothing. And then this happened." She took the moment to spread her arms and turn in a circle with her hands way out at her sides.

"She got that shit all over her, Honey," Gregory remarked. "It's gross."

"There are worse things," Ginger said. She then reflected that it had been grosser, for example, when Rydell had looked at her for all of ten seconds earlier in the day at the park and then picked his nose and wiped a booger on the underside of the bleachers, his mouth hanging open as if he were developmentally disabled.

"And why did this happen?" her mother pressed, Gregory's prurient interest creating a new wave of her own. "And where's Rydell?"

"He's at his other girlfriend's," Ginger said, thinking it was a special calling of her mother's to ask ludicrous questions with no foreseeable decent response. All her life, such questions came, but a quick, logical, irrefutable reply was usually the best answer. "This happened," Ginger said, meditatively, staring at her silver, at her shine, "because I wanted it to." She pulled a satin ribbon through her long hair, luxuriating in her arms' movement and the resultant sensation. "It happened because I was meant to glow!" she then said, warming to the idea. "I always hoped I'd be special. Now I am, Mama. That's why! It's a rainbow-touched miracle from the mercy of the grace of God." The last part was a catch phrase from one of her mother's televangelist shows.

"You're not fucking special, Girl," Gregory replied, taking a swig from his forty, before lighting a menthol Camel and blowing the smoke toward the back door. "Who told you that you were fucking special?"

Ginger turned away. "I think I am special," she said. "I know I am."

"Shut up," Gregory replied. "I know you're not. Not in any way."

"Yeah, you're special, all right, Ginger!" Petey chimed in, entering the living room in his dirt-smudged uniform. "Special Ed!"

Though she wanted to say, "Shut up, Petey! You can't even bat!" or, "Be quiet, you little thug," she remained silent. "More to be pitied than censured," she said to herself, as if it would soothe the shame of his meanness. She looked down at her metal stripes. "Petey, be nice to me," she said, like talking to a slow boy. "Because I'm nice to you."

Petey pulled a face. "Ginger-Schminger, you're the family loser," he said, in a tone frighteningly like Gregory's. "We never even wanted you. Why don't cha go find your own father? You don't even know where he is, you freak!"

At this, Ginger ignored Petey. She grabbed the phone, ran down the hall, and called Shelley. "So, Shell... Can you come out? I've got these metal stripes all over me. I need you to look at them."

"No way!"

"Way."

"I have to see them," Shelley said. "Meet me at the end of the block. What color are they?"

"Gray... No! Silver."

By the time Ginger arrived, Shelley had already maneuvered her wheelchair under the giant fig tree on the corner and settled to eat a cheddar-and-mayo sandwich. She'd tucked a napkin into the collar of her white poplin blouse, squinting toward Ginger's house, holding her sandwich aloft, before shouting, "Look at you, Ginger! Holy freaking cow! That's amazing!"

"I kind of like it," Ginger replied.

"I way like it," Shelley said. "Gorgeous. Are those, like, blades?"

"No. I don't know. But they're poking out more now."

"Neat," Shelley said. "Can I touch them?"

"Sure."

But Shelley cut her finger. "They're fine when you stroke down, but don't go up!" she then said, using the napkin at her throat to staunch the blood. "Those things are sharp! Ginger, you're like a shark! How neat! How'd this happen?"

"I don't know," Ginger said.

"But are you going to beauty school like that?"

"Do I have a choice?"

Shelley looked longer at the shiny stripes, before saying, "You think you can do hair like that, all cutty-slicey?"

"I'm going to try," Ginger replied. "Wish me luck."

Later that week, Ginger went alone to the trade school to pick up some registration papers. When Rydell came to retrieve her, he touched her clothed arm and said, "You're too weird for me now."

On this day, she wore a series of wrappings covering all but her face and palms, which remained unaffected. "What?" she asked.

"You're too weird," he said again. "I thought about it and I was willing to sleep with you when you were fat, but this silver thing... It's too much. I came here to break up with you. Was gonna do it in the car, but you can't get in like that. You'll tear up the leather."

As she walked to the school that morning, the sharps

from her skin must have sliced the fabric because she now looked down and could see glinting metal through her skirt. In fact, all her clothes were holey, from her shoulders to her toes, her leather shoes showing slight rents.

She walked home. Halfway there, her shoes fell from her feet. She left them on somebody's lawn and felt fine; the loss of Rydell was only a little disappointing. *I wonder if I'll be like a superhero*, she thought, then. *A naked, metallic superhero. This is like the first fifteen minutes in some movie—where the superhero loses everything to discover their quest. Do I have a quest?*

She went home and studied herself in the bathroom mirror. She noted with concentration how the metallic pieces now extended from her flesh by a good three-quarters of an inch. They covered her breasts and pubic region, almost like some kind of armor that stretched from her neck to her toes. "I am so sexy!" she said.

In the places where her long brown hair had fallen over the ends of sharp new growth, whole chunks had been shorn and were missing. With her index finger, she tested the edge of a piece of metal below her breast. She pressed harder. It made her bleed.

From the living room, her mother, as usual, practiced half-assed Pilates on DVD and explored every financially advantageous angle regarding how this new "predicament" of Ginger's could make them rich. "What if the metal is platinum?" she asked Gregory, who sat on the couch high-lighting his racing paper. "We could strip and sell it."

"Heck, yeah. I'll pull the shit off," Gregory agreed. "I've got some pliers. It might be worth a bundle. You could quit your job!"

"I'm not sure if it would injure her," her mama said.

"Naw, it won't," he argued. "But it's probably not platinum."

Ginger got in the shower to avoid the living room.

The water felt excellent. She emerged glistening, regarding herself in the steamed glass, wondering if she should walk out in only her natural armor or wearing clothes to be instantly shredded. Naked, she didn't feel indecent. The growth of the blades had all but covered her nude skin—so would her presence in this way, largely silver, be considered obscene?

She was surprisingly unafraid, even contemplating her new superhero name: Blade Girl? The Silver Streak? She laughed. Fearlessness was new. Her whole life had been fear. Now, her family talked about ripping her apart and, even without apparel, she felt sanguine.

Moments later, when she ventured into the living room and Gregory came after her with the pliers, she still felt calm, calm even as he pulled hard on one piece of metal below her left breast, though she yelped in pain, and said, "Stop it. Please, Gregory!"

"We need the money from that metal," he replied.

"You don't even know what the metal is," she said. "Mama called it tin yesterday! It's worthless!"

Lucky for her, her mother was observant as well as greedy because just then she said, "She's right, Gregory! Look! Ginger's tarnishing. Aw, man! That metal's not high--end."

For different reasons, this was terrible news for everyone, but especially Ginger. "I'm tarnishing?" she asked.

"It's yellowing below your thigh," her mama replied.

Ginger looked down at the metal. There were traces of other-than-silver color, like she'd peed herself.

"Maybe we should get the un-yellow parts quick," Gregory said. "Before they go bad."

"No!" Ginger replied. But as he came closer, she did the only thing she could think of, which was to wrap her metallic arms around him. He writhed and shrieked, self-cutting on her blades as he attempted to free himself. "Stop struggling," Ginger responded. "Stop now."

She wanted to say, "Shut up, you pussy. You wimp. You low-life happiness stealer who has held me down so long I had to grow metal to protect myself!" But she wasn't sure of the reason for the metal's connection to him, not sure enough for such an announcement anyhow, so instead she said the mildest thing she could conceive, which was: "Gregory, if you'll calm down, please, I will let you go, but I cannot allow you to use those pliers again."

"Let me go! Let me go!" he shouted, hitting and kicking, but she was shielded by the silver. He didn't try for her face.

"I'll let you go when you stop fighting," she said. "Let me see you calm." Holding him tenderly as if to give the care or nurturing he'd so often refused her in childhood, she allowed his struggles to cause wounds. "Tell me you won't come near me again with those pliers and I'll open my arms," she bargained.

"I want to kill you, Ginger," he replied. "I've always hated you." He cried more and shrieked as his blood dripped down his arms and legs while he struggled, refusing to say what she asked, and his refusal was oddly satisfying for Ginger, as much as she wanted to let him go. She realized she actually enjoyed holding him like a baby bird as he struggled, wept, and cursed because he was so newly powerless, so she said then, quiet as a librarian-in-training, "Just stop thrashing. Gregory, stop. It will be then that I release you."

He stopped moving. When she let him go, he was bleeding all over and fell to the floor.

"Oh, Gregory! Oh, Gregory!" her mother said, tears welling from her eyes, black eyeliner flowing in jagged streaks. Her mother took him to the hospital, praying, "Please, Jesus! Please, Jesus!" and Ginger replied to the quiet air in the house after they left, "Say, Mama: Gregory don't have nothing to do with Jesus," before she walked to the bathroom and showered again.

Afterward, both parents left her alone for several weeks. Even Petey was pretty quiet.

When Ginger sat on the bleachers at Petey's games, some regarded her with fear, but none were cruel any longer. Maybe they had seen the headlines about Gregory: *Local Man Hospitalized for Three Hundred and Fifty-Three Cut Wounds Caused by Razor-Edged Stepdaughter's Flesh.* Either way, her peers at school avoided her, she had no test customers willing to let her work on them, and each day, she called Shelley to bemoan for hours her lonely state.

In the throes of her isolation, she began to doubt hers was a superhero talent after all. The scales were great, but how would she ever touch somebody? Could she touch Shelley, she asked, but a hug given with one person sitting very still while the other wraps careful arms around them without tightening toward the torso can hardly be called a hug—and hardly solved Ginger's exile from her entire community. To make matters worse, she felt growth on the insides of her cheeks. "Shelley," she whispered. "I think the metal's growing in my mouth! How will I eat? Or talk? I have to get rid of this!"

Shelley thought long and hard. "I have an idea," she replied. The two of them sat under the fig tree. Between bites of another sandwich, while Ginger listened, Shelley expounded. "You're like a biological nightmare at this point, Ginger. Don't cry. I'm thinking maybe that metal is iron. You know? From your blood. And I'm thinking this whole thing is some sign meant to protect you from yourself. Think about it. You never say a mean thing to anyone, have never said a mean thing, and maybe you should. That family of yours is horrible. Maybe you're like a lizard or some other creature that adapts. You won't keep yourself well-defended, so your body does it for you. Test it! Say what you mean for a while," Shelley said. "Even Gregory can't hurt you! You've seen that. So do what you want for a change. It may be the only way."

The next morning, after Petey dumped her cereal bowl on the table, Ginger started to say it was fine, she'd clean it up—almost said, "Don't worry. I'll get it," but the razors inside her mouth felt poised to grow, so she said, instead, "Petey, please clean up that mess you just made and get me another bowl."

Petey laughed.

"I mean it," she said.

"Shut up, you loser!" Petey replied.

"Do it," she said, putting her soft hand on his shoulder. "Now."

He was about to refuse, staring at him decently as she was, but her wrist must have glanced his shirt because a red bloom flowered on his shoulder. "Oh, Petey," Ginger said. "I'm sorry. I cut you. You're bleeding. You'll have to change."

His injury wasn't severe, but the blood made a dramatic stain, so when Petey stood up to view himself in the mirror above the dining room table, he began wailing.

For an instant, all metal on her body seemed to shake and quiver. "I'm sorry," she called down the hall again as he ran, but Petey did not reply. Still, within an hour, he was back, had cleaned the mess on the table and brought her a new cereal bowl, alternately avoiding her eyes and looking at her like she were more terrifying than his comic book villains.

Not long later, when Gregory said, "Ginger, get your useless ass off the couch and grab me a cold beer," she nearly did exactly as she was told—but stopped. She didn't need him.

"Get your own beer, Gregory," she said. She also went to the beauty school and returned the paperwork to disen-roll. She had other options now.

Her mother was furious: "You dropped out? Why?

How could you?"

Ginger thought about lying, but instead replied: "I'm going to the University of New Mexico, Mama. I was accepted for the winter quarter and am applying for emergency aid." She decided she would soon move, maybe even before the quarter began, and leave this household behind. The metal that had begun to feel like a hard shell seemed looser now, though no less dangerous. The layers appeared to rise and fall, fluttering. "I'd like your support, Mama," Ginger went on, "but I don't require your money." She'd been saving for two years from her high school jobs. Besides, she could find another job. She was a good worker.

"The metal does feel a little thinner," Ginger admitted to Shelley that night. "Maybe you're on to something."

And when she ran into Rydell the next day, she discovered he'd been dumped by all three of his other girlfriends. He told her, like it was a favor, "I'll take you back on one condition: Don't tell anyone we're going out," but she did not agree. He was not, she decided, good enough.

She looked through him, opened her mouth, and said, "No, thanks, Rydell."

To aid in her recovery, she became less self-effacing, but even after another week, when the razors still clung to her body, she was beside herself. "Shelley, it's hard to be so honest all the time. I'm doing what I'm supposed to and the metal thins, but it won't go away."

Though Shelley was comforting, in the quiet hours of Ginger's new insomnia, Ginger began to ask herself questions like: What would a razorblade make love to? How would a razorblade have children? If Ginger wasn't destined for family life after college, what should she be doing with her new and incredible state? Would she be a parade dancer? A government assassin? Had her real dad gone through anything similar?

"You're unlearning a lifetime of being too sweet,

sweetheart," Shelley said. "Keep going. What else did you always want to do before you left home? Maybe that's the answer."

That night at home, mama went on and on about various scenarios for "disability for life" while Gregory watched NASCAR and Petey flung a plastic sticky toy at the sliding door, which *thwapped* the glass continuously like a palm smack-smacking a young face.

With her new policy of confronting problems rather than avoiding them, Ginger tried to be helpful. "Standing behind a car at Wal-Mart and hoping to get hit is not a good idea, Mama."

"Then I wonder if I could get disability for life by drinking some chemicals from under the sink at the dry cleaning store. Wonder how many organs it would injure," her mama said.

"I have an idea," Ginger replied. "Tomorrow morning, follow me, Mama; I'll help with your original plan. I think I can make you happy."

Upon reviewing the fervent glimmer in Ginger's eyes, eye-glimmer a big persuader in her book, her mama agreed. When the sun came up, Ginger and her mother left for the dry cleaner's. "You know how to do all of this?" her mother asked, after opening the store, pulling groups of cleaned clothes into plastic bags until the hangers poked from the tops. She rubber-banded them together, before saying, "Keep watching me, sweetheart. That college thing may not work out, and then where will you be?"

It was hot in the store. Ginger felt sweat drip down her side. "Get that gray sweater," she told her mother. "It's on this ticket."

Her mother moved the machine. Ginger handed the sweater to a customer.

The store was empty for a moment. "Now put your finger in that hole where the hanger goes, Mother," Ginger said. "Remember, do it without fussing."

Her mother did.

"That's good, Mama," Ginger said, "Now, push the GO button." She spoke calmly and sweetly.

"No," her mama said. "I can't. I couldn't possibly."

"You know you want to. Do it," Ginger replied. "All these years of talking about it, are you ever going to? And when will it all be good enough? Disability for life! Stick your whole finger in now! Do it, Mama. Push the button. Do it for Jesus! Jesus will love you forever." She maintained eye contact with her mother, staring deep into her squinty green eyes. Her mother's resolve wavered. "Hit it!" Ginger then enthused, and her mother, as if mesmerized by a snake charmer, some streetwise vagabond, slammed her opposing palm on the round dial.

There was hollering and copious blood.

"Go tell Aunt Rhody," Ginger sang, ripping the plastic from the sweater package and wrapping the soft part of the denuded garment around her mother's hand. "Go tell Aunt Rhody. Go tell Aunt Rhody—the old, gray goose is dead." She told her mother to keep singing the rounds until the ambulance arrived. "Hang in there, Mama," she said. "They're coming. I do hope you're right about losing a finger. Do you want me to hide it so it can't be reattached? Tell me, yes or no?"

"Give me my damn finger," her mother said. It was surprising how very docile she grew—seated on the cement floor, weeping, with an odd smile emerging from her pained face every so often—when Ginger handed over the finger. Docile, and determined. Ginger knew her mother's next move would be to call one of her talk radio or TV shows from the hospital.

Just then, before the ambulance came screaming up, a little old lady with silver-violet hair walked in carrying three pairs of brown slacks. "We're closed for the day," Ginger said, grabbing a pretty purple dress from a nearby hook, one that nearly echoed the rinse-dyed shade of the customer's hair. She looked at her mother again and walked out, hollering back, "I'm looking for my father, now. See you later!" The old lady still had not left. Her mama would play the scene for attention, Ginger surmised. Sure enough, an animated conversation went on behind the counter before Ginger even turned the corner, but as she walked into the afternoon sun, she felt lighter. There was the sensation of butterflies cupped by hands fluttering on her skin. Not long afterward, the metal began to fly free, detaching strip by strip as if it had only been tinfoil, jettisoned by fate and flung piecemeal into the wind.

Her skin felt new and scarred at once. There was blood on her hands—her mother's blood. But not enough to write home about. Not that Ginger could define home.

Home began to seem like the wistful amble of a homeless man, searching distant train tracks he'd never seen, hoping to find some undeniable connection and sense of purpose along the way. "Daddy, I'm coming to find you now," she said. "I need to know some things before I leave for college."

If she didn't find him, she decided, she'd find someone. The wind was blowing hard and hot as small streaks of residual metal that clung to the creases of her skin began to loosen and fall away. A moment later, a long breeze swept past and the rest of her silver took flight while she ambled toward the train tracks, before pulling on the borrowed purple dress from the cleaners and buttoning it to shield her renewed vulnerability, feeling all over a delicious unowned tingle like a heightening of desire or expectation, as she thought about disability for life, said, "Disability for life," and kept right on walking.

GODIVA

Godiva climbed on her horse in the bank parking lot between Mission Boulevard and the Zanzibar café, wearing a rice-paper dress airbrushed to look like the American flag. The night sky was lit with fireworks from SeaWorld, and Garnet Avenue had begun to crowd with bodies: Perfumed bodies, holiday bodies, bodies with piercings, and bodies wearing garments the size of scarves, with slits that threatened indecent exposure. "Love me, touch me, adorn me," she said, practicing her spiel. This was what she was born for, yet it had begun to bore her.

Almost everyone was slipless, braless, and tan; those not were tourists. "Like peasants," she said, "Oh, for the old days," and, "Whoa, whoa, Stud Boy. Easy there."

Her smooth voice consoled the horse, who, in recognition of her dulcet tones, lifted his tail and let a fart fly.

It was the Fourth of July and late in the evening; club hoppers in rayon, girls and girls, boys and boys, and girls and boys were cemented to each other on this street, ducking into coffeehouses for a boost of caffeine after too many Mai Tais, readying themselves for the drive home in cars that sardined alongside the boulevard's slanted parking spaces.

The police would be out in force tonight, so her dress would come in handy. She could not get arrested too early. From her trip that morning, she'd noticed that ratted and braided hair were out since her last visit, so she held Stud

Boy's reigns and used her other hand to flatten the mess on her head. As her fingers sifted through the strands, her hair flattened and layered, turning blonde with decorative roots, but in the dim lot, no one noticed. Then she made another change, willing her lips thinner and red, and said, in a new, deeper voice, "Trim," looking down at her Botticelli legs.

With a flit of her wrist, she enhanced their musculature, watching her tissue and tendons lengthen. When she noticed them tight, her shoes grew magically with her feet, half a size—in red stiletto heels. This altering was painful, but so repetitive she found the pain almost delicious, slicing all the way down to her toes.

"You deserve such pain," her liege, Leofric, had once said. "Being so beautiful has a price. It's prideful to show superiority, and you wanted such admiration, so now you'll do it again and again, alter and alter." Godiva hated the memory of his cocky, pocked face.

Thinking of him, she trimmed her nose, applying a slight ski jump to its tip, until her face was a mixture of all famous faces. This year's look was Nordic. Regarding herself in the bank window, she decided she liked it better than the Marilyn, the Twiggy, and the Iman, but "How long will this go on?" she wondered aloud. "How long must I suffer these tasks—and them with me?"

Though no one spoke, in the back of her mind, she heard Leofric say, "Forever, and your presumptive narcissism will punish you, but so punished will be every woman who sees you, for she will know perfection in your face and that it won't be hers." Well, Godiva remembered how he had sat her down on the midnight damask, muttering with a zealot's intensity, "You will change with their ages, so they will be blinded by jealousy—their pain, your legacy—because mediocre is not in your vocabulary, Godi. You will show them to hide, and that there is always something better than themselves, a glance of humility."

"I'm not bothered," she'd said then, laughing, "I'd rather be the exception than the rule." But she thought of the first day she bared her body, riding down the road, how the peasants had lined the street, heads down, knuckles pressed to cold cobbles. How shy she'd pretended to be, how serious about helping them, letting her long hair cover her until one man peeped, when she flashed him her nude nipple, not believing Leofric, until, as a result, the man had gone blind. The Peeping Tom, blind!

A miracle, they said, but he'd been half-blind to begin. And since then, she had been on this journey many times, changing beneath her skin, but she grew tired of stealing their sight for small pleasures. Nothing was good enough anymore to cause miracles. He had said, "Your crime is in knowing your beauty and unveiling it in the guise of something else... Please, Lady G. You wanted to ride that horse, nude, in pomp and circumstance. Now a man is blind due to your self-love and I shall have to recompense his family."

Not that he ever did, the cheap-ass, and he constantly upbraided her, but her first lifetime was still the one she longed for: She missed the food, the way a woman could stuff herself without fear, without diets, without compulsion to show a toned physique, and she preferred her complexion fair, but she could not stay behind the times, so she gave herself a tan. In a blink, her eyes shifted from hazel to blue. She knew she had found the correct balance of traits when the golden glow grew all around her as her horse's hooves *clip-clopped* on the sidewalk.

This glow had been harder to achieve lately—so many people, so many surgeries, so many cosmetic fixes for nature's original gifts—*and yes, how unfair*, she thought. But *c'est la vie.* The rich always bought more possibilities for their masquerades, more oils, more lotions, more gauze, and more gildings.

The rice-paper dress resembling the flag now clung

wetly and had started to dissolve. Already, she had attracted the attention of several men on the street, so she offered herself up as always, saying, "Lick me, touch me, feel me," and they did, with pleasure, until one star disappeared near her nipple, and a stripe fell away from her back. "You must remove the dress first," she said.

Several tried to climb Stud Boy's back to get closer, so she dismounted and raised her arms when a swarm of men jaywalked the traffic-studded road to stand before her. Stud Boy whinnied his relief at her dismount, not looking forward to the weight of the men's desire on his withers. "Take me, taste me, consume me," she commanded again, and the swarm followed, mesmerized, while she walked toward another throng.

Her horse kept his eye on her as the dress rapidly diminished, and when it was fully removed, she would blind them, but in the last century, this state lasted hours and then moments, never held for life anymore. Still, they always wondered: How could a woman be so perfect? Not a line on her face, not a sag, no mark, no disproportion, nipples the size of cherries, perfectly centered.

It was her nudity that won the moment. Many women could look fine in clothes, but without them? That was special. She strolled until she stood before the crowded café, beside the iron railings, a cluster of men in tow, Stud Boy sedately behind her. Many walked toward Mission Boulevard from the opposite direction, aiming for the beach, but when they saw her, they stopped. Some got rough as a mangling blur of hands grew insistent on her body, hands, tongues, some men licking her throat or chest, some attempting to fist or finger her as she walked, but, "The dress. Get it off," she insisted, not wanting intercourse—waiting for the crowd to go blind so she could ride away. When one man pushed to the front and unzipped his pants, then tried to block her forward motion, Godiva screamed, "No," and her crowd pushed him back.

Still, the idea to rape or molest her had set in, and fireworks exploded as the hands, more of them, invaded her
space. Godiva whistled for Stud Boy as the crowd got ugly,
Stud Boy who kicked a path toward her, then let her mount.
They tried to pull her off him, but he kicked from all sides.

Both men and women tried to grope her then, the
men pursuing her private areas with wet fingers, and the
women scratching and punching her stomach. Downcast
eyes were important, Godiva thought, to the semblance of
respect. She was a lady, but these people had no respect.

She did not like this place and these times. Her beauty
was an invitation, as was the flimsy garment she'd worn, and
the things she'd called out, hoping to rid herself of the dress,
had only incited more urge to plunder. If the women envied
her as they touched her, violence was their show, but from
her renewed position on her horse, she noticed a girl in
glasses at the picture-window table, shaking her head,
frowning, watching the crowd pulse around the horse.

"Shoulder and belly!" the girl called out.

It was then Godiva noted there were two strips of
dress remaining, one stuck to her abdomen and one to her
shoulder, and she reached down to pull them away, thinking:
Soon, soon, they will be subdued. The French grew
subdued, the English, the Peruvians, the Italians, too—and
these Americans would be no different at the sight of such
pure beauty. Then near-nude, Godiva moaned. She purred.
She yanked the strips free and looked around.

The crowd featured a glazed look, to be sure, but did
not wander off in a blinded stupor.

"Hey, Lady, you selling your body?" one guy asked.
"Or giving it away?"

"What a whore," a girl in the throng announced, but
the girl in the window shouted, "Run," as Godiva sat on
Stud Boy's back, and the rest seemed more impaired than

blinded as she glanced around.

"This is incredible beauty," Godiva said then, projecting a voice into the crowd with a tone as mellifluous as falling gold strings on a harp, "Be enraptured. Adore it," but, "This is America, Babe," some guy said, as the first hand went up onto Stud Boy's back, grabbing his reins, "Here, we either watch it, buy it, or fuck it," so she kicked her horse into a gallop, riding over several observers in the process. Their cries of pain did not trouble her.

She rode back to the bank parking as a siren rang out in the distance. To her surprise, the girl from the window was waiting in the lot, moving along the brick wall with one hand feeling for her next step until she heard Stud Boy's hooves and handed Godiva a sweater. "Put this on," she said. "Now." And Godiva had barely thrust it over her head when the girl laboriously led her back to the alley behind a vitamin store, luring Stud Boy with sugar cubes, then offered Godiva a worn pair of jeans she stripped off, the denim still warm, her own layered leggings revealed.

"They don't understand you," the girl said. "They are inured to loveliness and have come to expect it." But Godiva had not left her horse nor put on the jeans, and the girl was not looking at Godiva's face, her gaze instead fixed on a light emanating from a third-floor window in a nearby apartment, until Godiva said, "Thank you," and the girl's small chin tilted to the correct level.

"How does my own outfit look," she asked Godiva. "Does it look well? Are my pants too thin? I can't see myself."

Godiva heard the taint of a Transylvanian accent in the girl's shaking voice, and realized her rescuer's eyes had gone completely blind. A police car rolled up, Godiva pulled on the borrowed jeans while seated side-saddle and said, "It looks wonderful," as the cops got out of the car, its blue and red lights flashing. They yanked her from her horse, cuffed her, and pushed her head down so she could enter the back of the car. As the rescue girl regained her vision, which Godiva witnessed in her sudden ability to track faces in the ensuing conversation, the police questioned her, but when they turned toward another eruption of sirens, Godiva felt the pain of sudden powerlessness rush through her body.

Even her nudity had failed her. She altered her face so she resembled an old hag, one they would have been mistaken to have apprehended, and awaited the officers' return. Her skin stung, burning unmercifully as she imagined and created its new striations and wrinkles. It was painful, she realized, to create pain to engender ugly... So painful.

Via this act, a magic beyond her control originated.

When they finally returned for her, she had already turned into red liquid, the girl's clothes falling free, the cuffs slipping from her hands, and mutated from a liquid to a solid gold into skin and back again to gold dusted by ash—the same old gold Leofric had paid her in recompense for her nudity in public that very first time. "Here," he'd said, "Lower their taxes for yourself. I'll give you the lucre," and she had.

Now one cop said, "She gave us the slip," as he glanced in the backseat for the beautiful woman that had been there. But she was only gold, melted, smeared, and lumpish, coated with a fine layer of soot atop, appearing without symmetry or value.

One cop picked up her golden body, with the help of the other, saying, "This shit is heavy," and abandoned it in the trash beside the alley dumpster. Only the girl knew who she was, but Godiva could not speak through frozen lips, not that any anatomy was detectable in her current shape.

Still, she wished for the girl to notice her, thinking: *Use me; let me help you.*

Stud Boy then nudged the girl and tilted his head

toward Godiva. With the girl's help, they settled Godiva on his back like an awkward rock, ass up, and the girl mounted behind her.

Then they rode off onto the back roads as the last of the evening's firecrackers flared in the sky, burning a red trail from high to low, from heaven to earth, from the place where no one could touch the bright sparks, to the one where humans gaped at falling debris—their mouths wide open as if hoping to catch the ashes on their tongues, to make that holiday night's magic last forever, the magic they were slightly bored by that no longer served to blind them, even if it matched their very notions of perfection—though they would keep watching, because what else was there to do, just in case.

MY BROTHER, MADE OF CLAY

My brother was born with a patch of loam under his left nipple. When I was very young, I often asked to touch it, and Jimmy would pull up his favorite green polo and turn before me proudly like an older person displaying a new tattoo. The patch was the size of a quarter. My fingers came away smelling of silt. He died at the age of fourteen.

While he lived, Jimmy was charming and had many girlfriends. He was blond and handsome, with an endearing smile. Every week, I'd see him talking to girls on our block, smiling, dipping his head close to theirs as if to steal a kiss. I saw him steal a few. That year, I suggested he plant a bean sprout in his loam, but he refused because once a mustard seed had embedded itself in his skin and had been painful to extract.

I thought as long as he had the patch, something should grow there.

"Aw, Beck," he said, "I don't want something growing from my chest. You are brain dead."

"Am not," I said. "A bean sprout is not a mustard seed."

"Close enough. Just don't tell anyone about it, okay?" he asked. "Not at show and tell. Not anywhere. If you do, you won't be my sister anymore."

I did not tell anyone because I believed him.

When Jimmy was a kid, he had been an athlete, but as he grew older, he took to smoking dope with other kids.

At one time, he could throw a football fifty yards and hit an object the size of a number two on a jersey, but later he was lucky to make the hamper four feet from his bed. Still, he grew taller every year.

I looked like my mother, short and stout, but everyone said my brother looked like he'd come from someone else's family. He was then 5'10" and my father was 5'11" so my father became suspicious of mailmen. Often, he'd look a Nordic carrier over as if to ask, "Is this the one?" He and my mother slept in separate beds. At the time, I thought it was normal.

We lived in a three-bedroom house on Idley Court, two city blocks from children so poor they did not have costumes on Halloween. Jimmy got to know them and abandoned the kids from our street. He stayed out after dark. He lied, cheated, and stole.

He told me, "They say everything, but they don't mean it. Don't bother to listen. Do what you want." One night, after my parents fell asleep, I caught him in the basement with one of his girlfriends.

Her name was Patrice. She lived on the corner in the green house with red steps. They squirmed on the couch. Jimmy's pants near his knees, her legs, like stubby taffy, wrapped around him, and they moaned as his white buttocks pistoned up and down.

She lifted her flabby arm and pointed at me, standing in the doorway above the stairs, and Jimmy growled, "Go away, Little Sis. Don't tell." He had not taken off his shirt. Later, he told me not to mention what I'd seen and asked if I knew what they'd done.

I said, "No."

He said, "Good." He was nice to me after that, though his eyes were bloodshot and the odor of sage continually seeped from his clothes.

"Did you let her see it?" I asked.

"What?"

"The spot."

"No," he said. "Stop talking about it."

He showed me a locket he'd stolen from a department store to give her, but by the time he was ready to make the gesture, her father found out about them and would not let Jimmy near their house. Her father was a police sergeant whose squad car was habitually parked out front, a big, hairy man the neighborhood kids feared.

From the middle of the street in subsequent weeks, Patrice could be seen in her living room, staring out the window, her pudgy fingers pressed to the glass, her green, deep-lidded eyes wistful. She cried frequently and at random times, her eyes meant only for Jimmy; it was as if she thought by standing there Jimmy would find her and echo her sadness; then they could exchange long, house-to-house glances like thwarted lovers. Jimmy tried for a week or two —but suddenly began to kiss another girl.

One morning, I saw her unhappy family clustered at the doorstep of 1101—Patrice, with small suitcase in hand, the handle clenched tightly. They stared at each other with dewy eyes, and I saw them huddle as I ran to get the paper for my father. Her parents had spoken to mine the night before.

I remember I'd watched my father rip a check from his checkbook, and her father take it, followed by the quiet shutting of our door. The whisper was that Patrice was pregnant, but when she returned her eyes were sad, but her belly had not grown. Still, she hated Jimmy. She spray painted "Prick" on his bike, then pelted it with eggs.

Jimmy was unrepentant. Our parents reasoned with him, explained to him, and finally yelled at him: "Jimmy, why do you cause trouble? How will we pay for this? What were you thinking?"

Following a lecture, Jimmy always did something bad.

The next day, he stole a bicycle. My father tried to get him to admit whom he had stolen the bike from, but Jimmy remained silent. His eyes, once joyful, turned hard. To compensate for criminal activities, he was grounded and assigned a list of chores. He performed each with a maximum of negligence. He ran away twice that year.

At thirteen, he almost set the house on fire.

I'd watched him take a piece of newspaper to the stove, set it ablaze, and carry it burning through the down-stairs to light a firecracker, one of the quick-flaming varieties known as Ladies' Fingers. The firecracker exploded beauti-fully on the road, but Jimmy threw the singed remains in a trashcan beside our house. The trashcan was full of used briquettes, a broken-down cabinet, and paper odds and ends —so the flames rose quickly.

Jimmy laughed as they escalated, drizzling them with the hose, but did not spray them directly. The heat melted the can into a nubby ring on the pavement; then the neighbors, two Mexican men, ran over and doused the fire in earnest. They pulled what remained of the flaming can from the house as storm clouds gathered overhead, loosing a torrent of rain, but Jimmy wiped the smile from his face only when my mother arrived.

Standing in the downpour, she shouted, "Jimmy, how did the fire start?"

Jimmy shrugged.

"James Elliot Peter! How did the fire start?"

"I don't know," he lied.

"You need to take responsibility," she said, and then yelled at me, "Becky, what the hell happened here?" It was a good question: A portion of roof had been charred, and musty smoke trailed from the doused can, while the odor of singed plastic filled the air. Jimmy sent me a pleading look. He hissed, "Shhh," under his breath.

My mother shook my shoulders as if determined to

force the answer out, then asked softly, "How did it happen? Please, Becky, tell me what happened."

My brother glared. "It's not my fault," I whispered. Rain pelted my face. I was freezing. My mother let go of my shoulders, holding her hands over her eyes, and the rain slid from her fingers like water from an awning. Both neighbors glared at Jimmy.

One said, "Your son did it."

The other said, "Do you see how close the can was to the gas main? The whole block could have gone up." They returned to their houses, shaking their heads.

Later, my father said, "Don't play with fire, Son. If I've told you once, I've told you a million times." Jimmy, long-adept at looking contrite, feigned sorrow. From then on, our neighbors avoided us, but Jimmy did what he pleased, and "Piece-of-shit son," I heard my father say from his den days later, still focused on Jimmy's wrongdoing. "What's wrong with him? Why does he make this the house of Sisyphus? I'm toting that damn rock up the hill, again and again." My father adored mythical matches for his troubles, but Jimmy then delighted in bringing home a worse element: Addicts from downtown and pickpockets from the bus station.

From my room, I often heard the *whoosh* of his window opening and the *click* of a Bic lighter. When he was fourteen, the police came to our door and Jimmy was taken to juvie. He had graffitied a fence, shoplifted from the drugstore, and stolen from our mother's purse—though the last crime went unreported.

His face aged. His high, Swiss cheekbones looked sharp. Stalking the house at night, he consumed all bread, lunchmeat, ramen and other quick-eat foods. It seemed he was always growing. He was 6'2" the last time we measured him. "Jimmy is eating us out of house and home," my mother began to whisper. She avoided confrontation.

Though our house was on the "good side" of the lots,

we were always broke due to fines for my brother's criminal acts, and my mother's resultant shopping. For hours following Jimmy's misdeeds she haunted the malls, so her closet was full of shoeboxes: "Shoes. The only thing fat people can buy in cute styles," she said once, and then, as if wishing for a different reality in the near but unforeseeable future, bought clothes sized to fit the terminally anorexic: 0, 0+, 1½. My mother was a short Sally Struthers with a pear-shaped figure.

Furious, my father held the diminutive clothing up to her bulging waist and said, "Who did you think would wear these, Dear? Your midget twin?"

"I have a right to my things," she'd say, and go out the next day, dragging more home. We learned not to question her. My father believed she was addicted to the friendly *hello* of clerks and her own plastic purchasing power. It was three years after I wanted one that they bought me my first bicycle.

The same year, at the age of seven, I failed the second grade. No one at home seemed to care. "What is this book about, Becky?" my teacher would ask. All teachers looked the same to me, old with false smiles. I didn't reply. At recess I sat at my desk making loops and loops of spirals, nothing but lowercase Ls for pages. The other children did not like me because I lied all the time, but I could not stop.

"Becky," my teacher persisted. "Can you really expect me to believe a pet turtle destroyed your permission slip for the trip to the fair?"

"Yes," I said. "I used it to pick up his poop."

I had no turtle. When she called my parents, they told her they had forgotten to sign the permission slip—and why was she making such a big deal of it, anyway?

"Your daughter will fail," she replied. "How much help is she getting at home?"

"It's second grade, not brain surgery," my father said.

"If you were teaching her, we wouldn't have this problem," my mother agreed. "Obviously, she has picked up the lying in your class."

They were wrong. I learned it from Jimmy. When my father asked, "Jimmy, did you do your homework?" Jimmy always said *yes*. He got worse and worse, and my parents were beside themselves. "You children are turning out poorly," they announced—we would be criminals, whores, reprobates.

Strangely, after the fire, my father pushed their twin beds back together, and they spent hours communing in their room, as if on their second honeymoon. For the first time, I heard my mother's girlish squeals and the heavy clunk of their oak headboards meeting the wall. I believe my father reinitiated the sexual part of their relationship to curb her spending, but whatever his reason, it did not work.

Jimmy spent hours gelling his hair with extra-hold professional supplies. He had quit smoking pot, but moved onto uppers. Our parents were seldom home, and Jimmy then chased so many girls he used the phone incessantly.

My mother, unwilling to go without a phone herself, installed a private line for him. She also bought him a family-sized box of condoms. My father, deliberately oblivious, never said a word.

I kept tabs on Jimmy from the hallway, spying at his door. "I know, Gigi," I heard him say. "I miss you, too. Can't wait to see you. Will you come over on Sunday?" Jimmy's face, once smooth as a fresh peach, became pitted. When he hung up, he immediately dialed again. "Hello, is Carla there? Hi, Sweetie, what are you doing? How about Saturday? My parents are going out of town and I'm supposed to be watching my sister, but she's eight. She won't bother us."

As the months passed, his loam hardened. A sizable lump rose under his shirt. I thought it would be like a spot of dirt that could be rubbed off, and perhaps would finally

be gone, but when we moved the next year, his skin broke
out in a rash. The hardened lump appeared the size of a
tennis ball, then flattened. Twice a week, the dermatologists
tended the area, but no one could determine what should be
done.

The spot widened and spread across his chest.

My father said, "Jimmy, you have to take better care of
yourself," and lifted Jimmy's shirt, muttering, "If you bathed
more, this thing would die down." Then he dug his fingers
into the mound and ripped at it with his thumbnail.

"It won't die down," Jimmy said. "But thanks for your
support." He rolled his eyes and my father kept digging. A
rivulet of blood trickled slowly along the uneven terrain of
the dirt and down Jimmy's abdomen. Jimmy flinched. My
father looked disgusted.

"What are you looking at, loser?" Jimmy asked me. "At
least I didn't fail the second grade."

My mother said, "Becky, you need to be patient with
your brother. He was born with a deformity that makes him
angry." Jimmy's response was grabbing a crystal vase and
flinging it into the fireplace. My mother began to cry.

For years, I would remember these words: A deformity. Even now, at thirty, I remember the tone of her voice,
placating and fake. My father shook his head and swept the
shards. He said, "Jimmy just doesn't take to the *right* way,
and Becky will not learn, so perhaps the Lord is punishing us
all." He perceived himself as Job, and had many times
recited the bible in the hope Jimmy would change, but one
day, when Jimmy fell asleep during a lecture, I noticed he
had inserted earplugs.

We were gathered in the family room again,
debriefing style, on the plush, 1970, thrift-store sofas. While
my father spoke, my mother's eyes darted from object to
object, over the rusty Singer, onto the oak entertainment
center, and around the limp ferns in their tiny silver pots.

She had a black thumb, so several plants were dying, but she would not look at them, nor throw them away. Perhaps, she couldn't bear to admit she'd killed them, but glancing away from their ruin that afternoon, she touched her perfectly coiffed head and began to pull tendrils from the base of her scalp. I inserted my hand between the couch cushions to feel for a penny, or a pen, maybe an appealing piece of lint.

"...And what I'm saying," my father continued, "is that we need to work together. We are a family." He cleared his throat and said, rather ridiculously, "Together we stand, or united we fall! Emma and I did not raise you children to embarrass us. We want you to succeed. Jimmy? Jimmy! Are you listening?"

"He's sleeping, Dad," I said, though in hindsight, I now believe he was coming down, a bad amphetamine down that lasted days.

"Well, wake him," my father shouted.

"I need air," my mother said.

"What are you breathing now?" he asked.

"The scent of wasted words," my mother said. "Your lectures would put insomniacs to sleep."

My father sneered and left the room.

My mother grabbed her purse and walked out, saying, "There's dinner in the freezer, Becky. Heat it up."

Jimmy slept peacefully. He looked so kind when he was sleeping—not the boy who threw dirt at cars, or stole my parents' keys to make it with girls in their car. He looked friendly, like he was really okay, a nice kid. "Jimmy?" I whispered. "Dad's gone."

There was no response, so I poked him, but he didn't move. "Jimmy," I said, louder. Nothing. Sunlight filtered from the window behind the couch and he looked almost angelic. I pushed my index finger into the open space between his waistband and his T-shirt. I lifted the fabric. I had not seen the spot in a while.

On his chest, the swath of dirt wrapped all the way around and almost reached his sides. I ran a finger across. Dry as a dune, it crumbled. My finger smelled like plain dirt when I withdrew it, uncultivated, like a field rendered barren long ago. Beneath the dirt was a layer of moist, red clay. He awoke.

"You saw it, didn't you?" he asked. His eyes blinked open like a tortoise's, the bloodshot strings of broken blood vessels contrasting with his blue irises.

"Yes," I said.

He nodded. "It's growing, Becky," he said. "It gets worse every day."

I asked, "What if you watered it?"

"I take showers," he said. "Nothing works." For the first time in a long while, he was not arrogant, just honest. He gave me a measured look. I stared down at my purple shorts and bit my lip. He picked at a zit on his chin. "Becky, I'm falling apart," he said. "I've been such a fuck-up."

"What if you start doing good things? Right now?"

"I tried last month. I raked the lawn. I took out the trash. I tried to be nice to Mom. It still grew."

"What did Dad say when you did those things?"

"Nothing."

"Nothing?"

"Nothing." He scratched his head, and said, "I think it grows based on what they think. I can't go to school anymore. The patch used to be small, like a smudge of dark dirt, but now it's turning to clay—staining everything red. All of my clothes. The sheets. Everything." He looked at me and announced, "It's growing. I can't stop it."

I asked, "If you don't go to school, what do you do?"

"I go out in the morning and wait till they leave; then I come home. I erase the messages from the attendance lady and take a walk in the park on Holmes Street. I like to walk in that park. I don't even go for girls anymore."

He stared out the window and let a scowl settle over his features. He asked, "Did Mom go shopping?"

"Yes."

"And Dad to the den?"

"Yes."

"Status quo," he said. "Try to learn something at school. I'm going to take a nap." He did not get out of his bed for weeks. Every day, my mother fed him. She called the school to inform them of his illness, but they told her he had not attended in over a month. Because he was awake for only three or four hours a day, my mother did not have the heart to punish him. My father was too busy.

A dingy reddish-brown settled on Jimmy's face. His health worsened. One day, I went and knocked on his door. "Come in," he muttered.

My father said when we were in his room we were supposed to talk quietly, so I whispered, "Hi, Jimmy." I had gone inside to tell him I received my first A.

"Hi, Becky. What are you whispering for?"

"No reason. How are you feeling?" I said louder.

"Crappy, how the hell are you?" he asked.

"Fine" did not seem adequate. He was miserable and I did not want to appear less miserable. "Okay," I said. "I'm okay."

"You should be okay," he said. "You can walk around."

His sheets were coated with clay from his ankles to his neck. "I just came to visit," I said.

"Okay," he hissed. "You visited, now get the fuck out."

I left his room in tears. That night, my father called a family meeting. Jimmy was left in his room.

"Have you looked beneath the sheet lately?" my father asked, pointing toward Jimmy's room. We hadn't. He put on a serious face and said, "My son is turning to clay," and closed his eyes. "I am Job. I swear." No one paid him any attention.

My mother spoke softly, muttering, "I've tried to look under his sheet, but he gets angry when I try to raise it. It should be washed. It needs to be washed."

"He does not want you to change *the sheet*," my father boomed, "because *the growth* has taken over his legs."

"The growth," my mother repeated slowly, like noting the Latin names of flowers, then she wrote the words in a tiny black notebook, and started to cry. "My therapist," she said, by way of unnecessary explanation, "wants me to write down the things that upset me."

"Might as well just tape-record your whole damn day," my father said then, but while they glared, I figured it was a good time to announce my success.

I said, "I got an A in my spelling class today."

My father looked up with a grimace and replied, "Can you please focus on something other than yourself, Becky? Your brother is terminally ill!"

I said, "I'm sorry," as my mother wrote "terminally" and "ill." Then nothing was said for several moments until she murmured, "What will we do about *the growth?*" and my father hollered, "He came out of you that way. You figure it out."

"The growth must go away!" my mother shouted back, blood flooding her face.

"The growth," Jimmy then shouted from his room, "the growth, the growth, the growth, the growth," almost chanting from the musty darkness.

My teacher called the next day. She said something on the answering machine like, "This is Mrs. Nichols. I'm calling to let you know Becky has had a breakthrough and received an A on the class spelling test. If she continues this way, she may yet pass the grade."

My father's response was, "Of course, they can't flunk her twice."

My mother said, "What he means is that's great, Dear. Good job!"

"Bureaucrats," my father breathed. "They've got to cut red tape somewhere. Can't go around flunking everyone."

I went to Jimmy's room. His lights were out. From his window, the amber glow of a street lamp cast an imperfect arc over his bed. "You sleeping?" I whispered.

"No," he said.

"Dad says you're turning into clay."

"It's true, but now the clay turns into dust. From loam to dust to clay and back to dust."

I paused. "Can I touch it?"

"No!" he said, looking toward the yellow light. He acted as if I wanted to see his penis. "I heard the answering machine," he said. "It's good you aced that test."

"Thanks," I mumbled. I did not tell him that for the last month I'd checked myself in the shower for dust, for loam, for anything. "You should have planted something in it," I said. "Maybe it would have stayed in one place."

"Turn on the light," he replied.

I did and he pulled the sheet close to his chin, staring into my eyes. His feet, then uncovered, had turned to dust. "I'm trying not to move much," he said, his toes pointed toward the wall, perfectly formed like anatomical sandcastles. "Now, watch this," he said. He twisted his leg slightly, and his foot broke away from his ankle, the two parts separated by a thin, black line. "The dust reaches my chest now," he said.

"How can you stand it?" I asked. "How does it feel?"

"Like sand on the beach. First my body felt wet, but now it's drying out. I'm about to be gone from here, Becky; I feel it. Guess Dad will have a hard time explaining this one." He laughed harshly, then said, "Old fucker never liked me anyway. Before you were born, he used to say, 'You sure we had sex that month, Emma? You sure?' And I could always hear him." Jimmy paused for a second, reflecting, then turned to me and said, "You need to get the fuck out of here, Beck. They'll let you go. Just tell them Mom and Dad are nuts. Tell them neglect. Tell them anything."

He stared at the ceiling and closed his eyes. He immediately fell asleep.

The next morning, I peered in and his head had turned to sand. His entire body, except for the broken-off foot, was pristine. I stared at his sandy corpse for a long time. He looked handsome, white, and motionless. His clothing was the only splash of color.

My mother peered over my shoulder and fainted. She bumped her head on the bookcase and took some time to recover. My father entered the room and poked my brother's chest with his index finger.

The perfect facsimile of a ribcage crumpled. My father poked again. Jimmy's legs became mounds of dirt. As if to test the power of his pointed finger, my father glanced Jimmy's arms with his fingertip, and they too fell apart. He was about to touch Jimmy's head—the only thing left that resembled him—when I yelled, "No, don't touch it. The head is mine."

I took Jimmy's purple duffle, gently placed his head inside, and swept the remains of his hair into the bag with a hand-held broom. I took the whole thing to my room, but my parents left the rest of the body as if Jimmy would reappear, which he did not. When Jimmy's parole officer called, and my parents could not produce him, the officer came to our house. "He turned to dirt," my father kept insisting.

"He slept in that bed," my mother said. "Take samples from the clay. DNA."

The officer looked at my parents like they were crazy. "I think he ran away again," he said. "Teen rebels are crafty. Maybe the sand constituted an elaborate plot to make it look like he was sleeping."

My parents conferred. They looked as though his explanation would suit them fine, except they knew the truth. "Perhaps, you're right," my father said. "What do we do now?"

"Just wait. He'll show up."

The parole officer called once a week for many months. Suffice it to say, Jimmy never showed. My mother lifted the fitted sheet from his bed, with the sand rolled neatly inside. She deposited the whole thing in the trash. She cried as she did it, but once the evidence was gone, she acted as though Jimmy had indeed disappeared. She grew thinner, "from stress," she explained, so one by one, like irregular snow, white tags fell from her mall garments.

Other parents expressed concern, Jimmy's picture was plastered on milk cartons, and my parents were surrounded with support. I grew up with people saying my brother had run away. Somewhere along the way, my parents internalized the lie. Whenever my mother saw a mop of golden curls on a boy, she stopped and stared; her face went pale. The age of the boys she looked at never changed. Even in death, Jimmy claimed their exclusive attention.

Jimmy's room was left unaltered. I could go back today and see the football on the top shelf, the trophies, the model airplanes, and the dope pipe, made of foil, stashed in an old baseball mitt. My parents had frozen him in an era of innocent childhood he'd hardly known, a fabrication of their collective memory, and when they spoke of him afterward, he'd never aged past eleven, when everything was sunshine and loam.

Eventually, I went to college and earned a degree in horticulture. I landed a prestigious job, rented a nice house, and lived alone, speaking to none of my swanky neighbors. I did not know who they were, nor did I care. The duffle, carted through many moves, remained intact.

I had tried to plant a bit of Jimmy at every house I lived in, tried everything to make him grow. Sometimes, I caught myself looking at the dust, asking: Did he exist? Was he real? Was this sand, sifting through my fingers, once the skin of an adolescent boy who'd wooed a hundred girls?

Yes, I concluded: It was. There were only a few handfuls left, and I tried weeds, flowers, vegetables, and mustard seeds, but nothing worked. Finally, I succeeded with a Spartan Floribunda. The petals of this rose were coral pink. I sprinkled his dirt over the prepared soil and waited.

Rosebushes are not easy to grow. They require the right light, vigilant pruning, and almost-perfect conditions. Quickly, Jimmy's bush extended branches above the ground, but as I waited to cut springtime buds, I noticed none had grown. On each stem, instead, were thorns, gnarled and dark, with an almost patina sheen. Flowers never appeared. Leaves grew in sparsely. His bush was two-feet wide and three-feet tall—the largest rosebush in the yard.

My father, with whom I had kept in contact, came to visit one evening. He had recently divorced my mother. He did not call first, but arrived on my doorstep, and I led him quietly to the backyard. Once there, he pointed to Jimmy's bush immediately, muttering, "What's wrong with that one? It's ugly. A goddamn Goliath of ugly!" All around were vibrant tulip stock, Gerber daisies, Spanish moss, and zinnia. In the greenhouse, I'd grown several species of rare orchids. "Only thorns," my father said. He leaned in and pointed with his index finger, which brushed the tip of one. He quickly withdrew his hand as a drop of blood sprang to his fingertip.

"Don't touch that one," I said. "It's sensitive and has lost its bloom."

He moved on to a new part of the yard, sucking his finger and pointing with his other hand. He had the same weighty walk, older but unchanged.

As he strode the yard and twilight dimmed the landscape, I imagined my plants shriveling, one by one, fading and crumbling into dust. The shadows in his wrinkles appeared deceptively deep, like the crease between a sandy foot and ankle. "Would you like to go in, Dad?" I asked. "I'm not feeling so well. I'd like to get off my feet."

"Let's sit on the bench a while," he said. "You can tell me about your dead-end job. The bureaucrats, ha, they run everything these days. All of these state-funded operations are going down the tubes."

"The bureaucrats," I echoed, staring at Jimmy. "Actually, this business is privately owned... Let's talk about Mom. Have you seen her lately?"

"No," he said. He stared up at the Spanish moss and lapsed into silence, then said: "Your mother has not changed. She's still spending her way into a corner."

I yawned and asked, "Do you mind if we call it a night? I'm exhausted. Come back any time. Tomorrow, if you'd like."

Abruptly, he rose. "I'll do that," he said, patting my back in his version of a hug. "And I'll let myself out."

"Goodnight," I said, waving as he left, but I did not go in. I sat on that bench until the sky was so dark I could not see my hands before my face. There was nothing in my vision but the night sky and the glow of a distant street lamp, coming from the north.

In the dark, I could almost imagine Jimmy's roses blooming, or perhaps I forced myself to imagine them, but in that moment he was alive, real again—like the fragrant scent of silt on fingertips, lingering in my memory, both beautiful and grotesque. And that's how I remember him now. Jimmy does not change, though sometimes I imagine his body as a million grains of sand, scattered to the refuse of a city dump, or a large lump of clay on a red-stained sheet. Sometimes, I see him as a plot of fertile soil where nothing beautiful will ever grow.

Then, I remember the ruination that one straight finger can create—pointed toward, and rupturing, a heart.

COCK-SCULPTING

Art is never chaste. It ought to be forbidden to ignorant innocents, never allowed into contact with those not sufficiently prepared. Yes, Art is dangerous. Where it is chaste, it is not Art.

—Pablo Picasso

In her pale fingers during the last year, Verdana Lane had held three hundred and sixty-seven male members, commissioned twenty-three more, and was finally a phenomenal success. The gallery had, since she owned it, always been popular, but lately, supply could not keep up with demand. Though the poverty of her early days was far behind her, she distinctly remembered her first meeting with the dark angel—his first words whispered into her ear: "Verdana, Darling. I'll give you what you want, but you must promise me what I want. You know the rules."

Satan was a blond. At the time, barely able to heat her one-bedroom studio, she disagreed, saying, "I did not invite you. Get thee back to hell."

He laughed and said, "I live there."

She was unnerved. Bills lingered unpaid on her desk, a bag of clay sat beside her sofa, and she no longer owned a television. Fifty cocks adorned her bookshelves and windowsills, perfectly veined, unsold. Everyone loved them, but no one could see taking a perfect replica of a man's penis home. "Why not?" she railed. "Has there been anything more worshipped in all of time?" Despite her talent, her nails bitten to the quick, her face drawn in jerky mannerisms, her plain mug could not sell ice in a desert. Like an ad agent might say: Ugly doesn't sell.

Too bad, because her cocks were beautiful—designed to highlight each vein, each wrinkle, each curling strand of pubic hair. When moving them, she still remembered the names of the men—"Ah, this was Harry. Oh, this was Peter." To her credit, each agreed her vision of their organ was perfection though she added no inches and embellished not a bit, and when they saw themselves in clay, each was stupefied and profoundly grateful. Then she baked their cocks in a local kiln, replete with flesh-colored glaze.

That day, Satan shot her a measured look. "I can help you," he said. "What's wrong, Little Girl? You don't want any candy? Hell's the limit."

"Maybe so," she said. "But you don't live here, so get the fuck out."

"Foolish, Darling, do you want to live in poverty forever? Let's move to California." He directed into her brain an image of her future apartment stacked with thousands of unsold cocks: Cocks on cocks, misshapen cocks, foam cocks, festive cocks, kettle cocks, cocks and roosters. In this vision, Verdana sat on a couch, aged, practically catatonic, and a toothless man stared back at her, fondling his flaccid member. "You like it?" he asked.

She shrugged the vision away and decided if she did not believe in God, she did not believe in Satan. "You do not exist," she declared.

"You see me, don't you?" he replied. "But I sense your reluctance. If not your soul, I will offer you a trade. Flea bargaining... Fortune and fame for—" He paused, drumming his flat palms on her rattling table, "—a night in my bed, well, not technically a bed. I hate beds."

Verdana dropped the bills she held in one hand and the

vase she clutched in the other.

"Scares you, don't it? Ah, you prude! You are afraid? Okay, no S and M. No fire. No other women. Do you agree?" He raised his hand in mock-salute.

She exhaled and longed for a cigarette. Her ragged wardrobe and thrift store lamps would not protect her. She prayed to God, but there was no reply. No big surprise. Just as she thought, He didn't exist and if He did exist, who cared if He wouldn't help her when needed?

Snowflakes fell like silent erasers, gleaming in the stream of headlights, sending a chill through her windows. Her fingers ached. Satan made himself at home, caressing the cocks on her table. "Men," he scoffed. "So small, so ugly, so unlike me."

Verdana looked him full in the face. He wore a black suit embellished with mother-of-pearl. From his alabaster skin to his black eyes, he was every bit "God's most beautiful." Blue suede shoes with silver buckles tapped on the hardwood floor. Mentally, she wavered.

"I'll take the disease, too," he said. "Not a single bit of lupus will ever return. Do we have a deal, Verdana—or not? Don't say not."

From a neighboring apartment, the *thud-thud* of ghetto music intruded. "Yes," she whispered. "Yes." Pipes rattled in the walls. "We have"—the dial of the clock spun —"a deal." She stared at her phone as if expecting it to ring. "What do I do?"

Without listening for his answer she surveyed her surroundings. Already thin to the bones, she knew the lupus would take her within a year, and her work was not complete. The illness made her tired, so tired she often could not get out of bed—but if bums lived in the hedges, the nasty rap music created an aural Armageddon, and the all-night diner must be located across from her apartment— at least the low rent had kept her from homelessness time and again. Still, she regretted her consent as Satan made himself tea, his tea bag dousing murky brown in the cup, reminding her of the way water clouded when she cleaned her brushes. The cocks were true art, but her paychecks came from watercolor city scenes painted for tourists, the income slightly augmented by a rapidly dwindling inheritance from her paternal grandmother. "Do you renege?" Satan asked, and Verdana wavered. *Yes. No. Yes. No.*

These boring scapes could be painted in far less time than a cock was sculpted, but she could not live this way forever. She would not live forever with the disease. One night in Satan's arms, versus death and poverty... She watched him dip the tea bag in his water again and again, like dousing a kitten's head. The money would run out. Inevitably, money ran out, and cocks were her true passion. Her *raison d'être artiste.* "I don't renege," she said.

At last, he ceased dipping. "Isn't it marvelous," he said. "I love the scent of tea but cannot bear the bitter fruit." He dumped his entire beverage in the sink. "You ready? It's time for fun and games."

"Y-yes."

"Good," he said. "First, sculpt me with those long fingers; I want to see them at work."

She gasped as his cock sprang from his trousers, fully erect. Her fingers itched for clay. It (the cock in question) was, at the very least, fourteen inches.

She knocked the blowzy diner scenes from her desk, moistened her hands, and pulled a lump of clay from the bag. Then she sculpted without pause, kneading, shaping, trimming, and finally, held her work aloft. It was as though she could see two of him. "You have outdone yourself," he said, lifting her sculpture, and comparing it to others in the room. "Now get undressed."

Verdana trembled. She had not had sex in years, there were probably cobwebs where he wanted to go, and his size unnerved her. She hadn't even showered. He quickly stripped. When naked, fine blond hair trailed from his chest to his groin and two feathered stubs poked out of his back where it appeared broken bits of bone had sealed. *Feathers*, she thought—feathers that must have been white, but were now a dingy gray—and she ran her hands across them. They begged caressing. Once she started, she found she could not stop. He offered her his back, grinning, preening, saying, "Touch them! Enjoy them!" He sighed as he stood, fingering the replica of his cock, slowly enunciating his next words: "Dirty from the fingers of women," he drawled. "You are among thousands..."

She went to the window. His remark reminded her of an ex boyfriend who had thirty penile piercings and had told her they had caused three hundred and twenty-three orgasms before the last three he'd given her. In anger, she'd flung that man's clay cock against the wall. In the corner, the shards had lingered for months as if she had wanted to shatter him with the toss of her hands, yet fail to touch him afterward.

In fact, sculpting cock was a secret pact she had made with herself after this relationship; if she could make cock, fabricate it with the skill of her own hands, she did not need it. Satan smiled.

"Don't touch your sculpture," she said briskly. "It hasn't been fired. You'll ruin it and I'll have to start again."

He picked up one of her tools and made a deep hole where his urethra would be located.

"Release," Satan said. "It's gotta be there." Verdana looked away. "Now," Satan said, "get undressed." Despite his watching, she pretended it was a doctor's visit, pulled her cotton blouse over her head, and let her jeans fall to the floor. He stared at her imperfect body, her unbalanced breasts, and the stretch marks that marred her hips. A faint cast of disgust overcame his features.

She thought of Thomas, the married man who had
never left his beautiful wife for her—of his rejection when
he first heard of her disease. His cock had also shattered
against the wall. There was power in grabbing a man's cock
and making it explode into tiny fragments of shrieking deci-
bels. That sound, if nothing else, contented her throughout
many lonely nights.

Satan's face seized as if the recalled memory of an old
lover colored Verdana's imperfections so as to make them
bearable. "Stare at that man down there," he said. "Naked in
front of the window. Press your breasts to the pane."

She complied, though the cold nearly caused her to
faint. Her breath steamed the window and she avoided
bringing her lips any closer to the glass, lest they stick, but
her breath fogged her view. He pushed her forward until the
olive berries of her nipples pressed flush against the pane
and felt as though they might crack and break off. She felt,
for the first time in months, via the cold and the pain and the
uncertainty, a trace of desire.

Satan touched her softly. Warmth spread throughout
her body. His hands made her skin feel elastic; as he grap-
pled with her, it was as though disease fled. Her pain was
gone. His warm abdomen pressed against her back and he
lifted her easily to fit himself inside. Beneath the window, a
crowd gathered. She gasped. Catcalls could be heard and,
although aware of the men below, Verdana gave herself up.
"Good," Satan said. "Very good. Flow with me."

She was an apple cored by a mallet. She imagined
parapets and towers, she flew through a thousand towns a
second. Though his size was prohibitive, the pain was delicious. Never had she been so completely filled.

"Would you like to have my child?" he asked.

When he said these words, she recoiled. "No!"

"Calm down," he said. "It wasn't part of the deal." As
he slept with her that night, she dreamed of screaming, of

her legs splayed permanently open, and of baths taken in honeyed milk.

When he left the next morning she could not move. Her body was battered to exhaustion. Walking, even across the room, caused both torment and the delicious tingle suggestive of one well-sated. After two weeks in bed, she baked his cock and took it and her portfolio to a gallery in the fanciest part of the art district.

"Your name?" a snooty receptionist asked. This woman had high blonde hair pinioned to her head with an ornate chopstick. Tight, perky breasts bounced beneath a sheer chiffon blouse.

"Verdana Lane."

"Do you have an appointment?"

"No," Verdana said. "But I must show you something." From her sack, Verdana liberated the fourteen-inch cock.

"Jim," the girl called. "Jim, come and see this."

Within moments, it was agreed she would get a full room for her work and receive the standard 60/40 commission. Entering the taxi, she could not believe her luck. Within days, she was the gallery's hottest seller. She moved out of her tiny studio, and could finally afford a townhouse with her own gallery. The first display she set up consisted of Greco-Roman pillars with cocks on white platters. The only cock she would not sell was Satan's.

It became a keepsake. Each day, an eager throng came through the door, and she sculpted more. Each day, hopeful models disrobed and offered her perfect members to choose from—two hundred men lined up in her hallway wearing white towels, dropping them at once so she could peruse the goods. Untroubled by sickness, she experienced vigor and boundless energy.

Her now-tan body became toned in her indoor gym. Soothing balms refreshed her lips, and she had more than she could ask for, but this soon ceased to be enough. She began to know boredom. Unfulfilled by customers, she pursued the curators of museums and assured them her sculptures were worthy. After the first *yes*, the others were quick to follow. Verdana enjoyed social engagements, gowns, and fawning men—but she had no true love. Due to the fawning, she trusted no one. *Everyone wants something*, she decided.

That year, she was photographed in twenty magazines, received glowing letters, fielded calls from porn stars, and lived for her art. She became so famous she needed an agent, and was approached by several leading PR firms. The constant travel to give talks and attend exhibits tired her out. Two months into her contract, she developed a head cold. Meredith, her agent, rattled her line at five o'clock one morning. Verdana moaned a sleepy *hello* and dropped her head to her pillow, coughing. Meredith muttered, "Verdana, you need to be at the capitol building in one hour. Photographs with the senator—did you forget?"

"What? Cancel! I'm too sick to move."

"I am disappointed and unwilling. Drag your ass out of bed! Oh, and one more thing... we had a conference this morning and decided it would improve your image if you underwent a boob and nose job. We scheduled your surgery."

Verdana sneezed into the receiver. "I wouldn't be me," she said. "I'm sorry, but I can't comply." Although Merry may have said something to soothe her, something that nonetheless meant that Merry wouldn't change a bit of what was said earlier, Verdana fell into a fit of coughing and hung up. She wandered into her studio and thought about the head cold, how it reminded her of former aches, and then the phone rang again. "I'm sorry, Merry," Verdana insisted. "I will not chop my own nose or tits off. Nor will I blow them up!"

"Dana?" long-ago Thomas asked.

"Oh, it's you," Verdana replied. His Welsh accent caught her breath. She could envision the shaggy curls at his neck, smell the woodsy aftershave... Years. It had been years. She had once loved him very much.

"I've left my wife," he said. "Are you there, Dana?"

"Yes."

"I need to see you. I saw your picture in the *Times*, and you look so wonderful. Congratulations on your gigs."

"Thanks."

"Write this number down, okay? It's where you can reach me." As she would have so many times when they were together, she fumbled to do exactly as he asked, ached for him in a Pavlovian moment, until he said, with all of his old arrogance, "Did you sell my cock? Is it still there?"

"No," she shouted. "I hurled it into the corner! It's gone. You hurt me so deeply." Nauseated, she remembered his sneer when he told her he did not love her—that she was too plain, too mousy—that the disease would destroy them and he didn't have the inclination to wait. "You were not worthy of my love, or even my lust."

He ignored her, said, "I'm coming over right now. Where do you live?"

Silence. "I'll think about telling you," she finally muttered, "and perhaps I'll call you back."

"Verdana, be kind. You loved me once, remember?" he insisted. "You were always so kind. I'll pay you ten-thousand dollars to sculpt a new one."

"No."

"Do you have a man?"

"That's none of your business."

"I need to—" he began, but with pleasure, she hung up. *Of course he wanted her now. What man wouldn't?* She walked into the bathroom and scrutinized her pores, feeling strangely empowered until one thought, or a series of related thoughts, repeatedly occurred: *What if it was lies that made everyone love her? What if her cocks would never have sold?*

She preferred to think Satan had only opened a door— that the work itself would have garnered acclaim in a few short years—but at the time, she didn't have years. *Would she never know?*

This thought depressed her. "A nose job?" she muttered. "How about a life job?" She opened a bottle of Merlot and poured herself a coffee-mug full.

As if sensing her dismay, later that day, Satan dropped by. He wanted stroking. "Are you enjoying this?" he asked. "A little praise here." He wore a red smoking jacket and black tuxedo pants.

"Yes," Verdana said. "It's great. But this damned agent is getting me so many appointments, and I can only do one cock a day." Secretly, she longed for the old days when art was all that mattered, just herself and a friendly but ugly man in her studio as she made a replica of his manhood, fondling clay, scraping with silent tools to the industrial *chug-chug* sound of her floor heater. She hadn't cared what anybody thought.

"What will happen now?" she asked Satan. "Will this go on forever?"

"Until you die," he replied.

"How do I know if my sculptures are good? No one criticizes them. No one says they are provocative. I had a man come in with his teen-aged daughter; he bought one of her boyfriend for her birthday present."

"Provocative?" Satan asked, laughing. "Were they ever? Cocks? You sculpt human anatomy, Verdana. No more, no less. Nothing more common. Everybody has a cock. Every-body male. Besides, you wanted to be rich. Have I not provided that? You wanted to be famous. Are you not famous? I even had Thomas call you. A good touch, yes? I have him weeping with sorrow in the corner now. Do you

like that? Of course, he's been one of mine for a long time—
how I met you, actually. A friend of a friend." Satan smirked.

"I'm not happy," she whined.

"Is that my fault?" he asked, merciless in tone. "Stop
being a baby. Go out and sculpt cock. Come inside and
sculpt fruit. Sculpt pigeon shit or the hairy ass of a moth-
er-in-law. Who cares? They'll love you. Your audience!
Unconditional love. Can you dig it?" He sprawled on her
new leather sofa, kicking his feet over the armrest.

"I want to keep the gallery, but I need to see what
people really think. Can you do that?"

He extracted a toothpick from his smoking jacket and
picked at his teeth. "Why?"

The toothpick worked around his gums, one fissure at
a time, until she uttered, "Because if everyone loves what I
do—they don't love it because I am doing it. They love it
because you made them love it."

"So fucking what?"

"I want honesty."

"Honesty?" he said. "I won't do that to you. Not unless
you want to sign away your soul. Honesty? Fallen Christ,
what's gotten into you, woman? Artists disdain honesty."

"That's not me," she said.

From his pocket, after staring at her a while, Satan
retrieved a scroll and a feather pen with a razor tip. Specks
of dried blood stained the blade. "I'll take your soul for
that," he said.

"No," she said, "It's mine!"

"So you think!" he argued. "It isn't now and it never
was. All right! One more night with me and I will let the
public roar or rave. A completely honest reaction. This'll kill
you. Do you agree, Verdana?"

"Yes."

He sighed. "You artists think you want honesty, but
you really don't. You get into petty ego scrapes and bite each

other's tits off over trifles. You have skin no thicker than that on a bird's neck. No wonder you're always dying off. Suicide legion. Poor baby artist, needs so much attention. Honesty? Please. Honesty is a kick in the teeth while you're grabbing your gut. You still want it? Yes? Because honesty hurts, Sugar."

"Yes, yes! I do," she replied.

"Come downstairs," he said. "My limo awaits." He clasped her hand and issued a mirthless smile—reminding her of her father on an outing when he had clenched her hand the same way, and she had been en route to a dental extraction.

The streets swam with people. After they parked, Satan brought several blankets from the limo trunk and they rode an elevator up to the roof of a high-rise. "Here," he said. "I will take you here."

Verdana stared at the crevice between the roof and the ground. "The fall would kill you," Satan said. "But you won't fall."

The starry night beckoned. Windows on the adjacent building looked like a fly's eye—so many frames, so much sheen. He stripped her clothing from her body and, as he touched her, she felt the worst pain she had ever experienced —like ripping open her foot with a rusty nail, like being told Thomas never loved her, like miscarrying that child, years ago, and watching, slowly, the blood leak from her body— for days. "This is what it is to topple," Satan said. "Is this what you want?" He touched her softly with his hands, but his nails were carving knives. She bled. "Decide now," he whispered. "Now."

Her heart seized. Beneath them, the city was alive, vehicles passed on the busy streets, and she felt dead. "Yes," she said, unsure but unwilling to admit her indecision. "I'm ready. Let me see the truth."

"Remember," he said. "You asked for it."

As he thrust inside her, his cock tore her apart. She took months to mend. Initially, with the honesty he had unleashed, religious groups cried out about her cocks, schools banned photos of her art, but it took years for her popularity to wane. From the time of the first negative debacle, Merry called her once a week rather than ten times a day, until finally her opportunities exhausted themselves; Verdana was no longer in demand. "If you just did something other than cocks," Merry said finally. "We could sell a new angle and get a buzz going. Why not try women's genitalia?" and so Verdana did.

The women did not grant her the same reaction. They seemed embarrassed to spread their legs, like they had something ugly down there, like she'd be revealing a nightmare. One even said, "So is that what it looks like? I've never seen it before."

"You've never seen your own anatomy?" Verdana asked, then realized she hadn't seen her own.

"The problem is," Merry told her. "Your looks don't move the product. You need to help me here."

Verdana finally agreed to a nose job, and returned to sculpting cock. Merry convinced her to sculpt in Day-Glo, and she warmed to the work. On the day of the showing, crowds gathered. Verdana wanted to bask in their affection. New nose and lipoed thighs, she looked splendid. *I am*, she thought, *so far from my modest beginnings, I can hardly believe it.* She filtered through the attendees, easily anonymous.

Her dress was a long beaded sheath the color of ripe peaches. "It's huge," one woman said, perusing Satan's cock. "I've never seen one this big. This is the only good one."

"You see mine every night," her boyfriend muttered. "Who cares about size?"

Verdana approached the wine table. "What a joke," a socialite laughed, touching the large diamond studs on her earlobes. "This is not art. It's public display."

"You wanted an evening out, didn't you?" the man replied. "Well, here we are."

"You have to wonder," the socialite said. "How many men she has... if you know what I mean?"

"More than a few," the man replied. "I bet it's her fee— a night in the sack."

"Wicked, you! I heard her nose has an ugly hook, but maybe some men like that."

"Kitten, you are cold," the man said, stuffing caterer's quiches into napkins and then into his date's purse. They sidled into the crowd. Everywhere around her, Verdana heard jibes. She realized her exhibit was only well-attended because Merry advertised it as a freak show: "A Night of Cock."

Uncaring about the others, Verdana grabbed the four-teen-inch cock from its pedestal and strolled through the double doors. A security guard detained her. "Uh, Miss, return the cock, please."

"It's mine."

"Look, Lady. This gallery belongs to Verdana Lane. If you don't give back that cock at once, I'll have to arrest you."

"I am Verdana Lane," she said.

"Yeah, and I'm J. Edgar Hoover."

"I am the artist," she shrieked. "Show me some respect."

"Let me see some ID," he replied. As a crowd gathered to watch the exchange, Verdana realized she had left her purse at home.

"Is Merry here?" she asked. "My publicist?"

"I don't know who is here," he said. "There are over two hundred people. But I can't let you walk off with a display cock and that's all there is to it. Listen, Verdana Lane is ugly. I've seen her before, and, Lady, be thankful you aren't her."

"I am the artist," she shrieked again. "And you are fired!"

Satan approached, carrying Verdana's purse. "Excuse me, Sir," he said. "You are addressing Ms. Verdana Lane. I should know—because I'm the subject of this cock. Which is to say, this cock is mine." Verdana grabbed her purse, men coughed, and women tittered.

From the back of the crowd, someone yelled, "Yeah? Prove it."

"More than happy to," Satan said. He pulled his penis out and held it beside the sculpture. Some gasped. The flash of a camera blinded them. Satan wheeled around, pointing his rock-hard organ like a gun at those assembled. "Everyone go back to the exhibit, please," he said, then re-holstered himself. As Verdana strode away, a bevy of women greeted him. "Yes, of course I like to be sculpted... See you later, Verdana," he shouted at her back.

She walked quickly, holding the sculpture to her chest. *She had sold out and was unrecognizable*, she decided. No question. She longed for the hook of her old nose. By morning, papers all over town would announce the penile flashing at her gallery. Her fame had turned to notoriety, and she would never sculpt to anything but ridicule again. So there was only one thing left to do—return to the place that would not hurt. As she entered the elevator, she expressed her resolution, "I've got to end it all," and strode across the roof, looking down at the city. Across the way, windows emitted a dull golden light, but the stars were fogged over and the night felt dim. "Only a short fall," she told herself. "And then it will be over. But I'll drop his cock first."

"I wouldn't do either, if I were you," Satan said, appearing beside her.

She strode to the ledge and dropped his sculpture off the side of the building. She watched it fall until she could no longer see it. "Why not?" she asked, imagining the sound of cracking porcelain, thirty stories below. "My life is meaningless."

Satan pulled out a tattered scroll and read, "Proviso 34B: If the human takes his or her own life, they are doomed to hell. You're mine if you do."

"So push me, instead," she said. "I don't care how I go." She stared at the fine fabric of her dress and flung her satin wrap into the air.

"Don't you see?" he asked. "I already have—pushed you, that is. Honesty, that's the problem. You wanted it. Kill yourself? Go ahead. Be dead. Dead is good."

She retreated and stared at the blunt edge of her heels. "I won't do it," she said, changing her mind. "I won't. I'll get through this."

"But, maybe you should," he replied, twisting his bow tie. "I can see two things happening depending on what you do tonight. Would you like to know what they are?"

"Yes."

"If you walk away, you will live to the ripe age of forty-five. Adrenal cancer will strike you, but not before you sculpt another eight hundred cocks. The originals will rapidly devalue. You will be considered a pervert and shunned by the art world, but will stubbornly cling to your vision and never give up. But, if you plummet, flying leap, you will die eternally famous. Only four hundred cocks will survive your death and they will increase in value. You will be martyred. The young artist struck down in her prime—with so much cock left undone. Ha ha! I laugh for you! Presidents will weep that you didn't get to wrap your hands around their clay members. Young people will praise your work in an avant-garde underground for the next two hundred years. You will live forever. So, what do you choose, Verdana?"

"But I will go to hell?" she asked.

"You already slept with the devil," he replied, winking.

"So what do you think?"

She touched the beads sparkling on her dress, peered down into the night, and let the wind sweep her hem over the building's edge. The dress was elegant, long, with a sweeping skirt. Not a dress for a kissed toad. Though it was the color of flesh, she felt invisible, a part of the night sky. The cool air whipped her hair into her face. "My memory will live forever?"

"Yes," he said. "Now, plummet. You haven't much time."

She entertained visions of a long and beautiful funeral. She imagined the faces of young men one hundred years later, marveling at her perfect cocks. She swayed on the ledge, and then, with a graceful dive, somersaulted down.

"She cut off her nose..." Satan said, "and all that jazz," but he smiled as her body thudded onto the pavement, and leaned over to watch the blood pool around her head and corpse. A moment later, at the bottom floor, he wrapped her purse strap around her wrist then shouted, "Oh my God! The famous artist Verdana Lane has just jumped off the building. Call the police."

To himself, he murmured, "Vanity—will they ever be less vain?" He picked up the shards of his cock, pointed to the sky, and said, "Again, Brother. You lose," then strutted to a pay phone. "Operator," he said, "I'd like to make a call."

"One moment, please. Where may I direct your call?"

"Hell," he said. "Tell them we have a new arrival."

"Excuse me?"

"Nothing. Kidding. Dial this number: 1 (540) 555-1212."

"Dialing and connecting."

"Senator Jones, please."

"Jones speaking."

"It's me."

"Scratch. How the hell are you?"

"It's time for the play, Harry. The play of a lifetime—
fifteen-thousand civilians screaming and hiding in hovels.
Push the button; make a future in politics—not many people
you know will die... What's that old expression about the
ladder to success being built on a tower of human skulls?"

"Don't know." The senator sounded a little sick.

"Nice talking to ya, Harry. Figure it out. Do as I say."

Satan left the phone swinging in the breeze and luxuri-
ated in the sensation of his fine linen shirt brushing the nubs
where wings once were, then returned to the party. He had
many acquaintances to cultivate and, numerous though they
were, they had so little time, so very little time.

PSYCHIC PIGEON

In every large flock of pigeons, there is one psychic bird the others turn to in weakness and in strife, for he or she can hear and absorb the worlds of other animals, including humans. The gene that determines this psychic trait is rare, and those born with it descend from select family lines and must migrate, like travelers, far and wide to ensure every large group of fowl retains a leader. In the case of city pigeons, this leader is also called upon to locate food sources, govern mating squabbles, and train the group with all extended knowledge that his or her innate abilities can offer.

It is imperative that he or she appears unimportant to the outside world, remaining hidden, like a decoy, amongst the cooing-and-pecking rest.

For the psychic pigeon to pass away or be lost would be to the detriment of all. A flock without guidance, Harvey, the psychic pigeon leader of the Park Oceanic Valley Mall and Office Structure, knew would soon disband.

But much as a rock star can entertain too much adulation, Harvey was tired of leadership, so he often entertained fantasies of telling his flock: "I'm not psychic anymore; fly away. Leave me alone. I just want to peck for seeds and scout for white doves." But he knew he could not since this sort of speech would disgrace his family, especially his Uncle Earl, the godfather psychic pigeon with all-black plumage whom all pigeons knew from infancy, and were taught to admire and pay tribute to should they ever visit the West Coast.

Earl would kill him. Earl would peck out his eyes with no remorse and leave his eyeballs on the ground as Harvey's only possible food source. Yes, Earl was that cruel.

It was not that Harvey hated worship: He knew serving as the lead pigeon was a long and illustrious tradition—but he fancied himself a sensitive artist, and the relentless task of dealing with the idiocy of others was one he would gladly have shrugged off. He could hear all day long not only the banal thoughts of the birds around him (*My toe itches. What happened at Trafalgar square? Who farted?*), but also those of the people in the buildings and stores in and around the mall, who strolled like giants above his minions, nearly kicking them out of the way.

He stood on the preferred ledge, observing his favorite pastime of head-shitting, turning backward to face the building with his rear feathers hanging over the ledge, then staring deeply into the brick before him as if to meditate and targeting the most offensive passerby thinkers. He waited and listened. Thoughts. Thoughts. Thoughts. None of them of interest.

All decent people thinking only of obligations and commitments. *I'm sorry for you*, he thought, *that your reflections are so un-soulful.*

Weeks ago, he had informed the flock, in the interest of maintaining his health, that he required three off-leadership hours a day, so head-shitting was his new favorite activity and this alone amused him to the extent of rising above the sound of a soft *coo*.

Men in expensive suits were his favorite victims, Harvey decided, preferably dumb men with wide chests and impressive jaws who worked at the larger department stores and wore silk and cashmere so they could touch themselves all day. These men were always thinking about the pictures of multiple half-nude women they flirted with, whose private messages were lodged like marital kill-bullets in their cell phones. These men also seldom thought of their wives as they strode by, and if they did, their thoughts were most often negative: *I should really pick up Betsy's excessive dry cleaning after I go see Angelina at the lingerie store and try to look down her shirt at those perfect D-cups.* Or, *Damn, I can hear Eileen bitching already and I'm not even home. I left the socks on the floor. I didn't clear my plate. Good-Boobs54 wouldn't hassle me with that duty. Maybe I should live with her. Nah, she'd start nagging, too—about two seconds after I moved in. But, she'd let me fuck her, I bet, if I went out to Wisconsin.*

Because these men were shallow and self-centered, they made perfect targets. Harvey pitied the Betsys and Eileens of the world. *I bet she'd like a little arsenic to land in your toothpaste,* he thought. *I bet she'd take delight in shaving your pubes with a dull razor and then dousing you with lemon puree.* But because the Betsys and Eileens would likely never know about the GoodBoobs and Angelinas until it was too late, Harvey took extra care at playing his part in universal karma and took precise aim at these men, hoping to see his shit splatter, if at all possible, down the backs of their shitty heads; down their fine shirts; and, in the instance of an extra-good hit, straight down their necks to the skin below their collars.

Some men, not many, he heard think of their wives in a positive way, and these he avoided bothering. "Carry on," he said aloud. "For the sake of your women, I wish there were more of you." After all, Harvey had decided, he was not only a champion of universal karma, but also a lover of fine things, beauty, mysteries, and enigmas. He did not love pain or violence directed toward the innocent.

Still, he protected himself. When those he shat on were angered, as invariably they were, he made use of his several advance-planned strategic getaways so his presence could be almost immediately hidden behind building pillars. "Don't stick out when you're in trouble," he remembered Earl saying long ago. Though Harvey figured the frequency of his head-shitting practice might make him a target, he also was no plebian park pigeon, carrying the gas-spill neck plumage and muted colors of a plain gray. He was black and white, like a cow, easily identifiable, so he made a studious habit of avoiding any individuals, nice or otherwise, that he could assume might be carrying a gun and may try to hunt him later.

Looking around, he noticed the mall was fairly empty this Tuesday morning. As he people-watched, he listened predominantly for women thinkers. Curiously, they thought as much about sex as the men, sizing up their fellow shoppers and making lewd internal comments, but were much quicker to attribute a love-related trait to a man or replace whatever provocative thought had occurred to them almost instantly with a mundane concern like what would be for lunch. *What a tight, hot ass!*, he heard one think, followed with, *I'd like to wake up to him making my morning coffee. Speaking of which, I should get a latté. I could use three lattés. Thank God for coffee.*

Unfortunately, a sad sub-species of women were also easily derailed into repetitive despair at the failure of past relationships: *His eyes are so pretty,* Harvey heard one reflect as a man in a suit walked near the opposite overhang, and then follow with, *They look just like Jaime's. Oh, how I loved Jaime. I need a bagel. I need a Xanax.*

But all thoughts he observed seemed to echo the same themes. *Humans and pigeons both*, he decided, perusing a new group of walkers for possible targets, *are primarily interested in eating and fucking. Why can't I be like them?* he thought. *But I'm not like a pigeon. I'm not like a human. I'm a half-breed of rational possibilities.*

Surrounding birds had thoughts far simpler in execution. *Eat. Fuck. Preen. Repeat.* Frequently, the cooing of procreating flock brethren filled the air. *It's obscene how often I hear this*, Harvey thought, preparing to shit on two newly selected teenage girls thinking only of parties and stealing the other's boyfriend. Staring at the same brick in front of him as if it were a meditation stone, he aimed and dropped his load. The two were dressed alike in the same tight red tops and black jeans. He turned to look where he'd hit, grateful his feces had landed directly between them, splattering the long blonde hair of one and the chubby shoulder of the other.

"Eeeewwww! Eeeeewwww!" they shrieked, shaking their hands in front of them as if it would remove the wet debris, and careening wildly around the other as they searched for something to wipe the shit off. *The food court is across the mall, Ladies*, Harvey thought. *Good luck.*

He flew a quick victory loop from the ledge because their reaction was so pronounced. *I would sing this joy if I had a good voice*, he thought, but his mood shifted. Staring up at the cloudless sky, he wanted to fly away, musing, *Obligation is terrible, to anything or anyone.* Obligation bound him even now, he decided, if not his own squabs; he was the father of few. Though he did enjoy sex when he indulged, he also failed to mate frequently with those near because his taste had never clamored for mall pigeons, but instead the pretentious and rarer white doves. Unfortunately, these were few and far between in urban digs like the mall. Wedding steeples often released borrowed doves, but it was difficult for him to get free very often.

Regarding mall pigeons, he also had no taste for the mating dance of fluffing up neck feathers, quickly walking forward while bowing, and sealing the deal. He did have needs, but although the female pigeons around him worked hard to entice, even chasing him or standing still rather than performing the standard mating dance of evasion, which they knew he disdained, his efforts lacked a certain zest.

And he was strange, too, in that he had realized long ago he wanted to be in love. From humans, he learned he should want more than a quick grappling on the ledge that ended almost as soon as it had begun. But he had started to feel that true love would never find him, even with doves on holiday. So: *Here I am*, he thought, *in the reckless yet endless summer of my discontent.*

It was not long after this revelation that he began to fly a larger perimeter outside the mall and office complex, stopping to peck at curious objects like streetlights and antenna balls, before getting closer to the spacious children's park he enjoyed. Going this far was not far enough to escape the flock, however, in that it didn't matter what he tried; when they needed him, the recalcitrant mob could always calculate his whereabouts, which he attributed to their magnetic pulse tracking. Maybe, unbeknownst to him, they also had a spy bird. Today was no exception. He heard the group calling from half-a-mile away.

"Harvey! Harvey!" they yelled. "There's a problem."

"What is it?" he asked, as they swooped in close behind him. But he didn't look back, busy as he was watching a handsome man and woman seated on a park bench across the street. The two held hands and gazed at each other like lovers. Wanting to hear their tender thoughts, he neared, landed on the curb of a busy intersection, and made the flock follow him across the crosswalk when the light flashed green.

"No moving on a red light," he had often warned. "Only people who think of offing themselves go into the road when that light is red and flashing. They think things like: *My head will splatter on that windshield and won't life be better? Green is good. Red is not. Stick with green.*"

He always had to break down his logic for them. He

let them follow as he approached the human couple, but the birds behind him had already begun remonstrating their needs before he crossed the street.

"Harvey," they said. "Come back. Our friends are dying. We need you. You have to give up your off-leadership hours today. Come back to the mall."

"No," Harvey said, continuing to amble toward the couple. "I don't give up my off-hours... And where did you get that idea? Besides, I'm not at the mall because I didn't want to be there. Would you stop following me? I'll be back, like always, around four."

"Sooner, sooner," they chorused. "Didn't you hear? Pigeons are dying. Lots of us."

"But pigeons die all the time," Harvey said. "What else is new?"

The flock was then smart enough to send a bevy of female birds to the front, which immediately set upon dramatic weeping, knowing how he hated to see them cry. "If it's their toes and feet falling off from the consumption of too much fast food," Harvey said, "I already warned those idiots. I can't keep them away from the junk. I told you: I can lead the bird to manna, but I can't keep it from eating shit."

"No, no," they replied. "There's a bird killer."

"A bird killer?"

"Yes, in that back office with all the big pictures and books on a desk, there's a man doing us in. A tall man in a dark suit."

He didn't believe it. Was this like when they thought the aluminum foil around hot dogs had become the devil's fruit roll-up? "Go away," he said. "Leave me alone."

Still nearing the bench where the couple sat, Harvey could hear the human thoughts and tuned out the flock. *If I tell her what happened, this could devastate her*, the man thought. *I didn't mean to do what I did; I just wanted to get to know her better. I do like her. Maybe I love her.*

Meanwhile, the woman thought: *He looks so serious. Is he going to ask me to marry him, to move in? What is he thinking? Is he thinking of making love? I hope so.* She licked her lips and fingered the hem of her moss-green silk skirt.

That other girl in Toledo was a prostitute, the man's inner banter continued. *A whore with three piercings on her twat. How dumb could I be? And then there were the tiny sores, almost like cold sores, but down there—did that mean anything? I hope not. I didn't use protection.*

Both the man and woman continued staring at each other with masked, tentative looks. The silence continued. The woman took the man's hand and rubbed it against her cheek.

"I missed you last week," she said, thinking, *He's held off from seducing me for so long. Is it love? He must really respect me. If so, that's romantic, but I would like him to take me to bed before I start to think he's gay. Sex. Now. Please. It's time he gives me sex. Maybe he is small. Like really small?*

"I missed you, too," the man said—deciding urgently: *A few more weeks and the tests will be back. I can sleep with her then. With no guilt.*

"Do you want to go back to my place?" the woman asked, finally laying it on the line. "I'd like you to see my room."

That would be nice, the man thought, *and she's right; I have to fuck her now or she'll lose interest. She already thinks I'm gay. I'll just use a condom. Speak! Hurry up, you jerk; stop thinking. Start talking. She's waiting. Say: Yes. Yes, yes, y-e-s, say it.* "Yes, Sharon," he said. "I would love to follow you home."

The woman pulled the man up from the bench and clasped his hand as they walked away together. Moved, he marveled at the complexity of the exchange. The things people said and thought were so oppositional—not like the simplicity of pigeons. With pigeons, "Let's mate" had a clear meaning, as did, "I'm hungry," as did "I'm tired." Their thoughts and speech were from the same tree. Not so with people. In fact, his attention returned more and more to the birds—because they had come to shouting at him.

"Bird killer. Some stinking bird killer," he heard the pigeons around him squawk. "Doesn't Harvey care?"

"Okay, a bird killer," Harvey said, returning his gaze to the amassed rows of scouts. "What do you mean? How is the purported killing happening? Also, extra points for anyone who can tell me what the hell you expect me to do about the problem."

"Follow us back," they cooed. "It's the corner-office man who always wears those fancy suits. You figure it out. Aren't you the smart one, Harvey?"

"Yes," he said. "The smart one. The psychic one. All right, let's go."

When he returned, he followed them from his usual ledge and around to the side of the building where it was possible to look into the offices. On one ledge, he saw fourteen birds, sprawled, cold, still as lead. He knew them all. Suddenly, the impact of what the other birds had said set in.

Tears welled in his eyes.

Some were young, barely out of squab phase, some he had mentored not so long ago. On the ledge was also a pale-blue series of pebbles. The poison. He looked at the man inside the office. He saw only the back of his head but listened to his thoughts.

I've got to get these dead birds off my ledge, the man thought. *Need to fill out a custodial services form. The visual won't be good for visitors when I have meetings. And this pigeon problem is out of control. Something must be done. How can I keep the mall clean if we don't manage population control? A good business is a clean business*, he thought. *The mall must present the look of something new, something bright and desirable. A good manager is one who makes sure it happens.*

The man walked around his desk and toward a bookshelf on the back wall. Large, framed posters hung above the lower shelving and boasted motivational expressions like: "Success is what you make, so make it!" and "If you don't give 120 percent, you should only get paid for 50."

This poison works well, the man thought. *Maybe, with any luck, I'll get rid of all the birds. But I should buy more kinds. Just to make sure it keeps working. I could put it all over the mall. Alternate locations.*

The man looked at a pie chart on his desk. *Sales are decreasing*, he thought. *We need to increase revenue and reface the existing storefronts on the north side... Increase loss-prevention measures. Bump up security.*

"What is he thinking?" the flock asked Harvey, observing him keenly. "What is he doing?"

"I don't know," Harvey said, but he did. He also knew this man was determined to kill them, had no love for anything but money and success, and that Harvey himself would have to do something about it. If his life had been aimless before, Harvey realized his current role as leader was imperative. He felt the weight and splendor of an altruistic goal against a suitably dire enemy drop onto his previously slacking shoulders.

"I will," he told them, "make a plan to get rid of this monster. In order to do this," he said, "I shall have to enter the building. Pass the word: No one eat anything but known foods until the issue is resolved. I am imposing a ban on anything other than garbage-can sources."

The flock gasped and tittered. "Garbage cans," they repeated. "You're going in the building? But what about the people?" they said. "You can't go in people buildings. Pigeons don't come back."

Those present gaped at the enormous human structure with seemingly endless glass windows. It was then that
Harvey noticed a woman outside the building, in a blue
dress that whipped with the breeze. She pressed her hand to
the glass. *I knew it*, she thought. *I knew what I imagined
would come to pass.*

"I'll be fine," Harvey said.

"You won't know how to get back to the ledge," the
pigeons replied. "You'll get stuck in the vents. You'll die,
Harvey! We can't lose you. We'll need a new leader!
Someone else should go. Someone less important. And what
will you do to stop the man?" they asked.

"I don't know, yet," Harvey said. "But when I get
there, I will."

The next day passed in somber preparation. In case it
would be his last chance to mate, since survival was not
certain, Harvey visited and sexed up four females, hoping if
he did die on his quest, there would be another psychic
member to rule.

He flew around the building's perimeter and listened
for how best to enter, how to get to the boss's office, and
how to get out. At 9 a.m. the next day, he walked in through
the glass doors beside a pretty brown-haired girl carrying a
briefcase, a purse, a cup of coffee, and a sack of lunch. She
did not notice him, and hurried to apply pale peach lip gloss
with a wand as she walked.

And if I never see him again, she thought, *I should not
care. He didn't love me. He never cared for anyone but
himself. I have to stop thinking about him. It's over. He
couldn't even once tell me he loved me or cared about me.
And I have to see the boss this morning. I'll have to tell that
asshole stores on my wing won't be renewing their leases.
He's going to have my head. What if I get fired? Unemploy-
ment? Play my guitar between checking want ads? Oh, fuck
it all.*

Harvey was charmed. She pushed back the hair that had dropped over her pretty wire glasses with a defeated air. She touched her earrings and determined both quartz briolettes remained in place. In her eyes was a faint trace of extra moisture that did not go away. *Be strong,* he heard her think. *Where is all that motivational thinking stuff about letting go I'm supposed to be practicing? And, should I feel guilty? If I hadn't spent six months talking to Tom and fucking off at work, could I have made these big chains change their minds? What will I tell the boss now? Not that I fucked off and "oops." And how will the loss of those stores impact the other stores? What about those jobs?*

Arriving at her office, unaware of Harvey stealthily walking behind her, she sighed and sat in her small gray cubicle. On her bulletin board were Hawaiian postcards friends had sent and little green-and-blue origami creatures she'd been given by a paper merchant. She had itineraries, too, for still-pending trips she'd planned for others. *I just want to be in love with someone who deserves me,* she thought. *I want to quit this job and get the hell out of here.*

I feel you, Harvey thought.

Another co-worker peeked around the corner of her cubicle. He was a thin man with graying hair; he wore a thrift-store suit, and a puzzled look. "Did you fill out that form, Nessa, on the coffee you spilled outside the staff lounge, so the boss knows it happened? We need custodial services."

"Not yet," she said, thinking he smelled like mothballs.

"Well, did you fill out the custodial request form to get them here?"

"No, not yet," she said. *This colleague,* she thought, *needs a life. She had not spilled a cup of coffee, only a few drops. Why was he trying to be the enforcer? And wouldn't she just, even if the spill were cleaned, spill a few more drops the very next day?* "Did you fill out that form to admit wasting time hanging around my desk when I'm trying to work?" she asked with an ambiguous, almost gentle smile. "Remember, you only get one fifteen-minute break during a five-hour shift, Carl. Are you taking a break?" Then she smiled, more sweetly than before, mainly to confuse him, and said, with a tired air, "I'm just kidding, Carl. I'll fill out that form for you today, okay, Sweetheart? Don't worry."

She logged on to her computer and sighed. *The big boss. Meeting with the big boss at 9:30. Think fast*, she thought, *faster than ever before: What the hell am I going to say about the loss of those clients?*

Harvey regarded her shoes from beneath her desk. He would, he decided, follow her to the big boss's office.

I need a plan, she thought.

I need a plan, he echoed.

He almost wished he were her human counterpart, hearing how closely her thoughts resembled his. If he were human, he mused, they might easily fall in love. Bird though he was, he felt half in love already.

He hated this Tom guy, whoever he was. *Tell her you care, Tom*, he wanted to say. *Is that so hard?* There were twenty minutes remaining until 9:30. Harvey snuck back out to fly the ledges on a scouting mission. So many thinkers were crammed in the building. Their thoughts told him all kinds of things, but not about the structure of the business or the building's layout. He did, however, learn that the boss drank too much coffee. He would store that kernel away, he thought, walking behind a fat man with ample cover as he returned to Nessa's desk. On her screen was a personal message from Tom.

Shut this bullshit thinking down, he heard her think. *God, it's pathetic when I can't even seem to keep myself from thinking about him.*

She opened her work e-mail and checked the history

of work-related messages. She scoured them for ones from
the two departing clients. "Ah!" she said, having found two
indicating the clients were leaving the mall due to raised
lease rates and corporate's insistence. She remembered she
had sent the big boss an e-mail ages ago, asking if he would
consent to keep their rates the same. He had declined.

My ass, she thought, *is covered.* Still, she did not want
to walk down those long corridors behind the storefronts to
his isolated office, where he would ogle and grope. Something about walking along the dark hallway in the daytime
with nothing but dumpsters and closed doors on the way to
a lascivious wretch was daunting.

"Greg," she said, when she dialed his extension.
"Would you mind if we do a phone meeting, instead?"

"No, Nessa," the big boss said. "I need you to come
see me."

Harvey, below her desk, sensed a tremor of fear and
loathing pass through her. As if to soothe her, he walked to
her ankle and brushed it with his wing's soft feathers.

She didn't notice. Resolutely, she stood. *It's time*, she
thought, clutching the e-mails she had printed as verifica-
tion, something she'd have as protection from whatever ludicrous thing Greg said. She walked to the door behind the
cubicles and entered the mall and offices' back area.

Harvey followed at a close distance. In the long
pathway, the floors were cement. Hearing his feet clicking
behind her, Nessa turned. "Oh, little pigeon," she said.
"Don't get lost in here." Harvey puffed up his neck feathers.
He hopped from side to side. "You're a pretty one, aren't
you?" she asked. He loved her petting, ruffling voice. "Fine,"
she said, "follow me if you want. I'm only going into the pit
of hell."

When she reached a door marked 40001, she knocked.
The manager's voice spoke through an intercom: "Come
in."

Harvey followed and managed, barely, to enter unseen before the door shut. He then hid below the lip of the manager's desk, beside Nessa's feet. *Okay, I'm here*, he thought. *What's my plan?*

Outside the man's window were Harvey's dead friends. On the bookshelf ledge, he noticed, the box of poison remained.

In the background, Nessa began to speak. The boss replied. They began a heated exchange, but Harvey wasn't looking at Nessa now, wasn't listening. He observed the pale blue sky beyond the window and the pale blue rocks on the ledge, and the way the big boss wore shoes that were so waxed all leather surfaces gleamed. Then he was listening to the big boss as he berated Nessa for losing the contracts and felt a growing hatred for the man whose face he now wanted to see, up close and personal, so he would not forget him.

He could feel the stress mounting in Nessa's blood, her heart rate escalate. He heard his Uncle Earl's advice, *We must know our friends, but also our enemies.* So, what was Greg thinking? Harvey maneuvered closer.

Greg stood behind Nessa at the window. Both looked out onto something unknown. *Ah*, Harvey heard Greg think. *Yes, just like that. Don't move.*

Since he saw only the back of Nessa's legs, half her arms and rear torso, and the back of her head, with Greg blocking his view, Harvey couldn't tell what was going on, but Harvey could see that Greg had draped his arm around Nessa's shoulder, wrapping himself around her so his hand must be dangling lower down her front. He wondered what the posture meant, if not an intent to grope. And where, Harvey was curious to know, were Greg's thoughts of business and success now? Ah, yes. They had switched tracks to flesh acquisition.

Finally, I'm going to do it, Greg thought. *Right now. I am going to fuck her. She's weak. She needs this job. She'll let me.* And Harvey watched Greg grab Nessa's shoulder and spin her toward him as he heard Nessa think: *No. No. But what will I do for rent? I can't lose this job. Okay. Let him. Surrender. I have no choice. I have no choice.*

As these thoughts grew progressively heavier, Harvey felt sickened as he watched Greg unbutton her blouse, take it off, and drop it to the floor, dead window-ledge birds staring with open eyes. Greg put his hand between her legs and rubbed her crotch before pushing her down to the floor and positioning her on the carpet, yanking her skirt up to her waist, pulling aside her panties, and shoving two fingers roughly inside. Greg then grabbed her left breast.

She winced.

Greg unbuttoned his pants with obvious satisfaction. "If you fuck me now, Nessa," Harvey heard Greg say, for through this Nessa had said nothing, "I won't bother you again. I'll get you that promotion in a few months... Every-thing will be fine."

And Greg took a condom from his wallet. He got on top of her, sat up on his knees, and put it on himself, whistling.

No. No. No. Nessa thought. But Greg again shoved his thick fingers in and out of her with a rapid rhythm and began talking more and more about how he was going to do her like this, do her like that, on and on, and when Harvey heard her thoughts then, he realized for the first time that a human's thoughts could be screams. Inside, Nessa was screaming. Harvey had no idea what to do, but he did know that the love-sex dynamic for humans was complicated. There were too many dark paths it could go down and he'd be safer and happier to simply mate with pigeons, as he'd always been told. In that moment, he gave up on his ideas of romantic love.

At the same time, he had no doubt Greg deserved whatever karmic lesson came his way, but what could he, a pigeon, psychic or otherwise, do to make it happen?

I don't want him inside me, Harvey heard Nessa think. *Somebody make him stop. Back here, he'll never get caught. How many women has he done this to? I can't be alone.*

And then Harvey had an idea. Since the humans were on the floor near the guest chair and Greg's coffee cup, still steaming, was on the nearby desk, he would fly and push the cup past the edge until it fell, splattering onto Greg's naked ass. But just as Harvey had this thought, Greg pulled Nessa up from the floor and kissed her. She was not kissing him back.

Harvey watched. He spied the poison on the bookshelf. He looked at the dead birds, their eyes open, on the ledge. He wished he could stop hearing Nessa's thoughts, for they were terrible. He wished he could stop hearing Greg's thoughts, for they were worse: Greg liked her crying. Greg liked to watch her tear herself apart and enjoyed taking what she didn't want to give.

Harvey flew to the poison.

I'll take this bitch and then I'll drink my coffee, he heard Greg think. *If I hurry, it will still be warm.*

Harvey grabbed two enormous clutches and flew back to the desk. He dropped both, with superb aim, into Greg's coffee. *With any luck*, he thought, *this will save the flock. I'll be a hero. Earl will be happy. Maybe Nessa will get a new boss. Already*, he felt like a better leader.

And Nessa? he wondered. *Should I leave her now? No, he would have to wait until the whole thing was over so that he could exit through the door when she opened it.* He listened again to her screaming thoughts, watching Greg ready himself, and then, Harvey performed an act of bravery. He flew up to the ceiling and allowed himself to be seen. He stared down at Greg, aimed, and shat on Greg's face.

Greg stopped what he was doing and spat. His face

flushed red. He wiped the shit from his lips and his eyes. "Fucking pigeon!" he shouted. "I hate these fucking pigeons! It's not enough that I see them in the mall, but now they get back here, too? I'm going to kill it!"

Nessa waited, staring.

"I might poison the others, but this one I'm going to clobber," Greg said. With the handle of a window-hook-release device, he started whacking at Harvey, who flew from here to there to evade.

As Greg chased Harvey, Nessa righted herself. "Poisoning them isn't going to work," she said, quietly getting dressed. "It's limiting the food source." But Greg still chased Harvey. "And I've got to be going now," she went on, buttoning and straightening her clothes.

"Don't open that door," Greg shouted at her, "until I kill this bird."

She glared. When Harvey veered toward the doorway, she opened it quickly so he could escape. He did. Then she said, "What? Oh, I'm sorry. Greg, I have to go now, okay?"

Zipping his pants, Greg ran into the corridor, chasing Harvey, but he could not find him. It was only a few moments later, when Greg returned to his office and Nessa left to walk quickly back to hers, that Harvey dropped from a recessed lighting ledge and fell again into ambling behind her.

She was crying. And then she heard his feet on the concrete and turned. "You, little pigeon," she said, smiling with a sheepish look. "Thank you. Follow me. I'll get you out." Instead of taking him back to the offices, she walked to an external doorway illuminated by a green *exit* sign. "Go be free now," she said. "Be safe."

Harvey landed on her arm and nudged her neck with his head, before flying up and away. It was with no small amount of sadness that he watched her continue to adjust her clothing and wipe her eyes with her sleeves, before she moved away from the external door and entered the building where the cubicles waited, where the coffee stains and irritating coworkers remained, where some man named Tom had broken her heart, and her boss had molested her, and where her life would now return to an endless chain of obligations.

Somberly, Harvey returned to the flock. "I have," he announced, "attempted to poison the bird killer today. I do not know if it worked. But I have emerged unscathed."

"Huzzah!" they shouted. And the day went on. And he heard them procreating and eating and bickering. And he liked it, how simple they were. At least pigeons are basic but truthful, he thought. We don't hurt each other on purpose, or doubt what we do.

He was sad, still, for Nessa, but if the poison had not worked, Harvey was not done with Greg. Now that he knew who Greg was, he decided he would watch each day from various ledges, turn to face the appropriate brick, and aim and launch. It would only take so many weeks of being hit before the man would loathe himself, finding himself splattered so often with white puddles of shit that no suits would be left unmarked. And this thought made Harvey chuckle. *For you, Nessa,* he thought. *For the flock, and for you. If I were human I may have loved you—but now, at least, I shit upon our shared enemy.*

This struck Harvey as poignantly poetic. He thought it often as he flew above the heads of hundreds of mall-walkers in the coming weeks, people engaged in buying and selling and returning things.

When the murmur of their thoughts became a roar of human need, he heard his Uncle Earl say, *Hold steady, Harv. The roar will clear and then you will have peace. Wait for it. It'll come. Lift yourself up and away if you need to, where the birds go, and your peace will return.*

Harvey flew higher and higher, looking for that small

aperture of blissful silence from the hazy blue sky dappled in cirrus clouds, and then he floated, circled, dipped, and danced, mid-air, above it all, until it did.

FEAR OF SNAKES

I should have known it wouldn't work out when Mark told me he was afraid of snakes. Because I am a snake. Well, only while I'm sleeping. But the paranoia of dating a man who fears snakes—one whom you adore but can never sleep in front of—it is too much.

Who can you show all your cool skills to? We took a trip to the desert and I was dying to sidewind for him. It would have been a delayed-reaction sort of conversation because I wouldn't have remembered sidewinding or been accessible in the moment he saw it, but he could have seen it, and then we could have chatted about it the next morning. As it was, I started an argument and then went over the dunes to sleep. I came back to him in the morning, apologetic, as my human self... But this caused unnecessary drama. I hate drama. And if he weren't so afraid of snakes, I could have shown him my full self in all my majesty.

My snake self has a fantastic rattle. It is my snake self I carry through my dreams; I am a special kind of powerful in dreams. I can slither anywhere. I can slither up a skirt or under a sofa, through a mountain or across a sea. I have seen my rattle in mirror dreams, too. You know those dreams—the ones where you are a baby viper, then you are an old snake, and then you are a hungry viper, middle-aged, who hasn't eaten in months? Mark would have made an incredible mate, if it weren't for this snake thing. We liked hanging out at coffeehouses. We liked reading books by

Korean guys. We liked calling out, "Gotcha!" when we told a big fat whopper the other believed, and we liked pistachio gelato.

It would be nice to know I could sleep beside him and use him as a heat rock. I would never bite him while I was sleeping, and even if I did, I am not poisonous. Just large. Imagine how it feels to have a lover rub up against you at night; it's a snaky feeling already. Only, with me, he'd have to accept a five-foot long serpent girl in his bed and the occasional partially-awake flit of my tongue that would feel exactly like a child's Eskimo kisses. I have seen my snake body; always see it while first waking. I know he would see it, too. I have scared a lover before. It took me a month to convince Peter from the accounting pool that he had a nightmare when he saw me as a snake in a sole instant of napping weakness after a quick bout of afternoon sex. Finally, he believed me, because he wanted to. But Mark. Mark was so cute and so smart. I loved the way his hair had just begun to gray, and his efficient way of walking. Mark was kind, so kind. He watched me shop for dresses! What a guy!

I wanted to be with him until I died or he died or we died. But I couldn't because of his fear of snakes. And I had brought up snakes before. Each time, he recoiled, acted like, "Why are you mentioning snakes, knowing they are my phobia?" I think he thought I was a closet-sadist for the re-mention, but I wasn't, really. Just a part-time snake, in spite of myself.

I had ingested chemicals as a child. They made for transformations. They were in the cat food. It was recalled after a few bags came into my house—Snacky Catty was the brand. I was one of few humans affected. I was only three; yes, I had been eating quite a bit of it. Who doesn't eat cat food at three? It's tempting, right? You're low to the ground. It's there. "Go play outside," the parents shout and you are playing outside, but you're also hungry. No one ever told me not to eat Mrs. Snickers and Dr. Knockerdoodle's food. But, no, the cats didn't turn into snakes—they did seem to hiss more, though.

And about Mark, I wondered: What should I do? Really, just imagine the fear and pain I'd already endured regarding this snake thing, the slumber parties I'd missed, the naps I'd foregone while on tour buses, the friendships that could have merged painlessly into the friends-with-benefits realm, but did not, because I knew I could get drunk and pass out and those friends might tell on me because they knew other friends would find this transformation interesting and it might not take much to get them to share the nature of my serpentine ways, flip me over and sell me out, if I let myself relax—because as beautiful a snake as I am, all green and yellow with dazzling gold tones, I didn't really want to out myself to the hordes of unsympathetic normals.

But I would have to do something about Mark and I knew I would lose him. "Why can't you spend the night?" I remember he kept asking. Initially, I made excuses. I told him I had a cat to feed, which I didn't because I would have eaten that cat while I slept. I told him I had a hydroponics set-up that needed monitoring in the mornings, which I did not because the last thing I'd want would be to get arrested and be a snake-sleeper in jail. I finally told him: "I am afraid of intimacy. Commitment. I don't sleep over."

Then, he brought me a basket of mums and some delphiniums. He sang me three love songs he wrote *just for me* while strumming his golden yellow classical guitar. He got naked and on bended knee and said, "I love you. Please, please stay with me."

I thought: *You don't know what you love. You know what you hate. I belong to the latter category. What do you love about me? What?*

But he was so endearing. So I did what he asked—I stayed with him all night, pinching myself so as not to go to sleep, letting my eyes trace his body a million times. This wakeful presence worked for the first five nights he made me stay. But then he would say each morning, "You look so tired. What's wrong? Not sleeping well?" And he noticed I needed breaks between nights of togetherness, and grew suspicious there were other men.

"Why can't you be here every night?" he asked. "Who else are you going to see?"

"You don't know how I am," I told him. "What if you hated having me here at night?"

On the sixth night I stayed, I forgot the caffeine pills. I fucked up. I'm not sure if this fuck-up was my subconscious telling me it was time to test his love, but I fell asleep. I turned into a snake and my snake self moved extremely close to him to be warmed. My snake self was so happy! Then he woke up. He started screaming.

His screaming startled me and then of course I lost my snake-form. But he kept saying, "All this time, you've been a snake? Why didn't you tell me you were a snake? A big, green snake! I could handle anything but this."

And I said, "You said you hated snakes. Why would I tell you? I'm only a snake while I'm sleeping. You said you loved me. I tried to hide my snakiness. I'm sorry."

He said he forgave me, but he didn't ask me any more to sleep over. And then he didn't call me. And then he asked me not to call him.

I said, "Whatever, Mark. I am what I am."

"I am what I am, too," he said.

I thought we sounded a little like Popeye, but it wasn't a funny moment. It was pretty sad. I touched his graying hair one last time. I did tell you he turned into a rat while sleeping, didn't I?

Well, yes, he did. Maybe that admission clears up a few things, about his snake phobia, anyway. Something about dog food and childhood, which I never held against him due to my own circumstances.

Guess it's a bit different when you're the snake, though. Oh, it's hard to be the snake. Too many bastard rats. Yet you keep being drawn to them, again and again. Some kind of biological warfare, I thought, when the rats are as big as snakes but still so fearful, so attractive, so endearing, so beguiling, and so wrong.

MEN LIKE CHAMELEONS IN THE DARK

I grew used to seeing Pano only at night because we worked so much—though it felt like months since we had truly seen each other. I worked two jobs, he worked three jobs, and we often joked that we'd be lucky to recognize each other in a crowd, much less make children, which, in any case, we both originally said we didn't want. Sometimes, I wondered why we lived together at all. Him with his black, shady wings that stretched between his forearms and his sides; me with my extra eyes on the back of my head. Mutants, all, these days. But we weren't even compatible mutants.

He could fly.

Granted, his flight efforts were confined to twenty-feet airborne, and he more often used a limited version for short hops between the coffee machines and the cash registers at his liquor store job, but he should have found another flyer, one of those women he could leap lily pads with or do whatever kinky things other flyers do. Not that I didn't love his wings—or how they wrapped around me.

When he fell in love with me, he told me because his wings were organic they carried much blood to their ebony folds, blood that was affected by his thoughts, and these thoughts affected their color, which had turned to a flushed plum. This was how he was sure, he muttered so early in our relationship, that I was the one.

I had extra sight. He liked how my back eyes could watch him from the shaved panel on the back of my head while I cooked. My back eyes remained open, even while I slept. It made him feel safe, he said, to have so much watching going on. My feelings for him softened as his wings changed color to match me. When they did, they felt softer, too, which I knew was because he let me stroke them with long, lingering caresses. Up and down, side to side, over and under. They were his most erogenous zone.

"Touch that part near my armpit, Babe," he'd say. "That ridge. Lightly. Lighter, now. Yeah. Okay. Trace your name on my wing!" As I did this, I remember he rolled and twisted in the bed in such a state of ecstasy I could hardly believe I'd caused it. But this was a long time ago. He knew my kink too.

Sometimes, I let him make up the eyes on the back of my head because a fluttering of those lashes caused a tactile sensation—almost like he directly stroked my brain. "Turquoise shadow," I'd say, breath catching in arousal. "False lashes. Big purple liner. Now—a mirror."

He did all I asked and more. But this was before he added the third job, before the night window that brooked no shared daylight. I don't need to tell you how rapidly things deteriorated. We lost the friendly silence.

A few weeks ago, as I lolled in bed, I saw him watching me, so I asked, "What are you looking at?"

"I'm just wondering," he said. "If we had kids, would they have only one extra eye, or puny wings that couldn't even fly?"

"Fucksake. What?" I was shocked, hurt, twisted the coverlet between my fingers to compress it. "You didn't want kids," I said, all eyes burning.

He turned his back to me, opening and shutting his arms, fanning his wings, not replying.

"Did you lie?" I asked. "Fucking flyboy mariposa, did you lie?" There was a butterfly ad for contraceptives we often passed in the zoom-car when we drove together to the grocery store. Its insect was puny. I teased him with it sometimes.

"Yeah, maybe," he said. "But not on purpose."

More weeks went by this ambiguous way, exhaustion taking its toll. Finally, in something men might think of as an irrational female gesture, I said, "If you don't want me anymore, Pano, move out."

"I don't want to move," he said. "I love you."

But I had a feeling he didn't, so I went to his day jobs one by one, taking a sick day from mine. At the liquor store, I could park backward and look in, so I did. There, they had hired another flyer. Pretty, brunette, petite—with one of those round faces that looked sweet and well-intentioned. As she flew from station to station, I noticed her wings were black and yellow. I noticed him watching her, though he pretended not to. I wanted to poke out the eyes in the back of my head. He and she tied their aprons the same way, strings flapping loosely on their asses as they walked. He was very chatty, curious. This curiosity rankled.

At his second job as a Laundromat and dry cleaner's cashier, he hit up a pert girl with blue gills on her wrists, but I wasn't worried because what would a flyer want with a fish? It's not like he could fly through the water or get freaky with her in the down low, but once, just once, during his shift, I watched him stroke her gills with his thumb and index finger. She liked it and darted off with a blush.

At his third job at the motor shop, the only woman around was a slider, you know the ones who roll here to there? She had long green hair and slid all over the floor like a hot drop of grease, but he didn't seem to notice her much for the first few hours, so this was fine by me—until he stopped her sliding past him with a wide expansion of his open wing and then, in a slow move, like a lover, brought her near and whispered in her ear. She laughed. He laughed. They both laughed.

Raunchy, disgusting laughers! I thought. But I went home so he wouldn't know I had been at any of his jobs. I waited for nine o'clock.

When he strode through the door, I laid on the bed, pretending to be sleepy. "I'm home, Twila," he announced.

"That's good," I said. I had to be asleep by eleven to get up for my jobs the next day. He knew this. He went to the kitchen to fix himself goulash.

When he finally came back, it was ten till eleven. I figured he did this so he wouldn't have to talk to me. I pretended to be asleep.

The next day at work, I started scanning the available men, wondering if someone watching me would think I were flirting in how I regarded them. I smiled, sure, but I'd always done that. I noticed especially all the cute, younger men with multiple eyes, even pictured having cute little multi-eyed children without deformed wings, and I started to hate Pano.

I had awful daydreams of him having flight sex with the other flyer, dreams that made me almost furious enough to seduce one of the young, multiple-eyed men out of spite alone. But then I remembered: I had no real proof. Pano worked three jobs. We were tired.

And I was older; what would I want one of these young boys for, if not an afternoon romp? Also, I loved Pano. He said he loved me. For years, we had loved each other, until there was no unloving to be done. For me, his wings had purpled, and I wanted him to remember. So the next night, I showered and shaved. When he came home, I said, all sultry with a bit of honey in my tone, "Pano, why don't you come lie with me a while before I sleep? I've missed you."

"Okay," he said. "All right."

But it was like there was ice between us. He elbowed me in the side. A part of him wanted to be close, I could tell, from the way he kept looking at me and shrugging something away, seeming tender, almost regretful. "Do my eyes, Pano," I said. "The ones on the back of my head."

"Okay," he replied, and he made them up so pretty I wondered why he'd never done such a bang-up a job before. They were rainbow, with blue, yellow, orange, and lime liner, adorned with faux rhinestone lashes. When he completed his work, I felt happy.

"Pano," I said. "Let me rub your wings a bit."

"I'm tired," he said, flinching. "Later?"

"Later I'll be sleeping," I insisted.

"Tomorrow, maybe?" he replied.

"Oh, Baby, just open your wings and let me rub them," I said, furious, but it was pretty clear he wasn't going to, even in the dark. His arms were pressed tightly to his sides and he would not budge. I nursed several escalating fears and then sidled up to him, caressing him, trying in vain to get him to open his arms, and finally, finally, when I yanked hard enough, he did. But they were colored differently, even in the dark. And their texture was bumpy and slick. "Is your blood okay?" I asked, considering disease. "Your wings are different."

When I turned on the lights, though he tried to pull them closed, I saw that his wings were stained yellow and blue and green. *Blood flow was love*, I thought? Plum because he loved me—because the eyes on the back of my head were violet?

His wings weren't purple anymore.

The most telling detail about this whole thing was that he'd touch me while his wings held so many other women's colors. Dirty fucking butterfly! It's not that I'd agreed to give him a harem! I would not have agreed to that! I wondered how he'd touched them or they'd touched him.

"Clean my back eyes," I shouted. "Now." I felt them blinking as he did so, pleasure mixed with pain, but these eyes had limited-functioning tear ducts, just enough wetness to keep them lubricated. They could not cry.

I let them glare at him a few moments before he left for his next job. It was only when he did that I turned to lie on my back and block their view of our room. I shut my other eyes, too, the ones in the front, which had always been blue. Blue. But not azure. Not the blue of small gills on wrists, fingered by indexes and thumbs.

Reflecting on the differentiating variation in hue, I opened just one of my four eyes as I watched the ceiling and thought about who would pack first and what would go where... I wondered which of his three other women held the strongest place in his heart. And then it occurred to me: It didn't matter.

I knew at his early flinch, before he spread his wings, that we had more problems between us than intimacies. Contact with other people can do that, the ease of new, unblemished relationships causing all kinds of unspoken, heretofore unfelt, resentments in those more tested. I could kill him for wearing those colors, for lying.

I rolled onto my side again, letting all of my eyes open and peruse our shared room. Pano was gone, working, always working, but I had started to piece it together, his every ambiguous act, the reasons for his small and recent oddities like skewed return times, longer shifts, talk about our would-be deformed children. So I knew more then, lying by myself in our bed, than I had known in months, though Pano had long been aware of his own subtle changes.

I rested in the dark, pondering, imagining the slow disappearance of my color from his wings and his subsequent hiding as the jaundice, ocean, and salad strains took over. It was no small weight upon my conscience that I should have enjoyed so much sight, all my life, yet have been so blind. But no matter how many eyes I had, or which could or could not cry over a loss, it remained my duty to comfort myself. After all, I could not have seen a color changing in the dark.

SAINTS AND BLUE BABIES

Millicent stood beneath the tattered Sun Villas awning on Abernathy, with Timothy slung across her chest, wearing a dress the color of milkweed and a frown that depressed the thin tilt of her nose, wondering what to do. In her arms, the toddler was feverish, and there were four seething blocks to go before she reached her destination. *I've done it,* she thought, *stolen a child.*

She hoped to bypass the throbbing heart of the city and reach the clinic quickly, and, to soothe herself, pictured waiting on the orange floral couch in the boy's apartment, imagining relaxing from pain that had accumulated in her neck and curling her knees toward her chest as his temperature returned to normal while she awaited the confrontation with his mother. *Positive thinking,* she thought. *Dear God, help me.*

Navigating past a deli, past a hopscotch game, a dry cleaner, and another intersection, Millicent hoped she'd get back quickly. Really, she had done this to help his mother, Keisha. Millicent hardly knew the girl, but she knew the elderly residents of the Sun Complex were not happy with the young black woman and her screaming toddler— Millicent had heard enough about the child in the shared laundry facility to write a short documentary—and it was only a glitch in Keisha's grandmother's original contract that allowed Keisha to inherit the unit (the same glitch that let Millicent have her mother's)—but even so, they couldn't kick her out, so they complained. "We have nothing against you, Girl," they told Millicent, whom they allowed to over-hear them, "but you're the good sort, easy to live with, and they're not. Not too quiet either. They need to go." Millicent hated the plotting and the whispers, which grew increasingly severe. "Can we find a way to change the lease?" they asked. "Can we get her to move, or ask her to go?"

That morning, as Millicent stepped out to buy milk at the corner store, walking along the dim hall and again hearing the toddler cry, she decided to take action to protect both mother and son.

Keisha's door was wide open, and the boy hollered, looking abandoned. She shut Keisha's door halfway. She stepped past, not planning to walk in, but the boy kept crying. No one responded. Millicent turned back.

"I mustn't be a busybody," she'd said, but when she called out, "Hello?" and no one replied, she rushed in. She touched the boy's head and called out again, but again Keisha did not answer, and the child was feverish. "Oh, Lord," she said, then. "Protect me from this fear. Send me Jerome Emiliani, or Philip of Zell, if you will..." She listed a litany of patron saints and prayed.

Her mother had prayed, too, like Millicent—addressing old saints as if they were old friends—and luckily, Millicent's answer came just as she touched the boy again: "Go," an emissary of God whispered. "Take that baby and succor him."

Still, it felt odd to stand in another person's home amongst their things when lately her own apartment felt like a museum of sorts, a reluctant shrine to those dead and gone: Her aunt's doilies atop cherry tables, her mother's crosses and pictures of saints bathed in yellow light beside the large Christ painting, and photo albums of generations of Pietàs trapped in the dusty drawer. Keisha's things were new, all less than ten years old.

The boy wailed again, so Millicent clutched her lapis cross, saying a quick *thanks* and swooping him into her arms, then out to the street. As she walked, his small body nestled in her arms, he picked at her cross while she touched it, wrapping his hot fingers around hers. The cross was a gift for her first communion, but this child had no such necklace —so she didn't know his religion, or Keisha's. Perhaps they had none, but she didn't blame the girl, nor did she blame her for not hiring a sitter, for she knew the woman loved her child, worked three jobs to support him, and could use some help as a single mother—and if there were ever a time for a stranger's kindly intervention to keep those biddies at bay, this was it: A fat blister ready to burst on the heel of an untenable situation.

Millicent pushed through a knot of kindergarteners on the sidewalk, jabbering and pulsing around her like a maniacal stampede, their lunchboxes beating her calves, her legs bruised by their roughness, but Timothy was safe at her hip. He peered down at them with interest, and she patted his head.

As his weight banged into her side, she wondered how she'd pay for the visit—a check from her rapidly diminishing account? She had only the remains of her mother's court settlement, so this act of charity would force her from her comfort too soon, but that would be her cross to bear. She could not risk his life by hoarding her money; it wasn't in her, but as he wailed more, she seriously considered her doubts, adding to them. Still, if she hadn't taken him from Keisha's, his death might be on her conscience, and that was terrifying.

Quieted by long hours spent tending sick women, she was unused to city streets beyond a one-block radius of the complex, so she felt stripped by the crowd's unfriendly stares. She would, she knew, find it hard to leave the complex later to find work (when her money came down to

dollars and dimes), and as she lugged the boy down the
jagged streets, she considered what job she might find. The
temp lady said she had no marketable skills. How they'd
laughed at a shut-in, seeking employment, with no experience in five years other than caring for the elderly.

Timothy grabbed her braids and yanked. His hands
glanced her ear, warm like tiny muffins from the oven, and
she was seized with panic: Did she remember exactly where
the clinic was? Should she have called the paramedics? She
would have, but she feared they'd hand the child to CPS if
they knew he'd been left alone, and perhaps, they'd ask questions she didn't want to answer: Was Keisha a good mother?
Maybe. Did the baby often cry? Definitely. Did Millicent feel
the environment of Keisha's home was child-friendly?
Maybe not. These answers could incriminate a possibly innocent girl.

How to fill a syringe for a diabetic, Millicent knew.
How too to fluff a sleep-flattened pillow. But how to deal
with officials regarding a child? She crossed Balboa quickly
to circumvent the flashing walk-box, and recalled she might
have told them she was his babysitter, but how would she
explain not knowing where Keisha was, or justify incurring
the staggering bill the call might cause? She did not know
Keisha well enough to guess whether this would make the
girl truculent, and she preferred to skirt conflict whenever
possible—ergo, this morning, fighting the crowds.

Tired now, she walked slowly; the boy felt plastered to
her side and though he resembled human contact,
squirming and warm, she'd never felt more alone. Since her
mother died, Millicent hardly spoke to anyone, although in
the last weeks, a new landscape had bloomed before her, rife
with neon lights and curried dishes, swimming up where her
mother's old shoebox of a life had shriveled years ago; it was
exciting, if unfamiliar, and Millicent, like a child rolled into a
dusky tapestry, was partially ready to be unfurled, but fearful

just the same.

Even the mailman, swarthy, fat Mr. Nickles, seemed different—one day, a greasy, old lecher, and the next, a tired gentleman in frayed navies. She thought of him as Timothy slipped from her grasp and almost fell, then reminded herself: *Pay attention!* His weight felt heavy on her arms, and no matter where she put him, he felt increasingly larger as the streets tucked around them, so she tugged at his bottom again, balancing him more steadily. He still felt like a microwaved bowling ball, hot and firm, and he cried as Millicent tried to soothe him. As if sensing her panic, or perhaps because of his cries, four Hispanic men in chinos noticed her and called out, "Hey Mamacita! Barbie Doll!" They made kissing noises at her back, and it seemed that one of their hands had stolen over her thighs as she passed, reaching out for an intimate touch she would never have allowed. *Still, don't turn back*, she thought. *Keep the baby up. Don't look at them.*

Her milky skin often brought unwanted attention in this neighborhood, and though she was pretty in her pasty way, more than pretty enough to attract casual attention, she'd been long accustomed to repulsing men's advances, so she wore her familiar, cold glare. The calls of hot dog and flower vendors assaulted her ears as families en route to the C Street bus station scurried by, but when she finally turned the corner of B, the clinic door was boarded. Wanting to lapse into horrified tears, she sat on the steps, calling out, "Doctor? Is anyone a doctor?" but her voice was like a drop in a well, and the masses hustled past, absorbing its fragile notes in a crush of unfamiliar faces and tapping feet. Abruptly, a girl with strong perfume winged Timothy's head with her hip, then his head collided with Millicent's cheek, but the girl did not stop or apologize. "You should have better manners," Millicent shouted, rubbing her face, and Timothy wailed. The girl did not turn back; Millicent's voice seemed to dissipate again, so she glared toward the bustle, and then peered into the clinic's empty rooms.

When was the last time she was here—five years ago when she and Derek were married—when she had been so close to carrying her only pregnancy to term? The horror of those days returned, and she saw herself, as she'd been, scared, foolish, memorizing the contours of her stillborn baby's face and the sterile basin that now haunted her dreams; her babe had been perfect, but still. Perhaps if Derek had not thrown her against walls, if their relationship had been kinder... Either way, the baby was born dead.

Timothy yanked her braid and wailed again. Worry coursed through her as she stroked him, but the past drew her in like a traffic accident. What if her child had been like this one? Would she be different? Would she have never gone into her mother's stale rooms, dressed like a convent nurse, to meet the old woman's needs? A horrible thought arose, which she quickly staunched: Had her own imperfect marriage and lost child been a blessing in her mother's book of religious tragi-salvations?

She felt shamed and ungrateful, so she tugged a strand of her hair from Timothy's fist to chew on. Even her braids bothered her now. Her hair had always been white-blonde but flowed in long waves until she'd gone to her mother's; since then it had been pulled back into the rigid style she wore today, two braids in loops, wrapped twice around her head. She sighed, touching the twisting mess, thinking of her ex-husband, how he'd said, "Goddamn hair's a liar. You're a cold girl. No woman should be so cold," but she hadn't meant to be, and she'd cried an ocean then, wanting to say, "Teach me. Show me how to be another way," but after his violence began, she quickly gave up the idea of secular fulfillment.

Anyway, that was an old wound, so she focused on the present—this day, this boy, and this struggle. She looked at

Timothy's flushed features, and he issued a gasping cry, so Millicent tasted her own tears with the salty, city air. On the floors above the clinic's door, pots with geranium corpses loomed and she saw the building's newest state: Neglect, lack of interest, perhaps blattoid people locked inside the ugly, brick facade where a helpful clinic had once thrived. Years ago, women and children had chatted over fire escapes as families moved in and out, but no one graced the windows now, several were boarded, and the office had been closed for a long time.

All that was left was a cheap placard above the clinic door, announcing fees and hours, dirty papers scattered inside, and orange tape ribbons, dust-covered items not draped with plastic sheets. The building seemed ready for the wrecking ball. She stroked the guiltless wall reassuringly, as if to say, "It's not your fault," but Timothy moaned again, so she kissed his ochre forehead and whispered, "There, there, Timmy. It's all right. We'll find something." She had almost decided to shout "911" until someone listened and called, but she didn't.

A homeless woman in an organdy dress threw herself into the empty part of the stoop, adjusting her voluminous skirt, saying, "That boy don't need no doctor, Lady." The woman's mouth held stubs of teeth like sunken stones on gummy hillsides, and Millicent wanted to pull back, fearing the acrid scent of sweat on an unclean body, but she hugged the wall closer, staring at the stranger. Across the woman's brow, moles formed maps of stars stenciled on earthy skin, and her brown cheeks sagged as if they'd once held too much food.

Millicent shut off her olfactory sense as the woman approached her; she then realized the woman did not smell like trash, but a crisp spring day or a patch of leaves. "How do you know the child isn't sick?" she asked.

"I know what he be," the woman said. "Sick once,

yeah. But sick no more. You got the blue stones, lady! Don't you know what the blue stones can do? *Sante de lapis?*"

"Saints of Lapis?"

"Sante—health. Stones of health. You hear?"

Millicent, transfixed by the woman's conviction, listened but stared at her cross until glancing over to Timothy, who had regained a sleepy child's demeanor. The woman smiled, and Millicent exhaled, praying her thanks as the woman stood up again, massaging her own back and tossing Millicent a talisman. It was lapis and larger than her cross, resembling a thick-skinned, headless woman with huge breasts. "A healer I see you are—" the woman said, then. "And you need a helper. So touch him—your first heal, child."

Touching Timothy's forehead, Millicent felt his fever gone, but—*Oh, Lord, Keisha!* she thought. She had to get back. Maybe his fever would return, but she had to take advantage of the break because the clinic was gone, and there was nothing more she could do.

"Fine, you take him home," the woman said, as if reading Millicent's thoughts. "But keep what I give you. You have a keening for a young 'un, you. I feel it."

Timothy's laugh was a boyish chime in the afternoon air, and the woman smiled, putting her dusty fingers in his mouth for suckling. She looked at Millicent who, stepping off the stoop, called out, "Thank you, Ma'am," and waved. *Crazy old thing*, Millicent thought. Didn't she know the value of lapis, and shouldn't Millicent, like the good person she was, have walked back the gift? *But not today,* she told herself. *Maybe tomorrow.*

"Walk," Timothy then shouted in her ear. "Me!" His fat arms flailed. As she squirmed from his disorienting move- ment, he said again, "I walk! Now! Me."

The streets seemed safer with his fever gone, and Milli- cent slowed her pace until they seemed to glide past the crowds together, then across the uneven concrete, swallowing city blocks in record time. "A healer," Millicent said to herself, thinking of the stoop-woman. "If so, only by accident."

As they rounded the corner to the Sun Complex, Millicent grabbed Timothy and ran, but Keisha was already there, gesturing through her window and shouting, "Thief! You stole my baby. You no-good piece of white trash—"

"He had a fever," Millicent said. "I only wanted t—"

"Don't you ever take my baby again!" Keisha shouted, yanking the boy away. She shoved Millicent against the hallway wall, standing over her, and crushing Timothy to her chest, so he was between them and squirming. Keisha's saliva landed on Millicent's flushed face, as she threatened, "Don't you ever come into my apartment. I know about you! Nut! Religious freak. Shut in!"

Millicent burst into tears. "You work so much," she said, almost inaudibly. "He was sick and, no one was here... He felt so hot." Millicent clutched her cross as if it were a lifeboat and collapsed to the ground, saying, "I was just trying to help. That's all. I'm sorry."

Keisha stepped back and cuddled Timothy, running her fingers through his nubby hair, kissing his arms and face, and then cried silently with relief. Still, Millicent didn't move to pass her until Keisha said, "I'd gone to the store to get medicine. I swear, I was coming right back."

"Please don't be angry," Millicent pleaded, nose dripping, and a hot blush creeping over her cheeks. "I didn't want the old ladies to cause you trouble. I wanted to help."

Keisha soothed her with a few rubs and said, "Hush, Girl, you getting all worked up for nothing. I'm sorry I yelled at you, Millie. I'm sorry for what I said. I know you didn't mean nothing."

"I didn't. Really," Millicent said, but she thought: *Millie. What a nice, warm sound, a nickname she never knew she wanted until she heard it.* "I don't have children anymore," she said, her voice trembling, "so I shouldn't have taken him, but he was so sick. I wanted to help. You see, I had a child once—but he was born dead, and that was terrible on my conscience. Born," Millicent reiterated, wanting Keisha to appreciate the significance, "dead."

Keisha gave her a strange look, but didn't seem angry, and when Millicent was sure there were no hard feelings, she walked to her apartment, her legs shaking, fingering the talisman the woman had given her. The boy was well, but herself a healer? She doubted it. She opened her apartment door and stared at her mother's things, her aunt's things, her father's things—where were her things? Had she any? Even the dusty door was stale and reeked of other times.

The air felt thick and heavy, so she opened a window and let her hair down, brushing it for over an hour until it shone. She worked out the knots and tangles, and then let it hang like a banner from the sill as she watched all manner of people walk past, some staring up at her silver-white locks, which fluttered like butterflies in a breeze. Men called up, but she did not reply. So preoccupied with feeling the wind in her hair, she forgot to latch and lock the window, but she had a marvelous evening, dancing with herself in the fading sunlight and lighting candles to dine by.

That night, after she went to bed, she was brutally attacked.

Several men must have come through the open window, crept into her apartment, then looked for her bedroom. Hands swept over her in the dark, she heard no voices, yet the rupturing pain was unmistakable. They grasped her legs and sank into her with speed; afterward, she saw her blood.

Though no virgin, it had been a long time since anyone touched her, much less by force, so she turned on the light when they left, waiting in bed, counting rosary beads until morning. She tried not to touch the damp spot beneath her thighs, and had no one to call, but staggered down to Keisha's apartment, and when Keisha opened her door, she said, "Last night, men came into my room, through my window, and they—they..." already sobbing, so Keisha yanked the door open wider, took one look at her, and pulled her into her arms, saying, "Hush. There, there. Quiet now, Millie." Then Keisha said, "You need to call the police and go to the hospital—"

"No hospital. No police. I don't want anyone," Millicent said. "The police ask embarrassing questions." Millicent knew this. How many times had she been asked repulsive questions while hospitalized after one of Derek's fits?

"At least go to the doctor, Millie," Keisha said, peeling her shaking body away from the doorjamb. "You need tests."

"I don't have money. I—" Millicent paused and remembered she did have health insurance her mother had paid for until June, so she sighed, blessing the old woman's foresight, and said, "I suppose I could go to the doctor."

"Good, let's go," Keisha said, grabbing her fuzzy keychain from the table, and guiding Millicent to her Buick. She put Timothy in his car seat, and as she drove, Keisha said, "Millie, mind if I ask something?"

"What?"

"Well, Timothy was sick for days, but since he went out with you, he's been fine. You saved me some money, so I meant to thank you. Maybe I could help..."

"No thanks needed," Millicent said, and though her insides ached, she said, "That's good he's well. That's very good."

At the hospital, doctors examined her, and told her to come back in six months. She declined. A man with a mustache like a broom walked her out. He said, "You must also consider that you may be pregnant," so Millicent stared from one nurse to the other, then at the two doctors beside them, and nodded, her eyes glistening.

Keisha waited in the waiting room and didn't speak as she drove them home. Timothy was surprisingly silent, and when they reached the door, Keisha asked, "You want to sleep at my place tonight, Honey?" stroking Millicent's hand. "You can stay on the couch."

"No."

"What if they come back?" Keisha asked. "Why don't you call the police? They should pay."

"I can't."

"All right, but you should stay here tonight, to be safe."

"No, thanks."

"Think on it, and give me a call, okay?"

"I thought about it already, and I need my bed," Millicent said. "But thank you for taking me to the hospital."

—

Millicent was pregnant, but her assailants did not return. She applied for jobs, and discounting her heaving morning sickness and the weight in her breasts, her life returned almost to normal. She found work in an elderly wing of a local, Catholic hospital almost immediately, so her salary was enough to squeak by on, and surprisingly, the work served her well. She loved earning money. The ward smelled like her apartment had when her mother was sick, and she loved the scent of antiseptics as she entered, walking past cabinets of gauze, and noting the crisply made beds.

At first, she was awkward with her patients, but soon tended to them easily as she had her aunt and mother. She prayed to Michael the Archangel and John of God. She prayed to Giles, saint of the disabled, and many other saints as each illness brought another name to mind. As her patients left, one after another, it was rumored that her prayers had worked miracles, or that she had provided a direct link to the Almighty himself, a portal to the very ear of God. Old people said she had cured them, and gave her trinkets from their hospital stays as well as checks, stuffed bears, fresh flowers, glossy magazines, half-read books, and bibles, too, so many bibles. Millicent collected them, carted them home each night until they filled and overflowed from her tiny bookshelves. Still, as her stomach swelled in a Catholic hospital, with no ring on her finger, the higher-ups avoided her, and it hurt when they passed in their starched coats, eyes avoiding her jutting belly—so by the beginning of her third trimester, she talked to almost none of the staff.

She had developed a fixation with her lapis talisman, carrying it everywhere, like a child might a rabbit's paw. If she left it at home in the morning, she repeatedly crammed her hand into her pocket, as if it would appear, then went home to get it during her lunch hour. She rubbed the round nubs of the figure's breasts as she prayed to saints, touching its smooth surface, and reasoning that this, too, was a form of prayer—a touch prayer to the body, the body feminine, and the more pregnant she grew, belly like a moonflower, the more she resembled the figure, and the more she needed it.

She warmed its stony facade compulsively with her fingers, but had to hide it more than she wanted to because she did not want it whispered that she was attached to such an odd thing. By then, at least, the doctors concurred she truly had healed the sick, so they took an interest in her progress, chatted at length or tried to, and stared at her hands as though they held the answers their own scalpels craftily withheld.

She did not trust them and did not feel comfortable in the glow of their interest, so she often scurried away on false errands. Still, word of her healing had spread throughout the city, and just before she left the hospital for maternity leave, when her belly made it impossible to work, queues formed outside the tall, white building, entire families thrusting their hands toward her, shouting, "Touch me,

Millicent. Please!"

They clung to her ankles, and pulled at her sleeves. She touched them, but said, "I will pray to your saints, but there is no guarantee."

On Keisha's TV, she saw her name had been mentioned in churches throughout the city, spray painted on walls with neon flourishes, and drawn on billboards with crosses—like the name of God; still, in her bed each night, the adulation worried her. She told Keisha she was disturbed, but Keisha didn't seem worried: "They think you heal them," she said. "What's the problem?" Still, as countless people leaked into the complex and found her door, having brought sick babies and ill friends, she wanted to turn them away and move. The old people, too, wanted her to move.

When she asked Keisha what to do, Keisha said simply, "Stop letting them in, Millie. Don't answer your door."

"But they knock and knock."

"Just say, 'Go away,'" Keisha told her firmly, and Millicent skeptically considered it, until Keisha said: "What's that thing you're rubbing, Millie? Looks like an African fertility goddess."

"A goddess?"

"Yes."

"I don't know exactly what it is, but it comforts me," Millicent said, flushed at having been caught. "I know it's not a saint, but my attachment to it grows."

"You and your saints," Keisha said, clucking her tongue. "You're obsessed with them. A bunch of dead people... But that doesn't explain why you keep touching a fertility goddess—unless you've hopped trees? Abandoned your flock?"

"Never!" Millicent declared.

"Calm down, girl. No need to get ruffled. Hey, I ever tell you I thought you should be a nun and wear one of those—dimple, rimple—whatever those black and white head things are?" Millicent rubbed the lapis absently as Keisha spoke. "Anyway, that rock is African to the core, and that's the God's good truth. Not Catholic. Not one bit Catholic. So maybe you need to lay it down."

"Sometimes," Millicent whispered, shaking her head, "I think the faiths are connected." Her eyes burned, electricity zoomed through her and sizzled in her fingertips, so she wanted to push out her feelings. "In all faiths," she said, "the chosen are brought close to God through suffering. Christianity. Buddhism. Judaism..."

Keisha regarded her oddly, then laughed. "Believe what you want," she said, snapping her fingers in the air, "but I'd rather not suffer. Praise be to the Protestants! That's my church, and we feel fine!" Keisha danced around her kitchen, and then said, "It's the Catholics with all that guilt. Ain't no shame in our game, though," whipping Millicent playfully with a dishtowel.

Millicent then said, "Yes. Suffering is a Catholic virtue. Like John Donne once said, 'No man hath affliction enough that is not matured and ripened by it.' I love his words. They are so comforting, and there are so few who think as he does."

"John who?" Keisha asked.

"A priest, a long time ago."

"A white priest?" Keisha asked, stirring ribbons of pasta into boiling water. "Why don't you quote a brother for a change?"

"I don't know any 'brothers' to quote."

"Learn some!"

"I've heard the 'I Have a Dream' speech; does that count?"

Keisha rolled her eyes.

Though saddened by her friend's agitation, Millicent felt aglow even after she left. Then she remembered the rest of the Donne passage, so yes, she concluded: Suffering was her rape. Affliction would ripen her and was a trial to overcome. Besides, she had often hoped to have a baby, and she'd received this blessing! She'd wanted a job, and she got that too. In Keisha, she finally had a friend, and that was a boon.

She thought of the people who believed she'd healed them and wished them well. The only thing that bothered her was that she had not scheduled appointments for prenatal check-ups, so she often wondered if the baby was fine, especially when it did not move as she prodded and pushed her stomach.

At her apartment, she continued to let in the sick, and was finally offered the free services of a midwife named Jules who was plain with a rough face, but whom Millicent trusted. Still, lying in bed, she felt tired. Her feet ached, and while looking forward to the birth, she also dreaded a baby born of rape: What if she saw an expression on the child's face that became the miniature of a violent man, or what if she could not love the child?

Often, she rested at her kitchen table and peered out her window to watch men walking past as if the guilty party or parties would look up at just the right moment for her to intuit their involvement, but this was ridiculous. She could not even say how many had been in her room that night and had no idea what the child would look like. Still, she'd do her best to love it, as if it had been conceived through love. "An African fertility goddess," she said, touching the lapis figure. "Well, you surely worked in that regard. But the stoop-woman was right; I've become a healer, so I'd like to heal myself."

She caressed her stomach and the talisman in tandem. "No matter what," she told the unborn baby, "I will love you. And I will call your conception immaculate, for I did not see a father, so God must have made you." She then walked to her living room and stared at her mother's portrait, saying, "If I can heal, my gifts come from you, child."

But the baby felt still the following week, hadn't seemed to have moved for days. When Millicent poked the lump of her stomach, her water broke, and she staggered to her telephone, clutching her abdomen. She dropped to the floor with the phone in her hand, saying, "Jules! It's Millicent. Please come. I think I'm having the baby."

—

Her labor was long, and though she was at home, in the quiet moments between contractions, collapsed on sweaty sheets, Millicent felt her familiar surroundings were altogether different. She did not recognize her family's possessions, which had altered to nondescript blurs like the pictures on the walls, which seemed to swirl with misplaced color. She heard the clock ticking unevenly, and she prayed. When told to bear down, she clutched the fertility idol, dreaming of release and whispering, "Anne, mother of Mary, pray for parents that they may provide loving homes. Pray for healthy infants, too—" but the end of her prayer was cut off by a scream. Her own. And another contraction.

Two hours later, the baby arrived, and Jules watched his head appear from between Millicent's legs, which were sprawled like the limbs of a wall-climbing spider, but when the infant crowned, Jules fainted. "Catch the baby!" Millicent rasped, terrified. And then, since there was no answer from the woman on the ground below her, Millicent kicked Jules awkwardly to wake her and screamed as she pushed again. Washed conscious by Millicent's blood trickling down her face, Jules crouched, wiping her eyes, and pulled the baby free with trembling hands.

She presented it to Millicent. Millicent fainted too, only to awaken to her own hysterical moans: "My baby is blue, blue as an ocean. A tear on the face of God." And the child was not just blue, but the indigo blue of a deep wax river,

blue as aquamarine paint once used to depict the robes of
religious women—blue as the talisman, or Millicent's cross.

He assumed the glistening sheen of polished stone, but
it was as though the color was toxic, a deepening hue
spreading from the springy locks on his soft pate to his
toothless gums, then extending beyond his lashes and into
his eyeballs... She felt him harden in her arms and chill—as
he chilled, he became heavy like a rock.

Millicent wept, uttering, "No! No!" until her voice was
so hoarse it pained her to speak another word. "Was this
because I worshiped the false idol, God?" she whispered,
looking up. "Am I then so punished?"

She heard no reply but felt a hesitant sorrow in her
chest, a weight on her heart, and lay back down. She cried
for what might have been hours, and then heard a voice that
seemed to emanate from the ceiling. It said: "Kill what is in
you that fears, that wants, that clamors. Only then will you
live for me; my saints must be selfless. Share your child with
others. Share his life with me."

The afterbirth, once steaming on the table, had turned
to stone, as did the umbilical cord, but strength flooded into
Millicent, and ten minutes later, she felt unaffected by her
earlier labor. Her blood tingled, and she herself was like a
glistening miracle, but she felt pain, too, emotional pain, like
her heart were dying. Her child was not alive.

She lifted him above her head before Jules and could
feel his hunger for contact. He was meant to be owned by
all. She had to take him out. He would know what to do
with the crowds.

They would reap solace from his body, and she would
smile sadly, already martyred. It was October 31st, her son's
birthday, and All Saints Day on the old calendar. Outside, the
weather looked frosty. Cool air trickled in from the half-
cracked window. She wrapped her babe in swaddling cloth
and kissed his cold, blue eyes, his curled, blue fists, and his

snarling mouth—the mouth that even then was twisted in rage, venting his silent fury on the world's deaf ear.

Already a pale glow wrapped Millicent's head, and a sacred heart arose from her chest. As this new heart rose, her own died, and the eyes of the saints met hers from the wall, consoling her, but despite her pain, she saw each of the pictures, so oft prayed to, as depicting real people for the first time. "We love you," they seemed to whisper. "You were meant to be here. Come join us."

She stripped off her bloody nightgown and put on a dress.

Millicent walked outside with the baby, through the open door, and onto the street. She held him in front of her like an offering, but did not speak. They would know who she was, and they would come, groping for her child, caressing his hard skin until his features blurred like the talisman's, until his rage was wiped clean by the touch of fingers, like a stone smoothed by river water.

Millicent released her braids. Her hair would be free while she healed, tumbling down her shoulders and blowing in the breeze. It would be what led them to her, a beacon, whipping around corners and heralding her arrival. Already, she'd gained the interest of a homeless man in the alley.

He toted a paper-wrapped bottle and muttered to himself, limping on sore legs, so when he saw her, she motioned him closer. He came, slowly. She waited and readied herself. He would be the child's first christener, so, "Come here, old man," she said. "There are 140 parishes in the archdiocese. I bring him here first. Give me your legs, your arms, your hands. We will heal you."

He closed his eyes as he reached for the mother and son, as if grasping for a piece of heaven from the frozen afternoon, and Millicent did not disappoint him, nor did the lapis baby, so furious, so beautiful, and still. They took away his pain, and Millicent knew his body felt new, freer than before, but when he glanced up to thank her, she was gone, had strode away quicker than the playful breeze could steal a piece of newsprint from the ground and carry it to the sky.

She stood at the corner of the alley, tilting her face upward, then looked sadly back and smiled, as if she knew she had forgotten to check for the proof of their ministrations, but she then realized she could hear that man's thoughts, his joyful fluttering of hope and private blessings bestowed upon her person: He thought of her green hem, which left his vision last, and her flowing tresses, flying across the mottled sky like a blonde, chiffon curtain. In his head, he composed a poem in which he imagined a pair of modern doves in the floating newsprint and the mournful worship of her eyes. He tried to incorporate the wild fervor of his gratitude, how it parsed with true faith, noting the golden glow near her head, the halo. But his words failed him. "She was the something—" he said, as she walked down the adjacent street and turned the corner, "the something, the something..." he went on, stretching his newly nimble limbs: "The something worth saving in everything."

Millicent heard, but had already reached a distant corner where drug-riddled prostitutes offered their services for little more than a single hour's fee at a hotel so they might get out of the freezing cold. She offered them her lapis baby this time, handing him over to the women who passed his small angry form from palm to palm or arm to arm, smiling and cooing like he was a real-life child, singing and crooning praises to his furious little face, the fury they well understood, their visages already softening as they handled him, already healed and beautified by his infinite mercy, by his something miraculous that fed the holes in their empty souls and mended their hearts, too.

She stood with the women a long while, before moving on. Her baby was happy here, she knew, where there was much for him to do. But "Millicent, Millicent," she heard so many voices call from the cavernous depths of the endless city, "Bring him, now. Bring him here, your infant, your savior child." And she did. She brought and she shared him with everyone.

THE ROSE LAMP

All personal belongings had been stripped, except those that could be auctioned off. Windows sat open to air out the rooms, which exuded a musty odor like sickness. At least now, the agent thought, they were no longer dark. Light filtered listlessly through the panes, illuminating the pale colors of the Tiffany lamps that rested, like small dogs, in positions they'd occupied for years. The wooden floors were well-polished from years of oil and care, but had gathered dust. In this house, there was an aura of mystery, of history. Relatives had come and gone. Daughters had squabbled over baubles. Upstairs, in a room with cut-glass vases and cheerful drapes, after suffering a strange, short illness, an old woman had recently died. And today, the auction.

Two weeks before, Stasie was told, sterile tilt-cups and tissues had filled the nightstand. More tissue littered the floor. The nursing staff enforced the unnatural quiet. Even the flowers could not be left alone; those sent by well-wishers were routinely ushered from the room.

The recently deceased woman had coughed and complained of fatigue, an inability to breathe, and the starkness of a summer-window's sunlight glaring in her eyes. At night, the help staff admitted, she had wandered through her house, hands hungry for the feel of her belongings. She examined the staircase for new shadows and the slight cracks in wooden doorway frames. Sometimes, she opened her window for the soft moonlight and delicious air. One day, she stopped breathing altogether.

Her name was Ginger George.

Three weeks later, an auctioneer wandered through the collection, which included a famous painting, a smattering of antiques, china, and linens. Pets were disposed of. Also, there was a burglar's-clutch of fine jewelry that had not been apportioned specifically in the will.

Ginger, an older lady with pale gray whispering through her hair, sweet though austere, was the kind of woman who would buy ornamental lamps. On this occasion, amidst the bric-a-brac and several other small fixtures, one lamp shimmered lustrously. There was no name visible, but its quality was obvious, and the rose crystal gleamed like a living thing.

The lamp was shaped abstractly like a woman's body, similar to a curvaceous dressmaker's dummy, with no arms or legs. A band of carved facets trailed its length. The lampshade was black and delicate. Similar to the bracelets and cuff links once made with hair, it featured a fine sheen of black threads, which suggested the illusion of opaque blackness to the old cream fabric beneath. On closer inspection, these threads were hair, perhaps from an Arabian's tail. No person had traced the lamp's history on the auction card; it appeared to be a simple rose crystal lamp, without model or make inscribed. It was not electric, but designed for candles.

By the end of the auction several had bid. Finally, for $2000, Anastasia Perrin—Stasie to her friends—was the winning bidder. She had come to purchase one unusual item... Buying things that required no upkeep could be satisfying. Her husband, Geoff, was seventy-five to her seventy-three, so she decided they would not get another pet. Besides, without a cat they could go on vacation more easily and travel like they'd always planned when Geoff sold the business. That morning he told her to attend the auction, with this very thing in mind: *Go buy something is what you said*, she thought. *That simple. Go buy something and everything will be okay. That's how men seem to think.*

Still, she had to admit, after her purchase, the day seemed magical. She pulled away from the estate sale with the top down on the green convertible. She found herself singing a doo-wop song as she returned to their beach house. She smiled again as the ocean air flooded her nostrils and she entered the drive.

As always, the sight of her house, towering majestically over the cliff, pleased her. This was the house she'd always wanted. After fifty years of marriage, she'd lived a wonderful life, the kind she always wished for other people. Geoff, though he worked his fingers to the nub in the beginning, had quickly capitalized on the elite's need for elegant plumbing fixtures and after a few rough years they always had more than enough. Stasie sighed, thought, *How many people could live the life I have?*

She was fit for seventy-three, and her body didn't pain her like many of her older friends'. She was happy. She didn't want to speak incessantly about her bowels. She was so happy, in fact, that the loss of a little brown cat was the only trauma that could set her out of sorts for weeks. She teared up thinking about Mr. Higgs, then wiped the wet away.

It was late-August, 1983. The coastal air was warm and dry. Seagulls flew over the cliff toward the waves. She grabbed the lamp from the trunk and walked up to the house. Geoff stepped out, waving.

"What did you buy?" he asked.

"A lamp."

"Good," he said, noting her smile. He didn't ask how much it cost. He didn't seem to care. "I missed you," he said.

"Do you want to see the lamp? It doesn't plug in."

"Yes, show me." She pulled away the tissue and he stared at the crystal for a moment. The outdoor sun speckled it with a bright glint of flashing pink. "It's pretty," he said. She set it on the table. Amidst the bills and junk mail, tourist pamphlets fanned the cherry wood and she saw he considered Berlin, Ecuador, and Tahiti. "Do you have a preference?" he asked.

"Yes, Peru."

They were planning on vacationing in October. Stasie's granddaughter, Bethany, would be with them in a week or two and would stay until mid-September. Stasie thought of her excitement to have a visitor and kissed Geoff on the cheek, before saying, "How are the rhododendrons?"

"Fine—the insect-killing squirt bottle did wonders."

Stasie's green eyes sparkled. "Stupid blight. Where will I put the lamp?"

Geoff paused. "Why don't you put it on the night-stand, where the lamp was that Mr. Higgs knocked over?"

"Splendid," Stasie said.

When she went to bed that night, Stasie fell immediately to sleep. She dreamed, for the first time in a long time. Since she'd gotten older, her dreams were less frequent. This dream was about a beautiful young woman with long black hair. The woman danced in a meadow, wearing a white cotton dress. After a series of leaps and twirls, the woman collapsed in a mock-heap and began eating tiny watercress sandwiches from a basket, handing some to Stasie. If there were conversation, in the morning, Stasie recalled only that she'd watched this woman and that the dream was not about her.

She wondered if her granddaughter's impending visit had spurred the dream. She didn't even like watercress. She could no longer dance—but she knew the joy of owning a startling future, of being the girl others watched. As usual, Geoff woke beside her and kissed her *good morning*. She pulled on her old khaki pants and went to the garden. The tomatoes looked good. In general, the vegetables looked better than the flowers. Stasie missed her cat. A lump came to her throat. Buying something was only a thrill for a few hours. She decided to call her daughter.

"When does Bethany get here?" she asked.

"Next Wednesday. She told me she can't wait to be at the old house. She can't wait to see you."

"We can't wait to see her!" Stasie replied.

Stasie and Geoff tooled around until Wednesday, and then picked up Bethany from the airport. She looked thin. Too thin. "Hello, M'girl," Geoff said. "How's college life treating you?"

"Great! I love it," Bethany said. Stasie considered her granddaughter. Something was off. She seemed happy—her pale, freckled face was smiling, but her eyes were rimmed with red. The black beneath her eyes had been hastily covered with light beige makeup. Her red curls looked messy, clothes rumpled.

"What do you want to do while you're here?" Stasie asked.

"Play tennis. Go sailing. Hang out with you old folks."

"Do you want to buy something?"

"What, Grandma? Why? Do you need something?"

"I just like to go buy something these days," Stasie said, remembering how she used to take Bethany out to purchase hair bows and long spiral suckers. "Maybe a cinnamon roll?"

"Sure, Grandma. I'll have a cinnamon roll with you."

When they dropped Geoff off at the house, Stasie said, "What's wrong, Beth. You look like hell."

Bethany smiled. "You don't mince words."

"I want to know," Stasie said. "I want my girl to be happy." She called all of her daughters and granddaughters "her girls." So far, there were three.

"I shouldn't say," Bethany said. "It's ridiculous."

"Tell me now, because I'm not getting any younger,"

Stasie replied. She paused, clutching Bethany's hand, before saying, "My cat died, you know?"

"Oh, no," Bethany replied. "Mr. Higgs? How sad! When?" Bethany's expression was truly sorrowful.

"A little bit ago," Stasie said, glad someone other than Geoff understood.

"My boyfriend broke up with me," Bethany said. "Last week. He was my chemistry professor."

"Oh," Stasie said.

"He said I was too young for him and our relationship damaged his professional life. But I haven't damaged his professional life. I haven't told anyone. I didn't even ask him to leave his wife. And I'm in the humanities. It's not like I'll be taking any more of his classes."

"Oh," Stasie replied once more, not knowing what to say.

"Let's eat a cinnamon roll," Bethany replied, smiling bravely. "I'm hungry."

The days streamed by as the visit continued. Bethany and Stasie ventured all over town. Every night, Stasie collapsed into bed, exhausted. She began to feel tired all the time. By Tuesday of the next week, she decided she wanted to stay in and rest though they had planned to take out the dinghy. The lamp glittered dimly. Bethany came in and asked, "Are you okay, Grandma?"

"Yes, I'm fine," Stasie said, which was true, but the dreams of the young girl in white kept coming. They had spoken now. Stasie vaguely understood the girl's name was Amarilla.

In daytime, the dreams came while Stasie napped, and at night when she fell asleep. They had begun to appear sequential. But dreams were difficult to pin down. Who knew in what part of sleep they arrived? A year in a dream could be five real-time minutes to a sleeper, Stasie knew. Despite Bethany's presence, these dreams had become increasingly important to Stasie.

Once, she was out on a lake, boating with Amarilla, eating tiny strawberries and drinking wine. Another time, she sat in what must have been Amarilla's house—eating dinner at a long, dark table. In these dreams she saw a man's hands, but never a face, though she sometimes heard him and Amarilla talking. One day she asked Amarilla, "What year is this?"

"1754," Amarilla said. In this dream, Stasie plaited Amarilla's long hair for bed. On the nightstand was a lamp that looked exactly like hers, except its shade was made from broken shells.

"Is this your lamp?" she asked.

"Yes, Shelley made it for me."

Stasie assumed the male voice belonged to Shelley. Stasie awoke startled. Geoff came in and dropped a second brown bag on the dresser. "Tomatoes from the garden," he announced. He offered to prop her up with more pillows, but she declined. "You coming outside to pick with me?"

"Not today," she said.

"You okay, Stasie?"

"Yes. I'm sure I'll be fine," she said, hoping to usher him out, longing to return to sleep to re-enter the dream. Was this lamp she had Amarilla's? Could these dreams be visitations, or was it simply that she was old and feeble, prey to imaginings? Geoff left, but Bethany came in and kept her awake by reading books aloud.

"Grandma," she said, "you've been in bed for two days now."

"I know," Stasie said.

"Don't you want to get out? I don't have much time left here."

"Have you ever had a dream," Stasie asked, "that you don't want to wake from? I know it sounds strange, but my dreams have been so real. They make me feel like I'm living them."

"Yes," Bethany said. "A dream that's like you're living in someone else's apartment?"

Stasie stared at the lamp. "Yes. And you know, this lamp was in my dream, but it had a different lampshade. Must be a flicker of the unconscious. I'm so tired."

Bethany left, but came in the next morning. "Grandma, do you think you'll be well enough to take out the convertible today? I'll drive, if you're too ill."

Stasie put her feet in her slippers, yawned, stretched, and looked in her closet. "Yes, let's go out."

As the road zipped past, the sea breeze was invigorating. Some of the previous days' fatigue left Stasie. She and Bethany joked and shopped all day. Beth's cheeks looked pinker and her smile more authentic.

"I think you're recovering, Bethany," Stasie said.

"Sometimes you have to go away to come back," Bethany replied. "I'm away, and I'm back!"

Stasie kissed her granddaughter's cheeks. "I'm so glad. Stay as long as you wish."

But that night, Stasie found herself wandering the halls with a groundless anxiety. She felt short of breath, and soothingly touched the afghan blankets on the couches. She wandered to the guest bathroom and picked up the shells that lined the upper flats of the tiles where the shampoos were lined up. Each of the shells represented a memory of a trip she had taken with Geoff, a hand-picked souvenir. She listened to the oceans inside them, the roar of the echoes sounding harmonious with the cold of the tiles at her feet. She imagined standing on the beach to calm herself.

The dream she'd had earlier that night was disturbing. She saw the man's hands again, but this time they gestured angrily at Amarilla. The girl shouted, "Get out! Get out of here!" and neither of them spoke to Stasie. The man's hands gestured to the lamp. Stasie heard him say, "I made this for you, Amarilla. It looks like you. Maybe I'll take it with me when I go." Amarilla threw herself in front of the door.

"Don't leave me," she said. Her arms laced around his neck and they began to kiss, hungrily, angrily, passionately. He lifted her body up against the door and they made violent love. Stasie woke feeling winded, then began her tour of the halls. She went back to her room and studied the lamp. She settled on her pillows again. Looking at it sideways, the lamp did look like a woman. "Are you," she asked, "are you telling me a story?"

"Grandma," Beth said the next day. "I'm worried about how much you're sleeping. Is this an ongoing health problem?"

"No," Stasie said.

"Well, I think you should see a doctor."

Stasie went to the doctor's and left with a clean bill of health. Her physician said she was fitter than ever. She took Beth to play tennis on the clay courts near her house. She felt awake, alert. Only when she stepped inside the house did she feel exhausted. "Now for a nap," she said.

Bethany, who seemed happy enough that she'd visited the doctor, went to watch television in the living room. Stasie fell asleep. She saw Amarilla in the field again. This time, Amarilla lounged with a man she'd never seen. A young man, whose voice wasn't like Shelley's. Amarilla laughed, waving briefly to Stasie. Soon, she wrapped her long black hair around the boy's naked back. He looked about sixteen. A *clopping* of hooves arose in the distance. Amarilla looked up, fearful.

Stasie heard a knocking at her door. "What? Who is it?" she asked, sitting up in a fright.

Geoff entered. "It's me. I came to check on you."

Though compelled to sleep again, the concern in her husband's eyes woke her up completely. "I'm fine," Stasie said. "Don't worry." She took a few deep breaths, feeling a diminished breathing capacity.

She rose and ate dinner with the others. "We must have a carbon monoxide problem," she stated. "Does anyone else feel tired? It's always when I come in the house."

Geoff looked at her strangely, and said, "No. I feel fine." As Geoff spoke, Stasie passed out, but when they carried her outside for the drive to the hospital, she woke up and began breathing normally. As the day lengthened, she sat upright in the living room and drank a cup of coffee. In the mail that day, a package from the auction had arrived. There was a letter of apology, a request for the lamp's return, and a $2000 check addressed to Stasie.

The missive stated the lamp had been sold before the auction occurred, for a lump sum of $60,000 to a museum in New York, but the paperwork had been misplaced. The lamp was handmade, one of the finest pieces crafted in the early eighteenth century.

"I'm not giving that lamp back," Stasie said. "I bought it and they sold it to me. They'll have to explain their mistake to the museum." She sat on her bed and immediately wrote them a letter:

Dear Auctioneers,

I am within my rights to keep the lamp I bought. You will have to explain to the museum that you made a mistake. I'm sorry.

She put her reply in the mailbox the next day, furious, explaining the situation to Geoff. He said, "Why don't you just send them the lamp? We don't need it. It seems strange to me, anyway. It has a peculiar glow. And what kind of hair is on that shade?"

Beth said, "Grandma, if you want it, I think you should keep it."

Stasie began to hyperventilate. She reached up from her position on the bed and fondled the lamp's carved surfaces. "Look how pretty it is," she said. "I'm not sending it back."

That night she dreamt she stood beside Amarilla's dresser while Amarilla lounged in bed, almost sleeping. Shelley's voice was yelling, angry. He said, "You make me so furious, Amarilla." His hands entered the dream. They approached Amarilla's neck and closed around it. It was as though Stasie's neck were also trapped.

"No," Stasie shouted from her bed. "Stop." In the dream, Shelley could not hear her. His hands squeezed tighter. Amarilla's head rolled back and forth on the pillow. Her long black hair writhed like a many-stranded snake. Amarilla opened her eyes. Her lips were open.

The next day, the day Bethany left, Stasie felt shaken and weak. She went to the airport with Geoff to watch the airline's steel beast ferry her granddaughter into the clouds. Upon returning home, Bethany received another letter— actually, a glossy portfolio regarding the lamp. Its owners since 1955 were listed: Gloria Edderly, Darla Peters, Nanette Pram, Clarise Dunne, Georgia St. Claire, Melanie Ryan, Vannessa Starlter and Ginger George. The pamphlet went on to describe the lamp's legend: A torrid love affair between an artist and his model, whom the artist had purportedly strangled to death, before her body was found in a wheat field, shorn of all bodily hair.

Stasie stood before the lamp. Her heart raced. She swore she saw Amarilla's long lashes blinking through the pink crystal, her dark head shaved close to bald, unevenly, and her eyes open, wider, then shut. Stasie's legs gave out and she braced herself with one wrist on the table, while the other flailed for the bed.

In doing so, her hand accidentally glanced the lamp to fling it across the room. It landed with a thud against the closet door and then broke into shards as it hit the floor. The shade hung grimly to the base.

Tiny pieces of rose crystal were everywhere. The

fixture separated from the stone and the inside of the vase was hollow. Stasie heard a strange sucking sound as if an enormous inhalation had occurred.

The crushed lampshade lay on its side. In the dented top, the hair separated from the fabric, and Stasie saw a fragment of shell shard and the split ends of black strands glued thickly beneath the smooth veneer. She thought of Amarilla's long black hair and the lamp that was shaped like her body.

The shade would have been her head.

One arm felt cold, so Stasie grabbed it with her opposite hand to rub. Upon doing so, she noticed a single strand of black hair clinging to her, stretching from her ring finger to her elbow in a twisted spiral, funneling between the tiny, light hairs on her arm like a black adder through a wheat field.

It stole her breath. She plucked it from herself, rapped her knuckles lightly on the wooden frame of her doorway as she focused on the stale air that would soon be replaced throughout the home's upper wing, and left the room.

THE BHEINDRIS

Some automatons were fashioned incomplete, so the new owner would need to purchase a few parts to personalize them—eyes, for example, voice box, skin—but Siola was one who'd been salvaged. Some time long ago, pieces of her skin had been stripped to apply to other robots; joints were removed. From her neck down, various turbines and motors showed. She was my lover.

She was my wife because no one wanted her, because no one wanted me, because I found her beautiful, and because I alone could fix her with the mechanisms that stood in Ted Grich's house on the day I claimed her—despite that my fixing her was limited to keeping her running. The polycarbonate skin scraps I may have added to make her seem less mechanized were scarce in these times, so she would likely never "pass" or look like a real woman again, not that I had seen a real woman in more than a decade, and not that her parts and presence weren't more soothing to me than anyone else's, dead or alive, even now.

"Stop worrying, Jarah," she told me several times as I fretted about how long I'd been unable to perfect her, unable to apply polymers to hide her exposed parts. "I don't need skin," she often said. "As long as I can move, I'll be fine."

Her hair was long and the color of honey. It had nearly no weight, and from the static of her metallic motion, almost always floated behind her as she walked, like a golden banner. Behind her, too, was a red goldfish bot magnetized to follow, an early model of the Robo-pet series now nearly extinct, which trailed her by two feet and always made the air she strode through seem as if it could be water. In the way of fish bots, it expected no notice and desired no contact, so though it was ever-present, she and I overlooked it almost all of the time, except when it fell out of the air and needed the attention of my gentle hands for motor adjustment or a fresh charge.

"Jarah," Siola would say if I went too long without doing so. "I must be followed. Fix my fish, Bheindri. Please."

She was cordial from the start regarding my love and willingness to appease her. If she possessed one fault, it was that she did not love me. She could not. The owner she loved most was dead. Two hundred years ago, she was born or, should I say, created, so I was never her first human love. The one who sculpted her face and designed her features held that place, saved it for himself until she passed out of use by allowing no robotic re-patterning module to delete his memory. She'd been coded so his care, his touch, his love, and his words were all that would truly content her, and these only upon reflection of the past. What a cruel act! Most programmers wrote code now to ensure that re-implantation could occur when a spouse or caretaker was switched.

In many models, override chips found one set of learned rules and, upon new ownership, rewrote them with the traits of a new companion. She was rewrite-enabled, but densely configured so all current companion knowledge remained in short-term memory, whereas Thomason, the man of my ire, was hard-wired and permanent. So, like I said, she was a broken toy. Wired poorly for her purpose. Unfixable. But she was still a joy.

"Siola, recite again the passage in Sartre's *Huis Clos* that I love," I could say, and she would read and perform, for it was a play, with an animated series of voices that echoed verisimilitude with human interaction, yet retained her dulcet tones.

Most days, within the walls of our shared compound, she walked to and fro, which was her great pleasure, ambulating with a squeaking sound so faint I had to listen close to hear. On my part, such close awareness of her was a sign of my attuned concern, my affection, my deep love—that I should note a thing so small and hold this listening sacred, as it embodied my acquired knowledge.

She acquired knowledge, too—lifting books from the shelves and running her scanner-tip finger over the texts therein. She could read an ancient book in minutes, for despite the fact that many small electronic devices had shorted out years ago, an abundance of paper books remained, and it was during these times that I found her most foreign, flipping yellowed paper rapidly, as a machine might, in her true robotic way—her absolute recall, years later, perfect as any robot that had never been mangled.

After she had absorbed a book, sometimes long afterward, I would request a specific passage: "Siola, recite the early work of Keats," I would say, for example, and she complied. When she had questions, she asked.

"Jarah, which years would you like surveyed?" she might say, and there was never an unwillingness to provide what I wanted. She was trained to kiss the hand that fed, the hand that oiled, the hand that kept her moving. She also was taught to thank. "Thomason thanks you for tending me," she sometimes said.

I hated this. "I would like for you to thank me," I sometimes replied.

"Oh, yes, I thank you, too," she then said. "You know I do." But my wants were secondary to her long-term memory.

Tenderly, I oiled her joints and made certain padded

cushions on which she could sit in the compound. After powering her down, I fixed and oiled her. Always, I provided her fuel and maintained the dwelling temperature on the thermostat at which she best functioned: Seventy-six degrees. Hotter, she moved slowly. Colder, her skin was not soft, as human, and she strolled with a lurching slowness that meant her finer pacing was thrown off. Her hands seemed frigid in mine. I was glad she still had false flesh on both palms, so it was a relief to hold her hands, but such simulated skin was missing on her shoulders and along her left side, scraped from her elbows, and partially removed from where the swell of her buttocks would have sloped.

In other places, her skin cover was slashed, too—just underneath her bosom, for example, between her pelvis and her waist. As she recited poetry or prose, however, I looked only at her face. Even the scavengers who strip-mined her skin would not destroy her crowning beauty. The whole of her head was custom: They could not take off her visage or any piece because she had been made without duplicates— pale pink lips and light blonde brows spaced like a real woman Thomason had known were hers to keep.

I had been her husband for thirty years.

In and out for food and supplies we'd traveled, her dressed in flowing silk caftans to hide her missing parts. But time had changed me. As she remained just as I knew her from the start, I knew she now perceived that I walked slower and soon would need a cane or a walker. My hair, once brown as chestnut, had turned white. I was only thankful she could not detest my aging as a human might, for she absorbed objects by their shapes and humans by the mutating sound of their voices and the outline of their bodies. Her algorithms were adaptive, constantly adjusting. I would be her Jarah until I died because she would watch my changes and note them as time flowed forward. She was the perfect long-term partner, never jealous, never unreasonable.

When I did not tend her, I fixed other things. Clocks, watches, and the like. For many, it was a time of solitude. Work was scarce. The food we ate resembled pellets, long-stored reserves we consumed when real food grew rarer. These were filling, if not delicious. Automatons accounted for a good sixty percent of life on the planet, and while humanity struggled along, bringing together organic mating partners where possible, and creating small patches of green scattered throughout our city blocks, the machines would outlive us, and we knew it. Sterile, my line would die with me. For this reason, I did not seek a human partner, only a reason to continue.

I found my reason in her voice, in the words of the people who came before me as filtered through her rosy mouth and tone. Granted, I was getting along, my memory suffering as my urge for nostalgia grew, and more and more I asked for Poe or Fitzgerald, or Melville—wanting dirges, sonnets, texts she could read that would sound, in the onset of my increasing proximity to death, like loving words or stolen kisses. I knew age would make her lack of love for me unbearable, that I would seem like her grandfather soon enough to those who witnessed us together in my dwindling years, for many people cosmetically aged their automatons to age with them—and granted, I would not likely live more than another decade, but one day, she disturbed me when she said, "Jarah. I do not mean to bother you, Sweetheart, but it is time you find me a new keeper. I fear you will soon pass."

My heart nearly went cold. Was I to die alone, I wanted to ask? Would she leave me for a younger man before I'd even gone? This was not unusual; to continue, automatons were built to seek new repairmen.

"If you do not find me a new keeper," she then said, very calmly and sweetly, "who will oil me? Who will keep me running? Can you work this out soon, please? Thomason and I thank you for your help."

"Yes," I agreed. I concluded I must find her a new mate. I thought of little but duty and errands the next few days, yet couldn't force myself to move forward on her required task. Worse, I found that every time I looked at her, a striking pain consumed my limbs. A fierce preemptory regret. I had accepted her. I had loved her. I had oiled her and cared for her, though she could not lie beside me and keep me warm due to her machine parts, though she could not, by virtue of missing padding in her vaginal area, give me the sort of pleasure I'd enjoyed when younger with real women—she was my machine, mine, and now I was to give her up as if I'd not endured such deprivation? The sting of her words didn't cease to bother me as she walked through the house, seemingly unfazed.

In the coming days, she did not ask again about a new keeper, assuming as she did that I would find her another husband, for she'd learned she could depend on me. But was I, to her, I wondered, already dead, a soon-to-end phase of her long, upcoming life?

Don't get me wrong, I loved Siola. I tell you she was broken, imperfect, beautiful, and kind. It was not that I wanted to leave her untended, but that I did not feel ready to release her with my age and the idea of giving her away before I even passed caused a pain in my chest that would not abate.

When later in the day, her Bheindri fish fell out of the air, it seemed to visually represent my own falling out of her atmosphere, falling away from her vivacity and joy. When I passed her in the library, I wondered what she would say about me after I died. Had she seen Thomason? Would she perhaps say: "New master, fix the old master, please"? But this was my invention. I knew she already understood the ways of organic matter and was coded to interpret that I could not be repaired. In fact, she might not remember me at all once I'd gone, lifting my corpse like a light bundle and carrying me to the trash pits for the new man.

I already knew, she'd have no legacy of my memory because I was to be rewritten. This fact rankled and recurred much lately as I regarded her going about her daily business, and I began to loathe Thomason so fully that I searched the history archives for his picture. Such an arrogant man!

"I make the best bots," he was quoted as saying, "because they are unforgettable and well-mannered, trained to love."

As usual, Siola walked and read. She moved and spun. After she had asked about a replacement, a week passed with me watching and finding her beautiful and horrid, because she intended to be the bot she always was, and though I had succeeded, in many intervals, with determining her more human in my mind as we cohabitated, it was as though I could now recognize only the heartless bot shorn of skin, the thing nearest me resembling a woman, whose face seemed much like one I had looked upon with joy for many years, except I was consciously reminded now, as my death neared, that her eyes could assess my every biorhythm, that she was finely tuned and accurate as any machine of her ilk, and that she would know before I did the day I was to die.

I knew, too, as the days passed, that the replacement issue would grow more pronounced, for Siola was built to preserve herself and would ask again about who next would provide her with care, for she was mercenary and practical, a machine capable of logic, so she was not only to leave me, but also to herald and handle my death.

"Jarah, take care of my future," she said on another day, not long after. "Please find my next keeper."

There was a young mechanic I knew. I told her I would call him. "He may not want another automaton," I said. But I lied. Who would not want this beautiful machine, for her voice and head alone?

"Good. Call him," she said. "I am a machine so I cannot continue without fuel or resources. I cannot fix myself."

"I know that, Siola," I said, staring the grooves on our tiled floor. Then I asked, "Do you know when I will die?"

"Do you really want to know?" she replied. "If you want the measurement to the hour, I'll need some blood."

"No blood," I said. And then I thought for a while. Changing my mind, I touched her honey hair, said, "Prick me. I want to know." Foolishly, I then reached for her floating fish, but it emitted a terrible shriek, which jarred me. I changed my mind again, stating, "No. I don't want to know, even though I do want to know. Or maybe I want to know, but only five minutes before I pass. Tell me, then. Can you do that for me, Siola?"

"Yes," she said, puncturing my fingertip with a sharp. "Would you like to hear something, Sweetheart? Rimbaud, Tennyson, or Coleridge?"

"No thanks," I replied. She placed a drop of blood on her fingertip. She wiped it clean with a towel, registering without speaking the data she processed.

I thanked her. And I told her I would pay the young man to replace me a visit. I left. When I returned, I told her I had secured a place for her to go. I put the telephone number on the databank, and instructed her that it was the one to call when I passed. But I had not contacted the young man. I had walked past his house without stopping.

That day, I went through my bookshelves, pulling free volumes I had not read in years. I bade her read to me, for each passage spoke of letters written by women to their beloved spouses. She did this for months. As always, I fixed clocks, small pets, kitchen accessories. She ambulated, her Bhiendri in tow. And on the day I was to die, she strode toward me, her beautiful blonde hair flowing behind her like a buttercup flag, her red fish its catch. "Jarah," she said. "You are about to die."

"It is time for some oil," I replied. "Before I go."

I spoke of how she must not forget to call her new keeper the moment I passed. I left explicit instructions for how she was to give him all of the replacement parts I stored in the yard compartments. All this I did in the moment before I powered her down.

I did not know who next would discover and take her, but decided it was better this way. I'd harbor no jealousy before I passed. Thomason may have made her love him permanently, but, for a time, it could seem I would take her with me into eternity.

Perhaps, we'd form a tableau of a rotting man's body beside a frozen, gorgeous bot. I did not know. But for the last instant of my life, it could seem that I could reflect gratefully, while I stared at her still face, that we had lived a long and beautiful life in the compound, that we had found joy in the other's company, and that, like any old human couple might have, Siola and I died in close succession. For I could then feel, as my eyes wavered while beholding her familiar and serene countenance, that Thomason had lost his insidious hold on her heart—and I had claimed mine. But more importantly I could feel, in the instant I passed from this dark place, that, in lieu of me, for her, there'd be no other.

A COMPANION TO MINNOW LAKE

—For Ann and Doug Bailey

Cecil sat on the train wearing his charcoal business suit, variegated socks, and his splendid silk tie with small green stripes, but the outfit was stuffy, he decided, and reminded him of his time practicing law. He hadn't worn this suit in some twenty-odd years. The last time was to a church luncheon, which, truthfully, he avoided whenever possible, but his daughter, Camille, had made him attend.

She was the wrong type of Christian, he thought, the type with an urge to convert or reform every person they met, the kind of Christian who would joyfully lead a crusade—at least, she was ten years ago when last they'd visited at length, but Cecil vigorously believed in the phrase "live and let live." In fact, because so many early decisions were made for him, now that he was old, he felt perversely glad to ignore convention. He hadn't been to church since he was fifty. He stopped practicing law at fifty-five because he hated it, hadn't decided to be a lawyer in the first place. His mother had determined it for him because his father had been a lawman and, in her words, a son should follow a father's lead.

"Father" was the term Cecil used to describe the man in conversation, but privately, he referred to his father as Papa. Father, as a term of address, seemed so cold. Though he wanted to call him Papa aloud, he kept the term a personal prize, his mother having intoned "your father" in so many of her tirades that Cecil's memories of Papa, as he remembered him, were guarded and stored. Cecil was never sure when their magical power would expire.

Sometimes, when the day meandered, Cecil considered his father's ever-present duality in his life, as though the same person maintained two identities—the cherished Papa in Cecil's head, and his mother's daunting "your father," imbued with rich and ruthless strength. The two could not be reconciled.

Cecil looked out the window as the train passed an undeveloped lot of clay-colored land. There was no change of scenery from his window for several moments, until a small green sign attached to a faded Ivory Soap billboard heralded impending arrival in Camille's town: Valley View, 10 miles.

Camille said Valley View couldn't run longer than ten miles, so Cecil supposed it would be like Crescentville, his father's hometown. His father, known as Greggo to his friends, died at forty-five from a stroke. His passion for the law, too much red meat, too many cigars, and too little sleep had tightened the noose. Cecil supposed, when thinking of their shared career, that he had lived longer because he ran his practice deftly, without sentiment. He'd toiled to succeed, despite his disenchantment, but had worked long hours to retire early.

Despite his practice's success, even working hard Cecil could never do enough to please his mother. When he was in his early forties, he took Emily to her house on Sundays. It seemed, at times, that the old woman was holding up some ruler of his youth against his adult productivity, as if to suggest he had done nothing, constantly measuring him against his father's achievements, though he could never better them. "Your father was twice the man you are," she liked to announce. "Bless his soul."

When the dead died, they became her saints, Cecil knew. A few times, Emily sat at his mother's with him, still as a doorknob, but when they returned home, she questioned him in her sweet way about why he let the harridan treat him so cruelly. Afterwards, Emily pleaded sickness from the outings and eventually stopped going altogether, confessing that she could not bear Cecil's mother's ritual of frigid degradation when first she would repeat the number of clients his father went through per week. Then, she'd repeat how prestigious it was to be a lawyer—and, finally, she'd reemphasize how, after Cecil graduated with a bachelor's in psychology, she had pushed him into law school and out of the psych doctorate program at NYU, before she rode him, goaded him, and shamed him into attaining his law degree—which was, to him, a mere piece of paper hanging on the wall.

His father's death bestowed a legacy of insurmountable greatness, but Cecil's peculiar failures in his mother's eyes had always been present and clear. Although Cecil tried to love her, the gifts she gave him as a child were strictly necessary items: Compasses, rulers, erasers, books, and thumbtacks. The gifts he gave her she never understood. These were the formative episodes he remembered from childhood that he later discussed with Emily, long into the night, everglued to the plangent details of his mother's misplaced affection.

Once, he brought his mother a bouquet of daisies. The next day they were in the trash, their green ribbon soiled by carrots and rotten chickpeas. Once, he painted her a picture. She gave it to his brother to color on the backside. Jude was four, then; Cecil seven. Cecil never forgave her for letting Jude maul the work because Jude didn't color on the blank side; he colored over Cecil's airplane. Jude was Mother's favorite. She pinned Jude's ugly yellow-and-purple crayon airplane on the refrigerator, saying, "Look at what my two boys made for me!" and patted Jude on the head. Even now, at seventy-three, Cecil felt shamed that his picture had been regarded only as the background image, while Jude's had consumed the refrigerator-door limelight.

When Jude died in a boating accident during a family vacation in Carolina Springs, Cecil was nine. He remembered standing in his brown funeral suit, a pink carnation tucked into the lapel, holding his mother's purse. The rain had pelted the pastor's slick hair, rolling off like hot oil. Jude was only six. He looked like a dead cherub, morbidly made up with blush. Into his open casket Mother poured herself, bawling and bawling, until she made no sound other than a rasping choke. Her makeup ran down her face. She reached behind her for her brown leather purse once, but didn't look at Cecil.

Only his Papa clenched his hand with any warmth, at work six days a week but present for the one-hour service. Afterward, Cecil had a toothache, but mother wouldn't take him to the dentist until three days later. He feared, privately, that she hated to look at him because she wished it were him who had died.

Mother initiated the move to the city after his father passed. She sold the house for a "good deal of money," but Cecil's Papa would never have moved. His house in the country was intended as Cecil's inheritance. The lake was to have been his. Both house and lake had remained in Papa's family for over a hundred years, and because his mother sold it, Cecil decided that she had never truly loved his father.

Though it was rare for his father to take time away, on the few weekends Papa took off work, he'd spent his days sitting beside the lake. Cecil's mother had no taste for it, busy as she was intervening in other people's personal business, so his father often sat alone, and Cecil watched him, hidden, crouched in the wheat grass on the periphery. Long tufts of smoke rose from his Papa's mouth, and Cecil was quiet as held breath, quiet as a leaf.

Cecil's father had stocked the lake with bass every year, fishing with his son during the summer. The trips started when Cecil was nine, just after Jude died. The first time, his father baited the hook, saying, "Watch me once, Son. From now on, you'll bait your own." And then he smoked. Cecil's father loved Cubans, and for some reason, much of the time, Cecil's mother.

Cecil's train ride was a jumble of memories. He found the older he got, the more he remembered about his childhood. Perhaps it was the knowledge that he was moving to the country responsible for such nostalgia, but it had been years since he thought about these issues and reacted with anything more than a sad shrug. He did miss Emily today. She was forty-two when she died. Driving home one icy night, her car spun over a cliff, rolling, and catching fire. Cecil had never remarried.

Jude. Papa. Emily. Mother. All family dead, except his daughter, Camille.

Cecil had attended more funerals than weddings in his lifetime. He thought of his days as many dark spots relieved by a few bright dahlias. It was his mother's eventual death, a follow-up to Emily's, that led him into early retirement. With his parents' money, and nearly half of his paychecks from the last fifteen years saved, he was finally free to quit his practice. But for whom, if not himself, would he now live?

He didn't want to attend church with Camille. He would refuse, maybe lounge about her property's lake. When Emily was alive, he spent a lot of time wondering about his father's sold retreat. Who currently owned it? Was the lake still stocked? Did anyone fish in it? He visited once and tried to buy it, just after his retirement, but the property had fallen into disrepair. A young girl lived there, with a few friends, the house like a commune.

He asked her if she'd be in the market to sell anytime soon. The girl nodded *no*, her dirty long hair spinning on her head, and she shut the door. He went back again soon thereafter and offered her a substantial amount of money, but gave up the notion when she firmly said she wouldn't sell her house to a lawyer. "I need to buy this house," he replied. "It's the only thing I have of my p—" He had to stop, several times, before getting his point across, due to becoming choked up. "My father owned this house," he then uttered. "I want it back in the family. My mother sold it. The house matters to me."

"Well, I like it too," the girl said. "I paid good money for it. And I don't want to move."

"But I'm offering you double the would-be asking price," he argued.

"Offer me triple, Lawyer Man, and I'd still say no," she replied. "I'm sorry." Her pupils were dilated and he watched her stare at the crack in the doorjamb, willing him away, her feet pointed apart like a ballerina.

Camille and Emily sat waiting in the car. He could make out their expectant faces watching, distantly, through the car's windows. "It's an ugly house anyway, Dad." Camille said. "All boarded up and rotting. Who wants that place? Look at the bums who live there."

Emily looked back warningly. "Don't worry, dear," she said.

Inside the vehicle, Cecil damned his mother again, and rubbed his forehead as he drove away. Later that day, he took another trip to the lake and parked alongside the road; the girl with the stringy hair floated nude on its surface, pale in the five-o'-clock light and resembling Ophelia: Poor, mad Ophelia, with small and nearly flat breasts, without a heavy gown, with a slight spacey smile neither happy nor distraught.

He watched her for a long time, not desiring her body, just watching. When she turned and swam to the lake's edge, her young shoulders rippled beautifully. Her face was clean and elegantly devoid of makeup, timeless. It might have been 1813, or 1613 for that matter.

This was the last time Cecil saw his father's lake—the last memory attached. That night, he returned to his hotel room and ordered a scotch and soda, and Camille, only six, had cautioned him against too many. "Daddy, you need to stop. Daddy." Even now, he feared he had failed her as a father. She was undisciplined, self-possessed, and vulgar in her demands, reminding him painfully of his mother, refusing to listen to any but the most practical of details. When he was dressed slovenly, she didn't listen to him at all.

Though en route to her home now, the suit he wore was his way of establishing the rules of conduct. First, he didn't need to be babied. Second, she would not open his mail. Third, he would leave the house when he willed, and fourth, he did not need crafts. Cecil was adamant on these issues, but he wasn't sure how his prim daughter would react. Perhaps there would be an unpleasant scene, and she would wear him down until he settled into acquiescence. He couldn't remember a conversation with Camille that had ended well. In this, too, she was like his mother.

It had been many years since his mother died. She'd outlasted Emily by four years, and he often thought about her, not because he loved her, not because he missed her, but because either Camille brought her memory back to him on a visceral level, or because he felt neither of these emotions —only a sense of overwhelming relief.

He remembered her funeral, which was sparsely attended. It was windy. As if through the oscillations of a ceiling fan, the pastor's eulogy was scattered to the wind, and he heard the holy words... walk through... valley... death... shepherd... pretending to agree... sainted soul...

lovely woman... nodding somberly at each rise in inflection.

Then Camille was twenty-five, but that was twen-ty-three years ago. Now, Cecil looked out the window again and searched for his daughter on the platform; whistles moaned, and the train stopped; Camille would probably be late. Even in a crowd, he expected he would find her easily; Camille was distinctive with her thin eyebrows and wide eyes. She didn't take after Emily, and possessed none of Cecil's good features, but was the rare kind of woman whose face assumes no age: Eighteen going on forty, or forty and virtually unaltered—blending in.

Her hair had never wavered from its original mousy brown, and her skin assumed a stretched, hanging look. When she smiled it was melancholic, and her teeth were slightly crooked. He had offered to buy her braces years ago, but she didn't want them. Camille had a sharp tongue, like sour crab apples; Cecil suspected this was the reason she never married.

Though one in death and one in flight, Emily and Camille had left him at virtually the same time. After Emily died, Camille drifted to Norfolk with her boyfriend, Tom. The relationship didn't last long. Tom was the cheating kind —but that was years ago, Cecil knew, and possibly many men ago.

Today, he was moving in with Camille, away from his apartment in Greensborough, next door to his fishing buddy, Doug. Cecil's doctor had prescribed a few months in the country after his apartment was robbed and vandalized; the incident soon followed by an acute heart attack.

If it weren't for the heart attack, he would have continued to see Camille at Christmas and on holidays, but unexpectedly, on his way to her new house, he found that he felt surprisingly good. Camille had tried to put him in a home after the incident, but couldn't afford the care, so instead reluctantly offered her own. Stepping off the train, he pulled his bags from the overhead compartment and waited for the others, feeling a tremor of anxiety before reminding himself he was not going to Camille's old apartment, which he would not have moved into for all the stars in North Carolina. That apartment stank of mold, and there was no elevator. Its rooms were sparse and ugly, and Cecil had visited just once.

Due to new employment, Camille had recently resettled in Valley View. Her new place was a red-brick colonial with white porches—three-stories high, she'd said—and only three hundred and twenty-five dollars a month. On the property was a lake. She'd written once, to tell him she might send pictures. She did not follow through, but this omission whet his appetite more than any glowing description could. Perhaps this would be his calming place. The lake had decided matters, and he moved quickly to ready himself within two weeks.

He vaguely remembered selling his furniture the previous week to the same family he sold his apartment to. The property had appreciated quickly as the years passed. He offered it at a decent price, which he sweetened further when he saw how pleased the family was with his little place and the bickering that went on between the petite wife and her husband. "We can't afford it," she said, as the children hid under the coffee table playing slap games, so Cecil dropped the price by five thousand, thinking they deserved a break when starting out. The furniture he almost gave away, but a few things he kept: A curio, a roll-top desk, a blown-glass lamp, and his mother's china. He signed all the papers, and the escrow was to close shortly; until then, they would send monthly rent checks to Camille's address.

His bank account was still plump, getting plumper all the time, and all he bought for the move were several boxes of fine cigars to support the new habit he intended to start. He rented a storage area behind the complex from the Hide-

Away lady, Ann, and liked storing his things, as if tempo-
rarily, as though he was to go on a long, semi-permanent
vacation, like a man of leisure.

He tried to picture the lake as similar to the one on his
Papa's land. With the luggage matter resolved, he sat on the
wooden bench awaiting Camille, smoking one of his
genuine Cuban cigars. Cecil tasted the fragrant smoke, and
felt as he did while kneeling beside his father. The odor was
familiar, if not exact. He rather felt like his father today, and
hoped to spend a few weeks at Camille's lake, reenacting
those shared quiet times. The first few puffs were strong,
and he coughed smoke through his nose.

A lady with a poodle snorted at him from the bench
nearest his. He poo-pooed her, waving, and considered her
reply-smile a good omen. He was tempted to put his thumb
on his nose and wiggle his fingers like a child. He smirked,
waiting for Camille, and passed the time with a shoeshine
from a white-aproned young man as another extravagant
treat. After this day, these fancy shoes wouldn't leave his
closet for at least another five years.

Cecil felt faint with pleasure. His mouth began to tire
from so much smiling. A flush of blood raced to his head.
He decided to smoke at least two cigars a day. His doctor
might be angry, but he didn't care. Cecil, pleased and dizzy
with smoke, regarded the crowd. A passel of children disem-
barked the train to nestle in the warm breasts of their
mothers, who chirped and twittered over them. A few lone
businessmen walked briskly toward the exit. Occasionally, he
caught a glimpse of a tottering older person and smiled. Old
travelers were Cecil's favorite.

This morning he'd combed his fine white hair in a part
down the center, and had the feeling of escaping on an expedition. An expedition to a lake—what better? If he liked it
well enough, he just might stay. Truth be told, he had long
desired a move, and he knew from Camille's letters that she

had more than enough room. Besides, he'd sold the apartment, and where else would he go? He would tell her in a week or two. For now, he'd try not to scare her with being saddled with her old dad.

Cecil checked his pocket watch and noted that she was half-an-hour late. He began to feel a slight headache, accompanied by a growing impatience, coming on. Finally, one hour after his train came in, Camille arrived. He was the only person left on a station bench.

"I'm sorry I'm late, Dad," she said. "Traffic was a mess." She pecked him on the cheek, and lifted his bags into her Volvo. They chatted as they approached her house. The first thing he noticed was the lake she'd described. It was about an acre long, and green in a limpid way. One end was kidney-shaped, the other round. Yellow flowers laced its edge.

Her car's tires rolled over the driveway gravel and seemed to be taking him past the lake from a panoramic viewpoint where he could see each angle, every side. Dragonflies, water bugs, and flies flew over the lake's surface. Cecil clenched his palms. "Is it freshwater?" he asked.

"Yes, Da," Camille said. "Water from Shanty Creek enters through a pipe in the bottom." Cecil noted a few willow branches that had fallen into the shallow end, which he decided to pull out the next day. He made a mental note to write Ann, to tell her to please send his fishing pole, because he had forgotten it in Greensborough; he'd intended to pull it from the rented storage cabinet, but, in the rush and hustle, had left for the station without it. He remembered its exact placement at the front of the storage room where Ann would have no trouble retrieving it. It was late spring, and if she were conscientious, he could have it by early summer. When they arrived at the house, Cecil settled his few belongings in his room and strolled out to the long white porch that surrounded the house's second floor.

Camille had made tea, which he sipped on the porch, casually ruminating on the lake's color. *Mostly green*, he thought, *with patches of blue where the sky hits.*

"Pretty day," he said.

"Hmmmph," Camille replied.

Around the lake was a wooden-stump and barbed-wire fence. The gate to this area was locked, but a grazing pasture ran right up on it, although he was yet to see any cows.

"They're in the far pasture," Camille said, as if reading his mind. Squinting, Cecil located them in the distance like tiny brown specks. "You should rest now, Da," Camille said. "You've had a long day. Take a nap."

Cecil did not want a nap. "Are you renting this place, Camille?" he asked.

"Of course."

"I am going to buy it tomorrow," he said. "Call your lawyers."

"I haven't any lawyers."

"No matter," Cecil said. "No matter." He looked at the lake again, wanting to own it with increasing ferocity. It seemed to glow with a new hue. Light nibbled at the surface, which scattered sunlight in circular patterns of moss-green, white, agate, and sepia, swirling with spun reflections of the willows and sky. There were no trees but willows around the edge, their weeping tentacles sweeping down and caressing the lake's liquid cover. Cecil was tempted to sit and smoke another cigar, but Camille bothered him with endless chitchat until, yawning, he went to his room. She followed him and confiscated his cigars, taking them with her to the kitchen and telling him he could have only two per week.

He sat in bed for a long time, muttering to himself. Camille found him the next day sitting at the window, looking out at the lake, and pulled him away, detailing small tasks he could perform to keep himself occupied. "Don't look at that lake so much, Da," she said, worrying the edge of a cream doily on the table. "They say it's haunted, people have died there, so no one goes near it."

"Ridiculous," Cecil said, still angry about the cigars. He penned a quick note to Ann about the fishing pole and included money for the postage.

Though he found the lake tempting, Camille led him this way and that on errands, his first few days filled with sightseeing and visits to her friends' homes. He took a trip to the local library and researched the lake, then read in old newspapers that the property had changed hands six times in the past twelve years. Set on his path of buying the house, he called to inquire who owned it and the land, discovering both belonged to the bank. Evidently, after dropping the price below market value for the land itself, the last owner still hadn't found a buyer. The big bank, Crestar, finally bought it. They'd planned to sell it to a tourist for an almost-negligible profit, and Camille was in no position to buy, but instead of letting it sit in this rural locale, and because it had already been on the market a year, they let her rent it for a minor fee, with the provision that if they found a buyer she would move out with little-to-no notice.

The manager told him all this over the phone, and Cecil went to the bank the same day to make his offer. They accepted immediately, asking if they should notify Camille that she should move out. Cecil blushed at how long it took him to say *no*. And besides, this haunting business was ridiculous. Cecil felt he had made an excellent deal.

The people who died in the lake were young and old, wealthy and poor, but mostly tourists. He suspected they came from a backwards place like California, where they hadn't many lakes. Poor swimmers, he'd concluded. Death by drowning was the cause all the newspaper clippings listed —as if it explained anything.

He watched the water whenever he could. Cecil was

an early riser from his years at the firm, typically waking at six from force of habit, but lately, since moving to Camille's, though he took several catnaps during the day and went to bed at 9 p.m., he still wasn't sleeping well. Camille guarded him zealously in his first few weeks, keeping him house-bound. "You need to rest more now, Da," Camille often said. "At least several hours a day. Can't go gallivanting into the wilderness. Give yourself a chance to recover."

But the days passed quickly, one into the next. When he slipped free to visit the lake one lazy afternoon, Cecil found the gate locked. Occasionally he experienced bouts of insomnia that left him staring through the large kitchen windows at all hours, wishing something unusual would happen to lend him some perspective on the final direction his life might take.

One such bout found him sitting at the window in the middle of August, when young summer had all but died and the grasses browned in the neighborhood and the annuals stopped flowering in the beds. A flurry of activity at the lake's edge triggered the floodlights and caught a woman in a pale blue dress sprinkling flowers over the lakeshore. She regarded him, trapped in the bright halogen directed at her, then walked hurriedly through the adjacent pasture and out of his sight. Cecil set his alarm the next morning for just before four, the same time he had first encountered the woman, and tiptoed to the kitchen to see if she returned. She had, and each morning she brought more clover. He noticed that a good portion of the lake was coated with green. Each morning, he turned on the kitchen light when he saw the woman trudge up, and they began to relate to one another through slight waves and gestures. If he turned the light on, she knew he was watching. If she gestured back to him, he knew she wanted him to see her. For several days, Cecil carefully followed her progress.

On the sixth morning, she sat beside the lake, cross-legged like a child, until nearly seven. It seemed she was waiting for him. When she stood to walk away, he fled the house to discreetly follow her, maintaining a fair distance between them. Her ritual intrigued him, but when he arrived at her house, he was disappointed to find that it was nothing more than an old peach-and-green Victorian in a perfectly normal neighborhood, where children played in the street and cats ran into and out of manicured shrubs.

He passed her window and saw her pale face staring out at him, but then her body turned, and she pulled the curtain around her as though to block the view of him from whomever she was talking to. When she turned to close the curtains, she mouthed "Go away," and retreated behind the veil.

Cecil could not fathom why she acted so strangely, but he was a newcomer who had followed her home. *But why,* he asked himself, *did she look at him so pityingly?* He went away, chagrined, dismissing the young woman's reaction as the need to be alone, but she did not come the next day, nor the next. She was either a mystic, or crazy, he decided. Cecil wanted no part of either.

When he rounded the corner of the street that led toward his house, he saw, striding in his direction, another older man wearing a dark green felt cap.

"Excuse me," Cecil said. "Have you lived here long?"

"All my life," the old man said.

"Do you know much of the topography?

"A fair amount," the old man said.

"There's an old manmade lake up near—"

"Minnow Lake," the old man interrupted. He pulled a pipe and lighter from his coat pocket and set a flame to the tobacco. "There's nothing really to tell," the old gentleman said. "Several people drowned there, but they were lost souls. Anyone with a firm mind needn't worry about it. There's nothing in there but fish now, mostly minnows and brown eels. You can fish there if you don't mind doing so in a grave," the man added.

"Thank you very much," Cecil replied, thinking the old man was just as strange as the woman. His impression of Valley View as a retirement community was beginning to shift. Cecil turned to go, tipping his hat in what he hoped was a cordial way.

"See you later then, Cecil," the old man said, also turning to go.

"Hallo! How did you know my name?"

"Everyone knows you're Camille's father down from the city," the man said. "We're a small town, Valley View." With that, he smiled and turned on his heel, before walking up the next bend, leaving Cecil standing with his white fisherman's cap in hand, in the middle of an empty road.

"So, what kind of fish are in the lake?" Cecil asked Camille later in the day, watching the ripples and puckers.

"Trout and bass," she said, chopping at raw chicken in flour on her cutting board. "An occasional bluegill, minnows, and a few eel."

"Have you swum in it?" he asked.

"Oh, no," she said. "It's far too murky." She asked him about weeding and mulching around the small tomatoes, before muttering, "You'd do well to stay away from there, Da. I mean it."

"I bought this house for us, Camille," he replied. "Did I mention that?" They spoke awhile of the transaction, and Camille looked at him with pleasure in her eyes, touched he was willing to share it with her. During this moment, he thought her unusually pretty. He didn't want the tight look to return to her face, so he avoided further mention of the lake.

The next day, while she was away on errands, he walked a quarter mile up the road to a small farm, and bought five milking goats. He lifted them over his head, goat legs kicking as he struggled with the height of the short fence, and the pull of the others tied to the rope, straining to graze beyond the place their mouths could reach. *Goats are a stupid lot*, he thought, but he knew he, too, must form a stupid sight—hefting goats over his head and dropping them into a cow pasture, but he wanted to prove to Camille that her superstitions regarding the lake were completely erroneous. As soon as he could find a tool to pry open the gate lock, he would sit beside it regularly, but for now his agenda was keep the goats alive to prove to Camille that she was wrong about any perceived danger, so when he went to the lake to sit a spell, she wouldn't babysit him.

Goats are ravenous beasts, Cecil reasoned, and the tender morsels of green around the lake's edge will prove irresistible. The cows were pasture cows. Camille said they'd been there before she moved in, and perhaps they were trained to stay away from the lake; Cecil's goats had never seen it before.

Goats are ornery. Goats are shameless. If goats will not eat around a lake, then nothing will, and conversely, if they will eat, as goats tend to, then to Cecil there was nothing odd about the lake. These goats were his experiment; if they nibbled at the tall grass at the water's edge without disappearing, this would disprove Camille's suspicion.

Many days passed without incident, until he saw the old, blind gray goat wander down to the edge and delicately eat. The others continued to graze on hay he'd thrown down near the fence. A few days later, the gray was missing, but he figured it had chewed through a distant gate or stayed far afield. Possibly it had been eaten by some other wild animal that had sneaked in through the gate. He investigated and saw no openings anywhere in the fence, but the field where they could roam was long, and perhaps what happened wasn't visible to his naked eye. He took a stroll. It tired him to walk to the field's edge, so his attention was somewhat thin by the end of his search.

"Camille," he asked over dinner. "Have you seen the gray goat?"

"Da," she said reprovingly. "Are you asking about Minnow Lake again? Don't forget you're here to rest, and all you do, day in and out, is stare and fret. Go on down and sit nearby if you must. Go on down there and see. Maybe you'll disappear just like that goat." Then she blanched. "That was horrible," she said. "I didn't mean it. Please forgive me."

Since he told her about buying the house, she seemed much nicer, and he wondered if perhaps he had been too hasty in assuming she was trying to confine him. "I am here to rest," he said, drawing himself up loftily, "but I am not as old as you think."

"You're old," she said. "You have flights of fancy—and a weak heart. Now more than ever. Stay away from it."

"I should go back to the city," he announced, not really meaning it.

"No, Da, please don't leave," she said. As a tear rolled down her cheek, he was pleased by her uncharacteristic softness. "You may look at that lake as often as you like," she said. "It's just a lake. Who am I to tell you not to?"

She sat heavily on the crimson couch, letting her head fall in front of her. Cecil ran his hand through her hair and patted her head, but early in the morning he walked down the path and came to the locked gate. He pounded the lock with a hammer from the shed until it cracked and popped loose. He walked around the lake's kidney-shaped end, where the willows proliferated, and felt pleased for the first time in many weeks. He brought out a cigar and puffed happily. The next day, he took the small, red wrought-iron patio chair and delivered it to the embankment. "Ha!" he said. "Superstition be damned." Rising from his seat, he looked into the water to see a small minnow zip by.

From her spot at the window, on a rare day off,

Camille regarded him. "At least he is happy," she said. "The belligerent old crow." She took him to his doctor's appointment. His tests and visit went well, and after that, Camille encouraged him to go where he liked. Camille also permitted him one additional cigar per week, which pleased him to no end. Many days he spent musing about his past, dreaming of his Papa, and wondering, in the placid scenery, if he had been too hard on his mother. Maybe if he had known how to talk to her, if he had said the right things, she would have softened as Camille had recently. "You silly old sap," he said to himself. "You just want to love and forgive everybody now." *And why not forgive?* he thought. *Why not?* He had even begun to imagine how it might be to see Camille get married, choking up at the thought of walking her down the aisle, a forty-some-year-old bride, finding it harder and harder to believe that there wasn't a man somewhere who would claim his aging, hard-shell daughter.

One late afternoon when the light trickled down with a pinkish hue over the willows and into the water, he felt stronger than he had in weeks, imbued by a burgeoning vitality that evoked his youth. He thought of Emily, how deeply she had admired his ability to hike, and how he missed her while walking around Minnow Lake. He thought of Jude, too, how he'd never given his drowned brother a chance. Reflecting, he glanced over to view an unusual tremble on the water's surface. Two green-hued boys played beneath it, and the murky bottom had resurfaced to reveal a green-meadow texture. He could see their tow heads bob and fall as they ran gaily, skipping and mouthing words to each other until they dropped below his vision near the lake's deeper middle.

He ran to the house, shouting for Camille, but it was a Sunday and she had only recently returned from church. "What, Da?" she asked. "What?"

"Nothing," he said. "Never you mind."

—

Several days later, Cecil bent over the lake, dirtying his cotton slacks to look again at the bottom. He observed it so intently, in fact, that he realized he'd been watching a single minnow circling a reed for more than five minutes, when suddenly, a little boy's face reappeared, staring up at him with fish-like eyes.

Cecil gaped. He brushed his fingertips over the water's surface, reached down, but felt nothing. When he retrieved his hand, the ripples continued, but the boy's face remained clear beneath them. He mouthed something that looked like "Who are you?" His small lips were crusted with sores, his eyes rimmed red.

"I'm a companion to the lake," Cecil said, watching the same fish swim in circles around the boy's hair. Cecil felt an odd sensation spread across his forehead, and had the strange impression the boy was causing it. The sensation was of a leather strap tightening around his temples.

"Don't you recognize me?" the boy asked. "It's me, Jude." Cecil stared at the face, before staggering back a few steps. The same morbid cherub stared up. In his hand, Cecil noticed a twig from one of the willows. Bruises and lacerations from the rocks he'd been buffeted against when he had died covered his face. "I'm a little hurt now," Jude said.

Cecil started from the water, his heart pounding, and ran to the house in a panic, leaning against the trellis wall and breathing heavily. "I am dreaming," he said, his nostrils full of the star jasmine that had not stopped blooming. "I must be dreaming." He awoke in bed the next morning with a slight headache. When Camille came in with two eggs and some toast, he said, "Thank God you're here. I had the strangest dream."

"Da, you need to relax," she said. "Especially after yesterday."

"What happened yesterday?" he asked, eyebrows

twitching.

"I found you by the trellis," she said. "You had fainted and bumped your head. I had to ask the neighbor to carry you up here. You gave us quite a scare!"

Cecil heard a young voice calling his name, accompanied by that of a woman. "Who's here?" he asked, rising from the bed linens in his rumpled shirt.

"Da, no one's here," Camille replied, irritable. "Or, me. I'm here! Your daughter, Camille. Rest a while, and I'll make you some tea." She bustled out and finally he drifted off to sleep, still seeing the green little face floating in the lake.

—

Camille returned just before evening. "The doctor is taking you off that new medication," she told him.

"What medication?" he asked.

"The one for your heart," she replied. "He called to say you must be having side effects and perhaps hallucinations. I gave you the last pill at eight this morning. I've been hiding them in your food."

"I've had hallucinations?"

"Well, yes, it's quite common," she said. "But don't worry, Da. The medicine should lose its effect sometime the day after tomorrow. I'm sorry I couldn't tell you. I knew if I did, you would refuse to take them." She touched the gold cross at her neck.

Cecil was at once angry and relieved, but he didn't speak throughout dinner, and the next day Camille announced she had to return to the office. She left him that morning with strict orders to sit and listen to the radio. "I have to go back to the office sometime, Da," she said. "Go and work in the garden, if you must, but nothing too stressful. I've got to go now, or I'll lose this job." She pecked his face in her traditional way, but her hand lingered on his wrinkled cheek before she rushed out the door.

All day he heard voices from the lake, and when he

could no longer bear it, he strode down to the water's edge, but nothing was there. *Tricks of the mind*, Cecil thought, but he remembered the face of the lake-boy vividly, and that boy had been Jude, just as Cecil now remembered from the day they dragged his body up, lifeless and cold, when waves of river water had spilled from his mouth as his chest was pumped. Cecil remembered watching Papa's face break when they stopped trying. The long, sad haul of Jude's body to the morgue.

For a few days, he puttered around the house, beginning to feel quite lonely, but on Thursday of that week, Cecil considered fishing. His pole had long since arrived. Camille was out of town until Friday morning, so Cecil unwrapped the paper parcel and decided to see what he might catch.

—

He felt himself again and decided the drug had caused those days of peculiarity. The lake was the same lake he had admired for countless hours before coming to sit beside it. Though his insomnia had dwindled, the experience of seeing the boy's face had created a minor resurgence and Cecil found, when he could not sleep due to the clock's ticking, that he revisited the kitchen and again sought the woman in the blue dress he'd seen before. She did not disappoint. Clover. More clover she carried. He even noticed how she got into the area, which was not through the front gate. She approached from the far pasture where the cows had been. There were two wooden poles without fencing between them. She shimmied through with a sideways step. "And the gray goat must have left that way, too," he remarked.

That evening, the season reaching well into September, he walked out to watch the willows sway and dip their branches, green moss and familiar ripples dappling the water top. The light was falling to give way to the pleasant hour of twilight, the hour when the sky is not quite dark, and the moon shows prematurely. That night's moon would be a blood moon, red as sunset over a darkening ocean.

He had just baited the hook and cast a lovely arcing distance, when he noticed an unusual turbulence under the water about fifty yards away. He reeled in the bait, propping the pole against a rock near the patio chair, and ambled closer to explore. It couldn't be a current, because the water was piped in and only entered through the round-ribbed pipe on the other side. Cecil quieted and watched. Rotted twigs rose to the top, and then the lake was almost still. The willow tree and moon's reflection undulated under his gaze.

Then he saw what looked like a brown rope surface in the water. As it elevated, he noted the fine round bubbles rising from it, before a mop of auburn tresses replaced his impression. It was a woman's head, a wreath of pale, purple African violets encircling the hair. Her face turned upward. Cecil realized she was not his mother, whom he had initially searched for, but Emily: Emily young again, stunning in her dewy beauty except for the slight unnatural green tint of her face and soft lichen in her hair. He stared at the freckles on the bridge of her nose.

"Emily?"

"Cecil," she mouthed, looking up at him with the same gray eyes. "Cecil?" The old man leaned closer, and her bloodless hands fluttered to the surface, white-fingered and delicate.

"Emily," he said. "Emily, you look so beautiful."

"Cecil," she said, her face surfacing just below him, "When you die, you choose which age to keep."

The painful tightening around his head began again. "How is it that you are here?" he asked. "I must be imagining you."

"Cecil," she asked, "Do you remember this dress? I wore it the night you knelt in front of everyone at that party and asked me to marry you. You were red-faced from the run up the stairs, and you were more than an hour late because your mother's car broke down. Do you remember?"

She looked down and lifted the dress's hem. It was the same white summer frock with silver embroidery that he recalled stripping off her behind the house she spoke of. It floated below her like a pale balloon, and he could almost make out the shape of her pale ankles. "Come in and dance with me like we did at the Percys' barn," she said. "Come with me." Her fingertips seemed like bleached rose petals reaching toward him, out of the water only by inches.

"I can't," he said. "I'm old now. I'm here with Camille and I must be dreaming. You're a figment of a figment, Emily. My head is on my shoulders and I don't see you. You aren't real."

He closed his eyes and willed her away, but as often as he reopened them, she remained. He touched her outstretched fingers, which were cold and wet. He pinched his face, and splashed lake water onto his cheeks. It smelled of fish and plants. He struck a match and brought the flame to his fingertip, thinking *wake up*, and still he watched her movements, gentle, fragile, graceful. Her frowning face dropped back under the water. The reflection of the flame flickered just below her left eyebrow. His finger reddened and he cried out sharply before plunging it into the lake to cool. The water that rippled around it did not distort her face. She wasn't an image on the water. She had surfaced again, slightly out of his reach. She was real—if only he could touch her.

"How is Camille, Cecil?" she asked, a look of vague distrust in her eyes.

"Camille is fine," he replied.

"We always loved her so much," Emily said.

"Right," Cecil said. "We did."

"I always did," Emily said. At this comment, her visage flattened to a flash of silver and became her face at thirty.

"She was sometimes difficult, you'll recall," Emily continued. "Our little Camille. But she loved God. And she loved you. I loved you, too."

"Oh, Emily," Cecil said.

"I'm here." Cecil watched her face flatten once more and morph to the younger face he had first regarded. A minnow flashed before her eyes. "But I have to go. Goodbye Cecil," she said, cringing as if she had been stricken.

"No, Emily!" he cried. "Come back!" but Emily sank further into the water until he reached in to grab the last tresses sliding into the muck. In his palm were a handful of eels that became river reeds when raised, dripping and grotesque, in his hands.

"I am going nutso," he said to Camille that night.

"Da, that's why you're here," she said. "The doctor told me you were under too much strain. Go and sit by the lake; you seem to enjoy it there. I was foolish to keep you from it."

He walked to the far end of the house and sat beside the fire, staring at it well into the early hours of the morning. Again, he could not sleep. He sat at the kitchen window until the sky began to lighten.

The next night insomnia and nerves revisited. At her customary time, the woman he had watched tossing her clover returned. She walked to the water's edge with two large tubs marked "LYE." She had carried these carefully to the side of the lake and poured their contents into the hissing water. The kitchen light was on. Cecil leaned out the window, and called, "Hey, there. What are you doing at my lake? I've been trying to ask you for a while."

She looked up from pouring to say, "I'm saving your life, old man, killing the lake's dark creatures. To cover them is not enough. They hear your trapped memories. They'll drain you for sport." The water sizzled and bubbled with her every careful dump. She waved, then turned and walked away.

"How do you know?" he shouted.

"The lake is hungry," she called back. "I sense it. It will fool you. Move back. You're a target, Cecil. Go back to where you came from and stay there. It knows you, now. It's made its mark. I can see it in your eyes."

A shiver jolted Cecil's spine. He quickly walked to his room and packed his few suitcases, placing them beside the extra white poplin comforter. His heartbeat fast, he felt dizzy. He tried again to sleep, thinking the next day he'd tell Camille he missed his old hunting buddy, Douglas, and that he was sorry, but he had to go. He'd tell her she could keep the house, his gift to her. He slept past her departure the next morning.

An hour before she was due home, he strode down to the lake again and knelt to look once more at his reflection. He walked to the other side, and looked into the water. "She's crazy," he said. "Blue-dress psychic woman. Maybe she's as crazy as I am."

—

Cecil took his afternoon medicine and checked the rooms for his details. In the guest bedroom, he came across a new picture of Camille and him seated in the great room. It was taken on the day she had that long-haired friend, Tracy, over. "Let me get a picture of you and your dad," Tracy had told Camille, and Camille had agreed. How happy they looked together, he now reflected, how familial, the hook of his nose visible on her face too, the shape of his ears and his eyes. She'd be home any moment. His eyes burned at the thought of losing her, considering: *When and how did I grow so very fond of Camille?* He was grateful for the development, despite not anticipating feeling this much sorrow at the thought of leaving.

"A father shouldn't be gone so much," he remembered saying to his mother as a child.

He clearly remembered her reply: "Your father is always leaving because he is not lazy. He has a purpose!"

"But my father stayed, too," he considered saying so long ago. His heart calmed a bit. He didn't have to leave Camille! He wondered if perhaps it was the lake woman who was causing all his fear! Nothing in the lake had been cruel or bad. Everything had been tendered with love.

Cecil retrieved his fishing pole. He went down again to the water to see if there were dead fish floating due to her poisoning, to see how bad it might be. Nothing floated. "I'm going to fish here because I want to," he told himself. "Maybe I won't leave. I'll stay for my girl." He closed his eyes, imagining his Papa's round, tanned face.

"A good call, my boy," a voice said.

Cecil followed the sound. The beloved face hovered three feet away, red and round, jutting from the water with its thick, brown, sun-dabbled beard as it often was during the summer.

"I see you've already been fishing today," the replica said. "But you haven't caught anything."

Cecil stood awkwardly, shaking his head. "Papa?" he replied. "I am so happy to see you." The phantom Papa wore his green fishing shirt, the one with the burn holes in the pocket from where his half-lit cigar had dropped its red embers long ago.

"I'm proud of you, Cecil," this Papa said. "Come closer."

Papa motioned to Cecil with an inviting bend of his finger, then walked out deeper, his face intermittently surfacing. "Sometimes you gotta go deeper to get to the meat of things!" he shouted. "Come on in, Cecil!"

Mesmerized by the familiar voice, Cecil rolled up his trousers. His blood thundered in his skull. He wondered how he could be so intent on the retreat of a lake-made imagining who was not even a real man, yet the farther away his lake-Papa grew, the more excitable and full of anguish Cecil became. He stepped in with one foot, followed by the other. The water was freezing. The entire experience was dreamlike. "Really, I am back at the house," Cecil said, convincing himself. "I have fallen asleep in bed. I can walk into this water and chase my father. I will wake up." Cecil began to shiver.

He looked for Papa and Emily, whose distant body now appeared just beyond his beloved father's. Both elevated from the lake, Cecil's heart raced. The hair follicles on his legs and arms tightened.

"This must be heaven!" he said. "I can see everyone. Everyone I ever loved is here." But he was so cold. And the faces and bodies seemed so far away. "I have to get out of this lake," he told himself. "I'm going up to the house. Right now."

He heard a car in the driveway. He stepped out of the lake and stumbled toward the gate, where his body crumpled. The blood rushed, pounding through his veins. He couldn't see his own body fall.

In his mind, he walked beyond the land where his body spasmed. His feet carried him nearer and nearer the lake's center, and when his head sank beneath the water, at last, the soft mouths of Emily, his father, and Jude kissed the oxygen from his lips. When he was too deep to resurface, his blood slowed, many visages then present in the lake, and as the profiles of those distant heads turned, he saw that their faces, half-coated with clover, were singed with lye.

His heart gave out completely not long thereafter, before Camille could retrieve him from the grass. As he'd exhaled the last oxygen from his lungs, submerged in his own morbid fantasy, he saw not only the familiar faces from his past whom he'd spoken with so recently, but also the strange visages of those he'd just seen so disfigured, and he witnessed every single one of them, in flashes of blinding-white light, transform into singular, thronging fish —a silver school of hungry minnows in a verdant country lake, like an enormous, pulsing tide of slender, biting mouths— coming for him, tearing at him, bearing down.

CHANNEL 59

Before it arrived, Channel 59 was advertised on bill-boards all over the city, atop taxis, on the walls of public lavatories, and even on milk cartons hosting the grainy faces of missing children, tiny green ads crammed just below the "Last seen" lines penned by grieving parents.

We bought into it; of course we did. A year before it arrived. They wanted us to. It has, as they suspected, changed the face of modern entertainment.

—

It's March. Channel 59 arrived last September. Cable stocks crashed in December, rendering cable obsolete except for a few local stations situated in the sticks where Channel 59 was not yet installed. Even there, however, gossip has spread like word of a good book, when people read books, back before the paper-goods museums and the ban on tree use. Now mobile country folk make trips to big cities to borrow televisions of urban cousins, and most employers have made it possible to wear a portable headset in order for workers to hear the programming. No one goes without.

Harold's employer is no exception. He says this to Evelyn to emphasize why he is happy to watch the set.

Evelyn hates Channel 59, because Harold speaks of nothing else and because it thwarts the libidinous urges that rage, unfulfilled, in her thirty-fifth year, blanking polite conversation with a ravenous hunger. Virtual chambers cease to be enough. It is 2033.

Evelyn fades into an anonymity she swore she'd never willingly allow as she asks Harold to turn off the TV each night, before leaning back and pulling closed her robe to go to bed.

Sometimes, he does. Other times, he replies: "Why?"

"It bores me, and I'm tired of it."

"Sorry."

"Hmph," she says, shaking slippers off her feet.

Initially, Channel 59 was the answer to expensive media broadcasts, actors and actresses charging a million dollars a line, bad dental hygiene, and even AIDS. When the president went on the late shows to play his tubaphonic harmonica to solicit viewers, its success was secured:

"If everyone will just watch this show," he drawled, a thick dollop of Southern wealth dripping from his tone like cream, "there'll be no reason for war. Hell, the nation will be unified and entertained! Life is what we make it, entertainment sprung forward like every innovation man has invented thus far. Better than the Internet. A paragon of substance to be modeled after and expanded. It's created by you folks, just good, country people! And God bless every American citizen. Bless you all. Watch Channel 59. Discover your destiny! The harbinger of the future will lay itself at your doorstep. It's called your remote control."

"Harold, will you turn off that damn set?"

"I'm watching it."

"Why not play a board game? Or, let's go outside."

"Stop speaking, Evelyn. You are blocking the sound."

Harold began watching two weeks into the initial broadcast, spurred by polls and friends proclaiming the societal worth of Channel 59. He furthered his addiction by watching more and more. At the time, it was rated with an entertainment factor of twelve on the Thirteen-Point scale of the National Standards Committee. It has just scored thirteen.

Since then, Harold has not slept well, and the hum of the television is like the ever-present buzz of a refrigerator, which is less-than-surprising to Evelyn, because there is no rest for the Static Television Addicts (STAs); every day is an eight-hour stint at the workplace, followed by eight to twelve hours of concentrated watching. Channel 59 bores her. What are they learning? They must be learning something. Or does it titillate like porn?

No matter. Evelyn comes to accept that Harold is helpless in the face of his needs, and nothing can be done.

Still, she keeps the house moving. "What would you like for dinner, Harold?"

"Chicken."

"We don't have chicken."

"Okay. Beef."

"What kind?"

"The cow kind."

"Ground or tenderized?"

He also has no energy to fulfill her once a month like he used to. His entire demeanor has changed to a watchful exhaustion and though she hopes he will soon tire of this nuisance (like he tired of law shows in the eighties, cop shows in the nineties, and the glut of emergency medical shows in the early twenty-first century), as yet he has shown no signs of diminishing interest.

"No sign of diminishing interest," she repeats, sometimes angrily flinging plastic bowls in the sink or punching pillows into shape as she makes the bed after laundry on Thursdays. She pastes the faces of network executives on her dartboard and takes aim. As the months rotate on her calendar, Harold vegetates, vacancy thick behind his eyes, and he is more and more muted with his addresses, watching and watching, dark and purple circles etching bruises near the bones of his sockets.

Where is my handsome husband who used to please me? she thinks. And Harold's lack of desire is all she thinks about, so she waters the garden for pleasure, plants red dahlias under the windows, and fantasizes about a time, not long ago, when her navel absorbed him as fully as the set.

Her journal becomes filled with repetitive entries. Days 1, 5, 17, 26, and 30 boast a running narrative regarding why, on weekends, Harold is inseparable from the remote.

On Day 12, she notes that every auto-setting is now locked into his selection of choice—Channel 59—but he continues to flip imperviously, his arm outstretched, wrist slightly tilted to avoid the encroaching interference of the rubber plant, remote duly leveled at the prime flip-zone: 59, to 59, to 59.

And she ponders in blue-scribbled lines, whether the brief cessation of sound from the flip is similar to a musical interlude or a mixed interference, which creates its own pleasant diversion. The headset rarely leaves Harold's ears. On a staid Tuesday evening, day 53 on the new calendar, she would rather talk about the impending visit of his mother, the cause of their latest tiff.

This being Tuesday, and Tuesdays holding the specific significance found in biorhythmic charts, are the worst possible days for Harold to irritate Evelyn. So instead of settling her head on his rounded stomach to listen to food digest as the clicker clicks, she emerges from the bathroom wearing a lime-green, chicken-feather stole with three pieces of matching, mirrored vinyl that resemble a bikini.

She will talk about his mother or she will talk about sex, she has decided, not that the topics have any paired rela- tion. Her outfit is held together by strings, the mirrors no larger than the faces of sparrows, with over a hundred reflec- tive surfaces in all.

She reasons he will find her outfit as stunning and different as she does, because it took her at least ten minutes to leave the bathroom due to the strangeness of seeing so many reflections of her own body, captured by decals and reflected back again from the larger mirror—a recursive loop of Evelynic reflection!

But, he does not. When he does not: "Harold. Look at me," she says.

"Later," he replies. "I'm watching Channel 59."

She rebuts, "We have not had sex in five months, Harold. Six days, 23 hours, and 59 seconds. Look at me."

"Channel 59 will slow population growth, which is a necessary good," he says. "Because that which slows population growth is that which saves the planet."

"I'm on the population-control shot," she says. "No danger here."

"I'm busy, Evelyn. Cut me some slack." He remains uninterested.

She wants to shout or hit him in the head with the clicker. But the thought behind her lime green extravaganza was that she vowed, a week earlier, to do anything to get him back—this vow propelling her into the White Electric cab and down to the oldest city district.

The exotic dancer store was her final destination, the only store left where nylon or natural fibers could be bought for hosiery and the salesgirls did your makeup by hand. Oh, the enthusiasm that could be experienced in antiquated things! How she loved them and remembered the scent of the perfumed drapes that lingered in her nostrils from the store where the salesgirl had assured her he would love her new outfit—or, if he didn't love it, he would, at the very least, deviate for a moment from that awful blank stare.

Evelyn felt sure he would be fascinated by the startling contrast between her own fish-white skin, the lime mirrors of her suit, and the gray flash of the screen. But she stares at him from her parked stance in the living room and he does not look up. "Harold," she says, shimmying back and forth with only the slightest shaking of loose parts, "I want to talk to you."

"Yes, yes," he replies and tilts one ear in her direction.

"Harold! You watch too much Channel 59!"

"Yes, ma'am, you're absolutely right, absolutely right," he says. "But please move just a little to the left. You're in my zone."

"No, I will not move out of the way," she sputters. "I will only move more in the way. More and more and MORE in the way!"

"There's no reason to get het up!" he exclaims, flipping over to his other tactic of diminishing or denying the problem. "It's only a hobby. Oh my," he continues, finally spying her from the corner of his eye, "what is that awful get-up you're wearing?"

Evelyn then plants herself squarely in front of the set and begins to cry. He approaches, as if to comfort, and wraps his arms around her, but spins her out of the way just enough to continue watching, murmuring, "I love you. I'm faithful. Tell you what, I'll stop watching an hour early tonight and we can talk. Is that all right? That's fair, isn't it?"

"Yes," she says. She wipes her eyes with her open palms as he reseats himself. Turning toward him, she stands at a forty-five degree angle to the set. "Or, how about if I talk to you from here, right now?"

He looks at her once. And then he puts both hands on his head, surprised. "Hold it right there," he says and, in this moment, gapes incredulously and gestures for her to stand still as he creeps closer to inspect her costume.

"Evelyn," he whispers, awed, focused on the lime mirrors and their reflections. "You're wearing it! Don't move." He moves as close as he possibly can without disturbing the myriad reflections, and marvels at the magnificence of her suit, muttering that it grants him a thousand little televisions on one body. "Evelyn, Darling," he says, but a commercial flash interrupts the programming:

"All STAs," the announcer drones, "please meet at the group council hall this evening at 9:00 for therapeutic support. All ST Addicts: Please meet at the group council hall for a new, therapeutic-support panel. Channel 59 will cease all programming for a twenty-four-hour period next week, due to system upgrades. This is your first and final notice."

But Harold is still looking at Evelyn. She is blissful. She revels in his gaze, stretching her arms luxuriantly upward, imitating the poses of Vegas showgirls and then, when he plants his hands firmly on her hips to keep them from moving, she stops altogether, realizes what occupies him has nothing to do with her, and is enveloped by cold fury.

The sight of Harold, fixated so intently on the mirrors and the way the Channel is reflected, forces her to slowly ball her right fist, approach, and vehemently strike the set. She does so twice.

On the second strike, the glass cracks, and shards of the screen form a jagged, unlit jack-o'-lantern smile.

Still, she is unsatisfied, so she grabs one of Harold's boots and swings it deeper into the hole while he watches, horrified, before promptly calling replacement TV shops, which have all closed for the night.

She awakens the next morning to recall the sound of cracking glass, and the moment the screen dimmed. Especially, she remembers Harold in all his noisy sorrow, beside himself over the television, curled into a ball on the couch, sobbing. But afterward, he came to bed. He came to bed with her and slept.

Into that ecstatic morning, she skips to work. On her way, she remembers staring at the thrashed set on the doorstep, a blaze of her thriving rhododendrons growing in pots at its side. She remembers Harold saying he felt sick, nauseated, and she remembers cautioning him:

"Harold, if you buy another television, I will never speak to you again." To satisfy herself further, before she leaves, she moves one pot of African violets dead-center inside the mangled appliance. She touches the purple petals fondly.

But Harold does not think of her when he awakens. He does not go to work. He is trying to break his addiction by removing himself from the normalcy of routine. At work, he can watch and listen. Yet his marriage must mean something more. He Sudokus and arranges wall art to distract himself.

Later that morning, he stretches his shoulders in the breakfast nook, looks over an old photo album, and touches his naked ears. The useless headset languishes in the drawer, and he begins to see each potholder again, each knife, each copper pot. His awareness of the tender variety in reality returns, all stimuli appearing in vibrant contrast to the gray-and-white fuzz of his channel. He awakens as if from a long sleep. He then spends hours stuffing his face into the velvet texture of the curtains, sniffing and sniffing the perfume Evelyn doused them with earlier that morning. He will smell every inch.

There are yards and yards to go, but by the time she gets home he will have made definite progress. She will be satisfied. He does recall her saying, quite early that morning, "If you need a replacement addiction, sniffing the drapes should comfort you. Because they're the same texture."

So, he follows her advice.

In the background plays an outdated disc on the old turntable. A bluesy jazz singer croons him into rhapsody as the afternoon light begins to fade. Then Harold rolls himself in the heavy folds of the drapery like a caterpillar. He misses Evelyn. He suddenly wants to make everything right between them, persuade her that their love is worth working on—but insidiously, also wishes he could watch the television on the doorstep, or buy another set.

He muses that rhododendrons bore him when he peeks out the front door and imagines, with a wistful flitter of his hand, that he is holding a remote, that he is sitting in front of the set again, only this time he's outside, and everything is calm. He goes and sits at the kitchen table.

He closes his eyes.

He concentrates.

With hardly any effort, he discovers that Channel 59 is still there, transforming his mental screen into the facsimile of the tube he once watched and now realizes he will no longer need. The clarity of his perfect recovery begins to fade, however, as a distraction appears in view from the kitchen window. A short, black woman walks with a noisy child, so Harold strides into the quiet living room to reinforce his imagining without distraction.

It works. Ah, the snow drifts and white noise filters in. How absolutely he can envision the gray-and-black flecks he has grown accustomed to, and their slow, downward progression across the screen. Ah, the calm, cool happiness of static in its purest form! He knows Evelyn will be angry, but he cannot help himself. He keeps watching.

She arrives home to find him exactly this way, focused on the opening in the entertainment center where the television used to sit, looking so happy and at peace that she settles in beside him for a few moments, stroking his hand, listening to the calm of his heartbeat, while he, in the same pathetic way as before, his wrist bent poignantly to avoid the ever-encroaching rubber plant, gestures with the clicker at the emptiest patch of shadow in front of the gaping hole.

THE TIME BROKER

When I finally met the Time Broker, he sat at an antiquated mahogany desk with no computer. He looked up and waited for me to speak. "Time for sale," his ad had said, and I was ready to pay, though I didn't yet understand how it worked. My first question was: "How does one buy a parcel of time?"

I remembered how I got there. The waiting room I sat in hours earlier was packed. The arms of two other customers, one on each side, rubbed against mine, which made my skin creep as all foreign contact does when the mind is prepared for the body to be inviolate. We sat in the waiting room in a large, old building, twenty people or more crammed inside the tiny space, with more waiting in the hall. Those with seats counted themselves lucky. Discarded issues of *Scientific American* and *Harper's* sat around the room—some as old as a decade. The man to my right stank of sweat and baby powder; perspiration fell from his face like irregular rain. He cooed to his hand, like he held an imaginary dove in his open palm, one with which he was intimately acquainted. "Soon, soon," he said. It sounded like, "Crou, crou."

To my left, a woman in a red wool sweater stinking of mothballs rubbed her hands together, blowing on rough fingers, and shivered gingerly, though it was warm. I had my number, 854, and an appointment time: 2:28 p.m. Her number was 901, the slip on her lap revealed. Those who could not sit stood clutching their numbers. From the time I arrived, 2 p.m., four people had entered the desired office. I saw none exit, and was thinking there must be a side door somewhere in the Time Broker's rooms, one you could leave through unmolested. Before me had gone three harried women and a tall, indifferent man. This man wore a scornful, masked expression, so I was glad for his sullen departure. The wait, while seated across from him, had begun to feel interminable.

The bell rang. I stared at the women in the room as we made idle chitchat between issuances. This chime, we agreed, sounded like a customer-service bell one would find at an automobile repair shop. Its *ding* was accompanied by a deep baritone, calling, from the recesses of the attached office, the next number. It was his voice; we were certain. The man who could deliver us.

The woman with number 853, Mrs. Tillie, a small Italian lady in an emerald housedress worn beneath an apron spotted with marinara, said she wanted to buy back at least an hour with her deceased grandfather— just one hour to discuss his last will and testament and make sure he had, for his family, his affairs in order. Those nearby thought it a lovely gesture, and we smiled with appreciation at her blank, inexpressive face, until she rolled her eyes, furious, pinching her thumb and middle finger as if to clench a small, cylindrical object, squinted while cracking a twisted smile, and said, "I would just like to poke him in the eyeball with my cigarette at least once, and get him to sign the damn thing as we rewrote it, the will, that is—then reinsert the cigarette, and let it burn a while."

The other women stared at her in terror, except Mary-Ellen Butler, 851, from Minnesota. "I'm from Minnesota," she had announced moments before, in a thick Bronx accent. She wore a sweatshirt that read, "Minnesota is the Place to Be," and after Mrs. Tilly's statement, Ms. Butler said, right away and with a high, nervous inflection, "It would go out, you know? That cigarette? In your grandpa's eye? It's not like you could keep it burning there. Did you think of that? A cigarette does not burn well in an eyeball!"

Mrs. Tillie rolled her eyes, and then Mary-Ellen thought a moment more, her gaze and forehead screwed up pensively as she chewed and spat handful after handful of barbeque sunflower seeds into a Dixie cup. They flavored the air with salt and hickory, which did not mix with the room's other untidy aromas of body odor, sewage, and perfume. When done thinking, she finished chewing a third set of seeds, and remarked, "And if it did go out, that cigarette, would you, you know, relight it? I'm just curious as to what you would do next. What if the old man would not sign?"

Mrs. Tillie regarded Mary-Ellen with a dour look. "Damn right I'd light it again," she replied. "I'd get him to change his mind from giving all the money to that bleeding-heart liberal charity, and then I'd go buy a new car with his filthy, dirty money, which was occasioned, in the first place, by his activity in the porn industry. Why are you wearing that Minnesota sweatshirt, anyway? You aren't from Minnesota—you fucking New Yorker."

"Witness protection plan," Mary Ellen whispered, and then announced in a voice that carried throughout the room, "I'm from Minnesota. I do live in Minnesota, don't you know?" as if her regional phrasing would make her statement fact. "Besides, leave me alone," she said. "I've got business here."

As it turns out, Mary Ellen wanted to buy a little extra time, just for herself. "An extra hour a week is all," she said, swinging a mass of walnut hair over her shoulders. "A little time to sow my wild oats, maybe. Enough time to move around unobserved and do small, delicious things. Perhaps, I could go back home... See friends." As she spoke, it became clear she seemed to think this purchased time would cause the rest of time to stop, like a frozen landscape, as if she could move amid people, possibly stealing their purses or rearranging their details on the tables before them at diners. Maybe, if given the chance, she would steal kisses and hugs, too, steal them from her friends and family, caressing oblivious cheeks and hands, so that only she would know she had enjoyed seeing them again. Beneath her sweatshirt was a flimsy club-top of some kind secured at the neck with slim black ties; these ties bedazzled with swirls of tiny gold stars.

"Well, the woman who referred me said this service is quite expensive," a man like my father said, shaking his head. He was balding and wore a pair of sunglasses with a tri-color GO NETHERLANDS spandex band around his neck. "Quite expensive."

"And didn't you expect it?" a woman in an ivory pantsuit replied, checking her watch before closing a maroon leather day planner and dropping a cell phone in her designer purse. "Time isn't cheap. But what I want to know is: Did your friend get what she paid for? Did this time broker come through—or is it all a bunch of hot air?"

"Oh, no—it worked," the spandex-sunglass guy said.

The bell dinged again. "Eight hundred and forty-nine," the baritone emitted.

"You say that," business-woman replied. "How well?"

"Apparently very well," he told her. "She seems to have nothing but time, now. Said the consultation did her good." He wore biker shoes that made his feet look elven.

"I would like six extra hours a day, every day, for the next three years," a young corporate Armani guy blurted. He wore a shiny gray suit with pink pinstripes. "With that, I could demolish my competition. I could get extra marketing done—read up on all the business magazines, reply to international e-mails, hire another assistant."

"You'd never be satisfied," yet another man said. "There is not enough time in one lifetime to ever be as successful as you'd like. You'll burn like a star—and then you'll burn the fuck out. Believe me. Before the heroin, I had it all. Now look at me."

We did. He seemed two steps from an addict's grave. Tattooed black rimmed his eyes. I had not noticed at first that this man was the source of the sewer stench, as though he had dragged in the gutter on the hem of his long, black trench; his skin was drawn with hard, deep lines, and his hair was dyed an artificial black—blacker than his faded coat. His face twitched as he said, "I would like three extra minutes a day after I wake up. Three thoughtless moments where everything is special and lively again. Fantasy moments. But they have to be good. Really fucking good. I want to live these few good moments to keep me going for a while, just till I get my affairs in order, and then I want to die."

As the bell rang again, the next customer shot forward. "Eight hundred and fifty-one," a voice called. *Where did 850 go?* I wondered. In the crowd's crush, I found my mind drifting. *And what kind of time did I want? Would the Time Broker give it to me?* I had found his flier on the road, dropped like something at a strip mall, or like a nightclub flier plastered to every windshield, but this glossy postcard was lying outside my house, by itself, on the sidewalk. Half-bent and a little torn, it rested between sweeps of winter wind. It read:

Buy time now. Stop bemoaning that life is not your endless summer. Hire a personal trainer! Do everything you ever wanted—Right Now! You have time. Or, you will when you BUY IT! See the Time Broker. Call and make an appointment. Or come in and see us! Go through the trees of the Igetsy Forest to the building near the back. 8th floor. He who hesitates—Well, you know the rest.

Don't waste another moment.

I knew the location well. The Igetsy Forest was a copse of trees within a larger urban park. I knew the building, too, for it had stood as long as I could remember, since I was a child playing in the park. It was not as though I could really afford the expense, but I had to look into it, for the idea would rankle and rankle, I knew, if I did not pursue it to its reasonable conclusion—because what was money in this life if not the currency of entrapment, exchange, or pleasure?

Truly, I had come to a point where I would throw money anywhere—via credit card, ready cash, direct-deposit advance, or out-and-out loan sharks—anything to find a new pattern because the one I endured felt stultifying. I was excited by the idea of buying time. Buying time! Someone was finally selling time? I dreamt wild dreams as I exited my car for the appointment. I had called in sick to work, mentioning I might be in later if I felt better. After I dropped the kids off at daycare and traipsed into the woods, it seemed the walk was endless. My legs had tired before I reached the building, and there was a moment when a bright, golden flash blinded and stunned me. Glare, I assumed?

But then there it was: The building. Shortly thereafter, I located the entrance and the elevator, which carried a fusion of scents so repulsive I could hardly identify them—though one was definitely semen—semen and vanilla, possibly with watermelon fruit-roll up spun in.

And then there was the waiting room.

And then the others and the numbers and the bell, and the fine baritone calling out our fates in soft, modulated tones. As I entered his office, I wasn't certain what I would find, but he was just a man, this broker. A brown-haired man with a bushy brown mustache that begged clipping below an aquiline nose and heavy-lidded, light gray eyes.

"Shut the door," he said. I did. "I know what you want," he said.

"You do?" I replied. I'm afraid I didn't have much else to say. I waited for him. I noticed his office, which was far larger than the waiting room, did have a second door, way at the back of a long wall that extended beyond his desk. Shelving graced the entire length of the wall.

"I do," he said. "The question is not whether you can have it, Lucille, but whether you want it badly enough to pay the forfeiture."

I noted a plaque above his shelving that read *Forfeitures*, and thousands of tiny bell jars lining that shelving, each filled with different items of a small enough size to be cupped in the palm of one's hand.

"This is what they gave up?" I asked. "Something small like what's in those jars? You don't take money?"

He laughed. "Baby," he said. "Money never buys time, not the money itself. Not really. Look at the wall, if you'd like. See what others gave up while you consider what you really want. But don't waste my time."

"What do I want?" I asked him. "What do I really want?"

"You know what you want," he said, shaking his head. "Just admit it."

Then I noticed the items in the bell jars were not static, but appeared to be moving. He waved me back toward them. "Go. Two minutes to look," he said, before officiously reminding me, "I have no desire to be rude, but I am, as you see, on a schedule—a very tight schedule." He handed me a small bell jar and muttered, "What you must give up will appear in here. If you want what you want and you know it, put your jar on the shelf as your signature and it will become mine. As fair trade, you get your time. Oodles and oodles of time. Hurray! But hurry!" he concluded. "Each choice leads to another, which then leads to another, and pretty soon your window for the first choice will have elapsed. You may need to visit me again." And then he turned away, documenting something on four yellow notepads spread before him by making large Xs along columns of names and social security numbers.

I looked at the jars, first scanning those at eye-level, but there were so many I found I had to focus on one at a time. In the first, there was a large plantation-style house, with an equestrian ring boasting four horses, three riders, and four trainers. The riders each walked in and approached a horse, exercising precision as they mounted from the left, and then let a trainer lead their horse into the ring. The fourth horse was led only by a trainer at the far side of the ring, yet all participants practiced the fundamentals of English dressage. *So this person*, I mused, *gave up all this?* Yes. It appeared they had.

The next jar held a white-haired old woman at a small window table, her chin dropped into her palm like a ball inside a glove. There was a note card and a pen on the table. She wore plain aluminum barrettes and bobby pins, and stared into the gray, chilled sky outside her apartment. Strangely, though it did not snow in my city, it snowed heavily where she was. A nurse came in and the woman said nothing. It was then I perceived a single glittering tear making jagged progress down the aged woman's cheek. One, and then another. She had discarded the pen.

I squinted to see what she had written on the card, but her handwriting was too small. Still, she was lonely; that much was clear. As we all are lonely, perhaps. I looked at her a long time, recognizing a trace of my own grandmother, but her sadness was so fulsome, I had to look away and move along.

Each of the jars was tiny, but the people and things in them appeared as detailed as in normal life, as if each jar formed its own universe, a window, perhaps, into what some person, seeking an excess of time, had given up. There were cell phones in some jars, computers actively surfing an endless Internet, and small, barking dogs. In some jars were children, playing, sleeping, or performing other activities. I put my small jar beside me on the floor, for it was then empty, and began to pick the others up. They were light, some as a clutch of ragweed or rye, and even the heaviest was no more burdensome than a gallon of milk.

In one, two tow-headed boys were playing on the beach, chasing each other and a Frisbee, with a woman who had to be their mother. The family fell laughing into the sand. In another were six children, all with black, curling hair, sleeping in two queen-sized beds that had seen better days, two of whom were flushed with fever, and appeared red beside the others.

In one jar, I saw an enormous room filled with books, boasting pens in a large blue coffee mug and reams of ink-spotted paper that held the scrawl of someone obsessively jotting things down. Another writer. *Dear Ada*, read the sheet topping this pile, *I do believe I failed you in all things. How can you forget, each time you forget, what a short dream we are all living? Return to me. Or, I shall return to you.*

The room was charged with an energy of wistful education stretched to span a life of near-solitude and frequent displeasure. But there was no person in this room. So this, I reasoned, this place was what was given up—but what for? Time? Some romantic trip across a continent to reclaim an estranged lover? I saw an aviary in another jar, filled with hundreds of tropical plants, butterflies, macaws, and other parrots. People came in to view the larger birds, some selected and purchased from a vendor outside the enclosure.

In some jars were paintings, rolled and sealed, or store-fronts, or the ghosts of others known and long-dead, doing things long-since done, who appeared green and filmy, not quite opaque, in their ghost-like worlds, though their hazy environments were just as complete as the others.

"Hurry up, Lucille!" the Time Broker called, interrupting my musings. "Choose soon!"

I moved quickly then, obsessively letting my eyes travel every shelf possible. Some of the jars were marked on the bottom with a black *X*. I went back to my jar on the floor and picked it up, for something like a moldering cloud had begun to grow inside.

"What is this thing in my jar?" I asked him.

"You'll see it soon," he said, without turning toward me.

I walked to his desk, jar in my hands. "So, whatever appears in the jar is what you give up? Do you give it up forever?"

"Sometimes," he said. "Why do you look so upset, Lucille? You wanted time, didn't you? Time to read and write and paint and act? Time to acquire fame or notoriety. You wanted all those things. But you built a family. That was your first mistake. Had you been rich starting out, this may not have plagued you. The times are right for women to succeed. Choose!" he said. "Time awaits you. The smooth wrinkle of many desires! Choose now! Your forfeiture is near-complete." And he looked down at my jar, which, to my horror, self-populated with a park filled with trees and spinning play sets, swings, slides, glistening towers. The very park outside this building! And there were children on the playground. The day was sunny as today was not. And then I saw my husband. He was calling to someone, two some-ones, who were last to appear in the jar, initially slow-moving shapes as gray and nebulous as the current fog, but clarifying and becoming solid, I saw them as exact replicas of the tiny darlings I had dropped, that morning, at daycare.

"Julia! Peter!" I called, repeating their names several times, but they could not hear me.

"Drop it on the shelf, then leave through the exit door," the Time Broker said. "You must leave through the exit door in the back. It leads to your new life, where you will have already severed unnecessary ties. You will lose a year in this transaction, but it will have passed before you go. You will enter your new world ready to embark, gaining at least 6.53 additional years to complete your life's work. It may not sound like a lot, but it is. That time, in years, includes only awake-time. A bargain, really. Put your jar on the shelf and leave."

I could hardly hear him. I kept staring at my children, my children in his jar—for they were mine and I had birthed them, worked hard for them—and though I couldn't hear their voices through the glass, I watched my beautiful little girl turn to her father and speak.

He patted her head. She started to cry. A woman appeared beside her. And my son then approached the two of them and flung his arms around his father. He shouted, but was already three years old in this depiction, his hair longer than I remember, darkening. Had time already advanced for them?

"Put the bell jar on the shelf," the Time Broker bellowed. "Don't look too closely. It makes things harder. Really."

"And what if I don't want to?" I asked, fingering the glass under which my miniature children stood.

"In the quest for time, you always have choices. It's the nature of loss and gain. If you don't want the time, then open the jar. Let them go. They can escape. But not five minutes from now. So walk away, back to them—if that's what you want. But do it. Make your choice. The time and decision factors are already changing. Ding, ding. And, ding," he said, pressing the silver bell atop his desk, calling out, "Number eight hundred and fifty-five."

He ceased to regard me, then. I dropped the jar, which shattered on the ground but fused together instantly, before landing, whole again, on his desk.

"Goodbye," he said. "Goodbye, goodbye!"

I ran free. The people in the waiting area were amazed to see me rush past them, back through the entry door. "Is it fair?" they asked. "Can you get what you want? How is he? What's the rate?"

In their desperation, for the room was full of it, they shouted questions quickly. But I was too busy running to answer.

I ran down eight flights of stairs and through the forest until I reached my car. As I turned my key in the ignition, I saw children, lots of them, in the park that surrounded the building, but I had to get to mine quickly. As I pulled away, another gold flash hit my vision, and I watched a black-
-haired boy in overalls disappear, and then a blonde-haired girl with a purple polka-dotted ribbon laced through her braids.

No one in my family would understand the phrase I kept repeating to my children between dinner and baths and book reading and bedtime that night—but it meant some-thing to me. It was a mantra of sorts. An admission made in the terrible melancholy of tenderness.

"I opened your jar," I kept saying. "I opened your jar because I love you and I could not bear to lose you. Can't you see how much I love you?"

The children had no idea what to say except to acknowledge that they loved me, too. But my husband, thankfully well-accustomed to my emotion, simply stroked my head as I sat on the couch beside him, saying only: "There, there, honey," and "There, there," and "There, there."

SCHRÖDINGER'S LOVE CAT

Theodora has a small plastic box marked *This End Up* in which, every day, a manifestation of Schrödinger's cat lives and dies. When she tires of looking at work documents, she asks Cat questions. Cat always is or is not alive inside his box. Cat is a gray cartoon feline lit by a small white bulb. Terms of life are relative.

His box, sleek and gray, sports a compelling nuclear power symbol stuck to the top, a warning sticker reading *This Box May or May Not Contain A Live Animal*, and poison symbols on the sides, which make it feel dangerous. Because her questions are dangerous, too, she has to make them important, and poses them often to spice things up. She learns to adapt even complicated biological and emotional needs into binary question structures, like: *Will I get laid soon, Cat?* What's more dangerous than getting laid?

She moves the box's sliding front door and scans for his state. If Cat's final position in the box is upright, with normal yellow cat eyes, that means alive, which means "yes." If it is keeled over on its side, dead, with X eyes, that's "no."

Cat said YES to the *laid soon* question, so Theodora pumps her fist for a victory moment, but rapidly drops her arm when a manager walks by.

She doesn't worry about yesterday's answer to the same question, which was NO. Cat has no-ed her many times.

Content with the current YES, she puts the box down briefly, contemplating peppering Cat with a volley of hypothetical names as by whoms—but such queries don't interest her enough just yet. Right now, she rides the fleeting high of even a small, false positive. She looks with longing to her right.

She knows exactly who she wants and he's one office over, wearing a green Chaps shirt and attractive black slacks, the latter appealingly tight.

Her job today is to track styrofoam purchase trends in east Long Beach and up the coast, but instead she stares into her office neighbor Gary's window hole, which is a piece of glass between their carpeted office walls. She gives Gary a random thumbs up, which he does not see and does not return. He looks busy. His screens are full of work. She began to ask Cat about him months ago.

Will I fall in love with Gary?

Cat said NO.

Will Gary fall in love with me?

Cat said NO.

"Fucker," she said, but then asked Cat, *Does Gary have a sizeable—?*

NO.

This was before Cat began to change in his box. Before the new fire entered it. If she didn't like the answer to the questions in these innocent times, her strategy was to ask another similar, but different enough, question. Sometimes this second question inspired whole other inquiries, but her tendency was to stop asking when she tired of either NO or pushing the sliding door aside.

Does Gary secretly desire me, even if we cannot call it love?

Is Gary gay?

Will Gary have sex with me by accident one day?

Is Gary really working in there, for all that time he acts like he's working?

What is Gary's work-life secret and should I mount a nanny cam in his office to find out? Bug his office instead?

Does he have a sexy girlfriend who is thinner, younger, and prettier?

There are four hundred thousand styrofoam plate units sold monthly in the southern district. This figure is down from last quarter. Oh my god, typing this in, she wants to die. She can go a few paragraphs more on the use of these plates, but not much more.

She picks up Cat again. When she starts getting too seduced by asking questions, when the use of non-degradable styrofoam is oppressive, she asks Cat impossible asks, like:

Who is Gary anyway and what does he think is the meaning of life?

Do you think he would date a pretty fat girl?

What will Gary's goals be in five years?

Theodora wonders if people who work tracking sales of the stronger plastic bags, now that the ones filling the oceans are banned, feel the same malaise her job makes her feel. Do they sense their existence is meaningless? Do they know it for a fact?

Le sigh. Consult the window hole. *Gary is so hot.*

Gary is 5'11 with dark black hair that curls at his nape. He has hazel eyes. He is ballpark thirty-two. He knows her name is Theodora since he once asked whether her parents were history majors and she was a next incarnation of a president. She said she was, but more attractive. She think he knows her last name, too.

Once he gave her a compliment on a pleather laptop bag, but he's hard to get facetime with. He doesn't eat in the staff lounge. Instead, every day, he takes out a homemade sandwich. Most days his sandwiches look like lunchmeat and lettuce. He drinks a bottled water. Recently, she bought him a glass container since it disturbs her to watch him drink plastic molecules all the time, but she hasn't gotten up the nerve to give it to him. It sits in her desk drawer. He leaves fifteen minutes later than she does, so they never walk out together.

If the styrofoam plant increases production but thins the plates and charges the same rate per package of numbered units, there's a better likelihood of profit, she types, expressing this and thinking that one main obstacle to her incredible passion is that they work for different units, and that she can't just, say, knock on his office door and chat about work. He's in purchasing. She's in quality control and sales. I mean those are two different worlds.

She finishes another mindless spreadsheet that looks like fifty some others she's made, deciding another obstacle to their love is her height. She's 5'4. He's 5'11. Normally 5'11 guys like girls around 5'6. Also, Gary has perfect teeth. Her teeth are not perfect. He's attractive and put together enough that she could, alternately, if he didn't work here, see him as an appearance snob, completely into deliciously stylish gay guys.

As the next work sentence she types details the conflict between profit and utility, she literally feels a small part inside her soul slowly die. She knows she needs another job but can't leave, can't escape, not until she figures out the mystery of Gary.

She better do it fast, she decides. Because life is short. *What if he has a girlfriend anyway? I better give him my glass water bottle before I'm tempted to quit now*, she thinks to herself, and she walks over to his office door the long way because going up to the shared window hole and shouting would be weird. She knocks.

"Yes, ma'am," Gary says. "Come in."

"Hey, hey, Gary," she says, opening his door. "It's Theodora." Announcing her own name when he already knows it does sound dumb, but she follows this up with a goofy smile. She walks into his space and then, after a pause, closes the door behind her. Glass water bottle in hand, she says, "I noticed you drink a lot of water from plastic bottles."

He rolls his eyes. At least she thinks he does. "And?" he responds.

She wants to say, "This is the beginning of my new positive place in your life. I will solve all your problems, but first, here is this cool glass bottle I bought for you while contemplating your cancerous daily intake of thousands of tiny pieces of toxic plastic and dreaming of the next fifty years we could spend together if you like me and happen not to die of environmental hazards. So, don't die, Gary. Please don't die." But somehow, happily, she stops herself. She knows this wouldn't come out right. Instead, she says, "I have an extra new glass one, here. Take it. Plastic ones are bad for your health. You know, like our product is bad for customers when they microwave it? So I thought I could share it with you, this glass one, for your safety…"

"Oh," he says. "Okay, thanks. Anything else?"

She hands over the bottle. "Do you like working here, Gary?"

"No."

"Me neither." They stupidly grin at each other, but this is a conversation stopper. It's difficult, she thinks, when you can't tell anything about true compatibility if people only answer in short bursts—when you have no good reason for asking more, and yet you're so compelled. This makes for blabbering. She blunders ahead, pushing past the awkward. "Yeah, so, we've been working side by side for a while now. You always look so busy." She steps closer.

He visibly recoils and windows are rapidly vanished or minimized. "Busy enough," he says.

"Oh, all right," she says, stepping back. "Okay, bye."

The defeat of the moment feels large—her lack of a

clue about what to do next must show in her deflated posture, and she decides this walk over was really dumb. She wants to smack her own head. Perhaps, she decides, her whole crush was better imaginary.

Except as he then notes her crestfallen look, Gary says before she goes, "I'm sorry. I don't mean to be a dick. I'm under extra stress right now. Having car problems."

She stares at him before saying, "No worries," then squirms with shame and discomfort, feeling wet underarms in her purple satin blouse, sure now she has visibly sweat into the armpit areas, so presses her arms tightly to her sides. She lifts her gaze to Gary, trying to look self-assured as she begins to back out of his office, and as they stare at each other, because he doesn't look particularly unhappy and there are no rings on his hands, she asks, "Would you like to have drinks after work, Gary?" She doesn't even drink much, is quick to slutty drunk actually, but every relationship she's ever successfully started has required some alcohol to numb or slow her down enough for falling into sheets.

"Okay," Gary says. "Yeah."

"Great," she says, gives him the first thumbs up from her he's probably ever seen, though there have been oh so many, and walks out.

It occurs to her five minutes later that she gets off work later than he does. It also occurs to her that she has not indicated exactly when or where for the drinks. She sends him an email. This says: Can you wait till I get off at 5:15? She clicks send and then turns a deep red. Poor phrasing. This is terrible! Can you wait till I get off? That's so dirty!

She's so embarrassed, she refuses to even look toward his window hole, instead typing, **The styrofoam bowl units have had poor feedback due to a flimsy lip. A lip on a bowl is more important than a lip on a plate. If the design team could re-vision this product, we might have a better market. Furthermore, there is no chance a younger demographic will go for—**

"Yes," Gary replies.

She decides that this is a brilliant reply on his part because it means he will wait for her in every possible scenario, feels it's minimalist and romantic, already imagines them naked on some hotel bed near some bar and him kissing her forehead after. She focuses again on the reinforced rim of the coffee service cups, which she's supposed to remark upon in today's focus group, suddenly mortified since there's something deeply inappropriate about how much she's already imagined their drinks, sex, and aftermath.

"Good," she types. "Meet me outside the front door of the building. We can—we can..." And then there's a lapse. She wants to get good and drunk. She wants there to be a hotel. There is no hotel near the office without driving. Should they take one car? Hers? His? Both? She's going too fast. She ends up saying something like, "decide from there."

"Jesus, Cat," she says to the cat box on her desk. "There's too much fumbling in real life."

The focus group meeting on cups goes well. Her boss, who Theodora likes well enough, is happy with Theodora's suggestions.

The drinks with Gary go even better. Turns out, he's had a crush on her. Turns out he's happy to go up to a hotel room and manages, with an efficient ease, to shepherd the situation into enactment. They take two cars. She drinks two martinis.

She notices he's an eye-closer during sex. He moans soulfully and whispers things like, "You feel so good." He likes the lights off the second time they do it. They do it about six times. Both of them really needed to do it, she decides.

They leave things simply, with a kiss.

They never talk about tomorrow. She exists in suspended animation.

But the next day at work, Gary isn't there. Theodora feels a blush creep over her each time she thinks of their hotel room stint. She gets somewhat angry because he told her nothing about not coming in, not even a text. She grabs the cat in the box, but this time the questions rush up so fast, she has to breathe meditatively and calm herself before deciding what next to ask.

What is Gary thinking? Wait, fuck, she remembers. That's an impossible question for YES/NO. She tries again. *Is Gary thinking of me?*

She pulls the door aside and something new happens. Cat, who clearly only had two unique poses since the beginning, has a new appearance, which is that of a gray cartoon feline, with a dopey smile, surrounded by hot orange fire. Cat on fire. Cat with closed eyes.

Hard to tell if they are Xes or not. They are curvy lines.

I'm seeing shit, Theodora thinks, trying another question:

Is Gary glad we had sex?

Cat's dead.

Theodora's furious at Cat. She wants to ask Cat why, why, why, but that doesn't work. Cat never answers questions about why unless they are YES or NO.

In her mind she replays every moment of her intimacy with Gary, how he held her thighs down with his forearms when he put his face between them, how he flipped her over more than once per act, how he happened to have ten condoms in his tight pants' pockets, how his anatomy was larger than mid-sized, how he smiled a mysterious smile as he left the room...

Does Gary want to see me again?

This time, again, fire cat reappears. But fire cat and his ambiguity pisses her off. Damn it, she thinks. What's going on with Gary?

She thinks about Gary nonstop, whose questions lead to fire cat, and any non-Gary related questions have standard cat, live or dead. So Gary made fire cat appear, she then thinks. Does the fire cat mean fire cat of love? Why that dopey cat smile? Why hasn't Gary texted or called? His silence, causal to most of her doubt, also causes a sudden sense of surreality about what happened between them and why.

She decides only Gary's next words will unlock what's happening here. Yet there are no words from Gary. It's not that the sex wasn't great, she soothes herself when pissed; if it wasn't great, we wouldn't have done it so very many times —simultaneously typing: **Customers find that their knives cut right through thinner styrofoam plates, so the thinnest parts should be the external border in a new design. Border design as particularly slender could be less significant than a slender base. As discussed, do not thin border lip design in bowls.**

But maybe the sex wasn't great, to be honest, she thinks. She wanted to think it was, though. And anyway, it didn't turn into love. Or did it? Was this love—this crazy waiting and wondering? Is the love cat alive or dead? Is the fire cat love or death? She asks Cat:

Have I fallen in love with Gary?

After this question, Cat does not stop at a single pose. It seems both standing and keeled over, shown doubly at once, in representation of simultaneous life and death.

A week later, she discovers that Gary was incinerated in a terrible, rolling car accident as he left the hotel after their tryst. That he's passed away.

It's because of our sex, she thinks. *And our drinks.*

In her mind, she hears her mother say, "Stop being so dramatic, Theodora! Everything is not about you!" This is oddly soothing until she begins to think: *I haven't even met his mother. Actually, I don't know Gary at all! He was just a huge possibility, looming, and partly realized. I just looked* at *him a long, long while, lustfully, through a working window hole.*

Well, you did bone him six times, she reminds herself. *Don't forget that. That could be a basis for attending his funeral.* But it's not like she's invited. She has no way of finding out more. As a potentially guilty party, she asks herself torturous questions like: *If we hadn't had drinks, if I hadn't asked him for drinks, if our sex took longer or shorter, if we'd instead been intimate one more or one less time, would that other car have never encountered Gary for that accident?*

It occurs to her these could all be YES or NO questions. She picks up the box even though her work phone is ringing or because her work phone is ringing. "Ok, Cat," she says, "Don't give me fire cat again. I need brass tacks. I need answers."

But the first question she asks after that—*Did I just lose the love of my life?*—is met by an empty dark box. She cannot see Cat at all, in any manifestation.

Cat does not reappear no matter how many times she slides the door aside. She has no idea how to disassemble the box to get at the light bulb to replace it or whether even replacing the bulb will solve the malfunction. Cat has left. Cat is gone, just gone. It's so very dark in the box.

Jesus, she thinks. *I guess I'll never know.*

LITTLE RED RIDING HOOD AND SUN TZU'S *THE ART OF WAR*

It's a little known fact that Little Red Riding Hood was a student of military strategy. The actual tales that involve her, fashioned and retold by spies, often vary in content but never mention her abiding attachment to the ruler Sun Tzu.

Why did they not address this? It was such an important aspect of her character. She says in her own diary that she loved him. The lost diary. One of many. Here's a passage from before the diary's wolf and granny episode; consider this like Season 2 of 12 the LRRH timeline:

1/12:

little hearts and flowers all around the border of an empty page Meh.

1/13

some ugly things that look like Teddy Bears or Ogre dolls

1/14:

Mom's a hag.

1/15:

Same.

1/17:

LRRH + ST forever! ST, you are genius about FIRE warfare! I want to set fires and try the different strategies, but they say I can't! Even as experiment. I'm so distraught!!!

Wish you were here!! I want to stroke your little black beard and touch your kimono! Wait. Is that what you wear?!

Turns out, obviously, no one answered, which is usually the way when you ask questions of someone you don't know in a diary. Still, back in Little Red Riding Hood's home village, it was well-known by her friends that she had a raging crush on the military leader, one that excluded local boys, or any boys, really. "I like my men grown," she'd say. "Sage and wizened. Seasoned with blood." Sometimes, with glee, she'd add, *"Dead!"* and she often began sentences with, "As Sun Tzu says," though this was also when her mother and grandmother frequently tuned her out, probably when they sent her walking in the woods, directing her back and forth between their houses on errands to get breaks from the rambling.

"Now, don't talk to strangers," her mother warned each time she sent Little Red off, but it could be argued that this request was to protect Little Red's listeners from unsolicited rants rather than to protect Little Red, who had a nasty way of punching and biting when challenged. In truth, no one in her village really cared about issues of laying siege nor determining the size of neighboring armies, since there were none, though many listened to Little Red's discourse out of a will for self-protection.

Never mind that she was mainly occupied with regurgitating ST rather than sharing her own ideas, it only matters for this telling that she believed she survived the predestined wolf's belly or did not survive the predestined wolf's belly encounter based on her perfected or lacked understanding of Sun Tzu's teachings.

It's time this cogent influential factor was highlighted by the record, and maybe it wasn't documented before because people tended to ignore what a woman said about a crush of the romantic nature, particularly if her crush was too oft quoted. OR these pertinent details of the LRRH story may have been omitted because European retellings frequently omit debts to wiser Asian cultures. OR such brevity in detail may be a function of the fairy tale genre itself, causing LR's worship of ST to be left out since the thoughts of fairy tale characters are so regularly abridged that it's a foregone conclusion that one will infrequently hear of the real obsessions tormenting and inspiring them.

Regardless, as discussed and moving forward, Little Red Riding Hood loved her some Sun Tzu. Here's how the whole wolf belly episode went down:

Once upon a time, in a village near some woods, there was a small child with a cloak and a basket, walking a path toward her grandmother's house. She was either seven or seventeen. She had either cake and a butter pot or cake and a wine bottle.

If she had a wine bottle, it was likely she nipped from it as she strode along, working on her new Sun Tzu song in unsuppressed glee, adding only "Where are you? Where are you?" to the words, "Sun Tzu, Sun Tzu," so far, and playing this sequence on 12 bar repeat.

If she had just butter and cake but no wine, she probably wished she had wine and wondered why someone thought cake went with butter, why bread wasn't sent. She probably took little nibbles of the cake. The song, in either iteration, went the same.

Regardless, her grandmother had been sick, so that morning Little Red's mother had said, "Go take these things to your granny, and do not talk to strangers."

"All right, mother," LRRH said, because she liked the walk. "Right away."

It was just as she freely traipsed along, humming "Sun Tzu, Sun Tzu, where are you?" and considering this fixed and primary chorus, that she either took some shrooms or a talking wolf appeared.

If a talking wolf appeared, he said, "What have you

there under your mantle, little girl?" and it was kind of
pervy.

About the talking wolf, LRRH thought of how Sun
Tzu's *The Art of War* said in Chapter Six that fighting could
be avoided by throwing something odd and unaccountable
in the enemy's way, so she just talked about her wine and
cake, or butter and cake, because they were at hand, hoping
to confuse or distract him when his gaze traveled over her
clothes. "I'm going to my granny's!" she then announced.

If she took some shrooms and there was only a halluci-
nated wolf, she did and said the same things, except twice
she dropped the cake and had to pick bits of grass out of the
spongy surface. She got distracted staring at the blades for a
while then decided she should be on her way. In either
version. Also, in both versions, he asked where granny's
house was and she told him it was: 1. fifteen minutes further
in the forest, under three large oaks and nearish the chestnut
trees, or 2. beyond a mill, at the first house in the village, or
3. found via either a path of pins or a path of needles.

In some versions, he told her to go pick some flowers.

Or he watched her traipse off and hoped she'd pick
some flowers.

Nonetheless, he went quickly to her grandmother's
house while she dawdled, sighing with pleasure at the
wonderful visions she had from the shrooms or the wine or
the flowers and having paused where such blossomings were
gathered.

"Life is so very beautiful!" she thought. "But why do
moms always give the tastiest things to their own moms?
Daughters get jacked! And why do I almost never stop in
fields of flowers to sniff them or hang out?"

Then, when she thought how her mother might scold
her for taking her sweet ass time, she recalled that Sun Tzu's
Chapter One on "Laying Plans" clearly stipulated that when
circumstances were favorable, one should modify one's

plans. So she kicked back even longer, determining that circumstances were favorable, and ate the cake for her grandma, too, feeling only a small bit confused or dismayed when she arrived at her grandmother's house and shouted "Good day!" but received no reply.

Usually her grandma shouted back, "Shut up," at the very least.

Then she noticed the freaky looking thing in her grandma's bed, which was either a wolf or a hairy ogre or an old repulsive man with his winky hanging out.

What, you might ask, did she do then? She made like he wasn't a stranger in her grandma's nightgown and she asked him questions about the sizes of his facial features, though her heart raced to behold his ugliness in her grandma's frock. Then, possibly addled by drugs, she inhaled deeply and remembered Sun Tzu's Chapter Two on waging war, which said, "In respect of military method, we have, firstly, Measurement; secondly, Estimation of quantity; thirdly, Calculation; fourthly, Balancing of chances; fifthly, Victory," so she tried to apply this doctrine, even if all of this was in her mind.

In measurement, the shroom wolf was the length of a bed, she decided. In estimation of quantity, there was one. One shroom wolf. By this calculation, there was no grandma. While she had a balanced choice of running away from this apparition to reach safety or coming nearer to discover the location of her grandmother, she determined her mother would be pissed if she didn't at least try to find victory in recovering her grandma, so Little Red neared the bed.

It was at this point that shroom wolf sprang out of the bed and ate her. "Fuck," Little Red thought, traveling down his gullet. Then she said, "Hi, Granny," since there her granny was, deeper in his belly.

"Hi," Granny feebly said.

Little Red held up the bottle of wine or butter pot, half consumed in the case of the wine and with nothing to go with it in case of the butter, and offered to share. "Want some?" she asked. "How we going to crack the fuck out of here?"

Her granny said, "Let's wait for the hot woodcutter," the idea of which Little Red enjoyed.

"Well, Grandma," she replied. "Sun Tzu says victory is not in assuming the enemy won't attack but instead on making our position unassailable. We are pretty unassailable here. We could wait or we could stab this wolf's liver. Or we could punch his lung sacs. What do you think?"

"Hot. Woodcutter," Granny said. "Let's wait. I made my opinion known."

So, in some versions, but not this one, they waited. The woodcutter came, and he cut them out. He became the hero. In other versions, she and her granny were stuck and died. But no versions popularly available have begun to fathom how the true story came to pass, which was LRRH and her granny's survival occasioned by LRRH's own cunning and smarts—because the real story is never told, which is why you are learning about Sun Tzu, and the true story now, which is also the tragic story of how an inappropriate true love for a dead man freed a fairy tale creature from an imminent carnivorous death and expanded her horizons.

So, there they were, in the belly. While originally Little Red had agreed to go by her granny's dictates and alternately scream for the woodcutter and wait silently, after five hours stewing in his stank digestive juices and yelling, she decided to recite the entire *Art of War*. She did this with great gusto, speaking most words directly into the wolf's kidneys.

Here and there, she also sang the chorus of her new Sun Tzu song, which you have already heard. One could say things then went quite to her and her granny's benefit. She had gotten through no more than one third of the book before the wolf began to shout, "Stop! Stop with the Sun Tzu! Stop it!"

This only served to embolden her and improve the recitation. She continued and he continued asking that she stop. But she did not. She continued reciting all the way up until the point where the wolf, like the whiney bulimic baby he was, put a paw down his throat and puked her and her granny up on purpose.

And just then the hot woodcutter came running up, but she and granny were covered in puke. So he killed the wolf but cringed as he beheld the women, perhaps even holding his nose for a second, and left the woods with barely a "Glad I came by."

Neither were cute enough for him, both decided later, while acknowledging it's hard to be cute enough, no matter how cute you are, when covered in puke, though as we well know the retold versions of LRRH's tale include neither her deep and abiding love for Sun Tzu, nor the role of wolf vomit in turning the woodcutter off, nor the reality that this victory was obtained by LRRH following one of Sun Tzu's most brilliant musings, which was: "If your enemy is of choleric temper, irritate him."

But seldom do fairy tales get anything entirely right or include the minutia of day-to-day living. So, anyway, broad strokes, Little Red thought, picking up her diary that night. And that's why she wrote all these things down, hoping that one day someone would find it.

After finding the diary I immediately went to spread the gospel of the real story. Yet though I've told others now, no one believes me that LRRH's story went differently. They don't want to change their read of it after all these years, liking how it was before, nor believe that Granny really was so lecherous or Little Red was that vigorous. Also, they don't like the evoked and unsanitized smell of puke from regurgitation at the end of the story.

But real stories aren't always pretty.

Hers wasn't. She kept living. The diary went on.

We paused on the wolf incident here, but I didn't even tell you about Season 8 of the LRRH diary stories, when Little Red went to go dig up Sun Tzu. At long last, after many months of searching, she found his grave and put a ring on his bony finger. Literally dug up his hand to do so.

And she had finally written the other verses of the Sun Tzu song begun in Season 2. Naturally, the "Where are you? Where are you?" part changed to "Gonna marry you! Gonna marry you!"

And she was wearing the most beautiful black lace wedding dress in the moment of the ring offering—as her granny wiped the dirt off the hand bones and officiated the ceremony.

DANGLING NOW, IN THE EROTIC CITY OF GHOSTS

"The first to arrive could not understand what drew these people to Zobeide, this ugly city, this trap."
— Italo Calvino, *Invisible Cities*

In the lingering Erotic City of Ghosts, no one does laundry. No one does laundry because ghosts do not sweat. In a blink, night turns into day, day into night. Citizens can appear at any hour and time travels like a star. Lust in the shade of crimson roams and conquers. The horizon is majestic. What do you see?

There is no use in saying you might refuse to look. The city scoffs at all who fail to look.

That type does not exist. Everyone looks. Even the blind. One could say they look longest.

As the history of any city accumulates, this city grows but does not shrink. There are many sights! Look, look there: Through that low-E, dual-pane picture window there is a girl in tights and a red leotard, lifting her leg up to the sky. Her thigh meets her cheek in an intimate slide. She lowers her lashes and smiles. In the sun, her hair is auburn flecked with gold. She continues at the barre, dancing for you.

Beside her house, there is an apartment complex wherein a man peers heavily at a book the size and weight of a small dog. Note his curling black hair, his quizzical expression, the wrinkles on his forehead when he raises his furred brow. He has asked you a question—but did you hear him? I think he said, "Shall we retreat into the b—" but a clamoring begins.

No, it is a clapping. It's a reaction to a dramatic performance. Someone offers flowers. Someone whispers, "You were unbelievable." Someone's hands slip into your jeans, from behind, not moving much, just cradling the flesh above your ass. Their hands are warm and unassailable in their mission, which is to hold.

It is magic! Or perhaps it is a teenager with a bracelet, standing in front of a library. He holds out this bracelet and earnestly entreats. He wants something. A promise of forever. He is a ghost who does not yet know what forever means.

If he did, he would not ask. Think on that.

This city has twelve libraries. The people are learned. This city might be mine. Something in each neighborhood appeals uniquely to me.

Surely, always, there is a rough part of town. This is the place where you may watch the bodies of athletes flex and contort as their forms glide over an asphalt court. A ball bounces and rolls into a wire-grid fence. This is the place where ghost sheets are dirty and the bills are ignored, where cars oxidize and small children wear shoes the price of fancy meals—a place where you fail to fit in but remember having enjoyed from time to time.

"Whatchoo doing here?" someone says.

"Waiting for you," you reply. There is no ambiguity in your look. Red surfaces in the other's face like a stop sign. To you, green means stop and red means go.

Browns and yellows dance, whites and blacks, pinks and tans. The Erotic City of Ghosts is a beautiful place, full of diversity. You can visit at length, be drawn to the tearful glances of the people who are all full of feelings. There are many tears.

Eroticism and Stoicism are unbalanced. This city is rarely Stoic.

Should you like a more subdued city, the Shameful City of Scant Offerings is suggested. There are many quiet people there whose tears have different meanings. They know more about nameless, continuous regret. "I could not go see you because... Changing my life would mean..."

These people abridge all charming thoughts. This is because they have never experienced the direct joy of Erotic Ghosts. They chose away from experience. In their own way, you may decide, they are ghosts as well. They are the ghosts of can't help you and never will.

They can be upscale and downscale, fat and thin, undeserving and unrewarded. Often, they make banquets out of solitude. Not everyone has a seedy side of town. In smaller cities, more often, there is a nook that resembles a dream or a diary. Sometimes, these cities are so small there are few inhabitants and the ones who exist there are better known than Bibles. The Erotic City of Ghosts does not discriminate on the basis of primary locale.

Religiosity is welcome here, especially of the sensual sort. "God, yes, god god god, yes."

Oh, my, the carnival. Streamers! A young boy reaches his hand into his mother's. One of the magician's assistants with fishnet stockings and a short lace skirt has winked at him. She holds a rabbit. Her smile pours into his veins, hot as confusion. Her shiny pink lips cause a fluttering in his heart. He will look for her, years later, in another tiny skirt. She will be warmly remembered.

If there is one issue with the Erotic City of Ghosts, it is that when it is overpopulated, it is hard to absorb at once. So many things will fade. The brick building that had five windows, in hindsight, has only three. The park where lovers frolicked, with time, has become an ugly place. There is litter. The higher the population, the less each citizen stands out.

If you blink in the Erotic City of Ghosts, you can be any age you wish. The sights will differ with your focus. The world's a mystery. *Touch me and I've no longer fallen. Fall for me or I'll die alone...* add your own rock song cliché. People are capable of anything. Definitions of sexy change by the hour. View the enormous wheel of need. Everyone spins it. Everyone plays.

There are those with whips in hand, clamps, chains. Those with flowers, rings, and chimes. "I want to break you," some will say. Be wary of these. They have dungeons. "I want to taste you," others will proclaim. Give space to these; you can never be made sweet.

I knew a girl once where her Erotic City of Ghosts held just one man. Her real world held just one man. This showed one can be living with one ghost in alternate locales. Her ghost in the Erotic City treated her so sweetly. He made her feel so fine. But that was years before. To regard her now, you might forget who she was and that another version of her ghost lives right beside her. It is possible to live with a ghost you enjoy who has only passed away in your head. Your ghost is yours forever.

Recognition is all, recovery.

She needs to recover him. In memory, she tries. But memory is tricky and self-serving.

In the Erotic City of Ghosts, she sees only his most engaging moments or most terrifying. Both their hair is white now. They hardly speak. Sometimes there are two places one can be at once—but to hold onto adjacent distances can make for tears.

Tears, I said, not sweat. Last reminder: In the Erotic City of Ghosts no one does laundry because there is no sweat; ghosts do not sweat. They wear only the shiny or sparkly outfits important to memory.

Ghosts dance. Ghosts beckon. Ghosts charm.

Ghosts make helicopter patterns with lower anatomy while laughing and drinking Malbec. You can fit them in your pocket or in a porous structure the approximate size of a softball. This sits on your shoulders. Enjoy it! Take time in its recall.

In the Erotic City of the Living, there is no recollection, only sensation, only the very moment that encompasses your now. Here is your warning: This turns quickly into death. Death of the moment is where the changeling ghosts are born.

You will notice, in the Erotic City of Ghosts, that there is no place for the careless hello. Conversations are more evolved, more charged. They have already happened and thus become more iconic, telling, or predestined. In a blink, night turns into day, day into night. There is no time for boredom.

The girl in the window, at the barre, in the red leotard, lifts her leg up to her cheek. The boy in the court strips his ribbed white tank and rubs it across his face. The man in his apartment looks at his lover then his book, then looks away. Ghosts are comfortable here, transformed to snapshots. They have one thing in common.

They all belong and all belong to you. Forever à la carte.

Or perhaps your city has a different view than mine, but each city will have one thing in common: In the Erotic City of Ghosts, one's skin creeps with the awareness of another's flesh. The owner is not indifferent. The heart pounds. Desire must exceed the experience of the lover and yet the lover's perception is constantly changing.

No one here knows how to say a casual hello. What rush is there in that? Though everyone here knows how to say: I loved you once, goodbye.

ABOUT THE AUTHOR

Heather Fowler is a novelist, short story author, play-wright, librettist, and poet. She the author of the novel *Beautiful Ape Girl Baby* and the story collections *People with Holes, This Time, While We're Awake*, and *Elegantly Naked in My Sexy Mental Illness*. Fowler's *People with Holes* was named a 2012 finalist for Foreword Reviews Book of the Year Award in Short Fiction. *This Time, While We're Awake* was selected by artist Kate Protage for repre-sentation in the Ex Libris 100 Artists 100 Books exhibition in conjunction with the 2014 AWP Conference. Fowler's fictive work has been made into fine art collaborations many times, and her collaborative poetry collection, *Bare Bulbs Swinging*, written with Meg Tuite and Michelle Reale, won the 2013 TWIN ANTLERS PRIZE FOR COLLABORATIVE POETRY. Fowler's stories and poems have been published in the U.S., England, Australia, and India, appearing in such venues as *PANK, Night Train, storyglossia, Surreal South, Short Story America,* and *Feminist Studies*. Please visit her website for updates on new projects and recent publications: heatherfowler.com.

OTHER TITLES FROM PINK NARCISSUS PRESS FEATURING HEATHER FOWLER

BEAUTIFUL APE GIRL BABY

A Novel by Heather Fowler

"Fowler has written something impossible and brilliant: *Confederacy of Dunces* meets *Mighty Joe Young* meets *Pantagruel* meets *Heathers*. I have never read anything like this book, and I'm always thankful for the few times as a reader I get to say that. So thankful for the funny, fierce, feminist words of Heather Fowler." —Amber Sparks, author

PEOPLE WITH HOLES

Stories by Heather Fowler

"Readers who admire any of the finest writers in the genre (Isabel Allende, Gabriel Garcia Marquez, Franz Kafka, Toni Morrison, and Salman Rushdie) should enjoy the flights of fancy within this book, and also be able to confront its darker journeys." —*Foreword Reviews*

DAUGHTERS OF ICARUS

New Feminist Sci-Fi and Fantasy

"Throughout, the authors explore themes of gender, identity, and autonomy, with characters as diverse as miniature clones, stripper vampires, aggressive mermaids, and mystical crones. Many of the stories focus on gender roles and the pull of relationships, whether parental, familial, or romantic, among all kinds of people." —*Library Journal*

CPSIA information can be obtained
at www.ICGtesting.com
Printed in the USA
LVHW081719110719
623803LV00018B/1011/P